Ugly Love

COLLEEN HOOVER

Ugly Love

**SIMON &
SCHUSTER**

London · New York · Sydney · Toronto · New Delhi

First published in the USA by Atria Books, 2014
First published in Great Britain by Simon & Schuster UK Ltd, 2014

34

Simon & Schuster UK Ltd
1st Floor
222 Gray's Inn Road
London WC1X 8HB

www.simonandschuster.co.uk

Simon & Schuster Australia, Sydney
Simon & Schuster India, New Delhi

A CIP catalogue record for this book
is available from the British Library

Paperback ISBN: 978-1-47113-672-6
EBOOK ISBN: 978-1-47113-673-3

Typeset by M Rules
Printed and bound by CPI Group (UK) Ltd, Croydon, CR0 4YY

MIX
Paper | Supporting
responsible forestry
FSC® C171272
FSC
www.fsc.org

For my two very best friends,
who also happen to be my sisters,
Lin and Murphy

Ugly Love

chapter one

TATE

"Somebody stabbed you in the neck, young lady."

My eyes widen, and I slowly turn toward the elderly gen-
tleman standing at my side. He presses the up button on the
elevator and faces me. He smiles and points to my neck.

"Your birthmark," he says.

My hand instinctively goes up to my neck, and I touch the
dime-sized mark just below my ear.

"My grandfather used to say the placement of a birthmark
was the story of how a person lost the battle in their past life.
I guess you got stabbed in the neck. Bet it was a quick death,
though."

I smile, but I can't tell if I should be afraid or entertained.
Despite his somewhat morbid opening conversation, he can't be
that dangerous. His curved posture and shaky stance give away
that he isn't a day less than eighty years old. He takes a few slow
steps toward one of two velvet red chairs that are positioned

against the wall next to the elevator. He grunts as he sinks into the chair and then looks up at me again.

"You going up to floor eighteen?"

My eyes narrow as I process his question. He somehow knows what floor I'm going to, even though this is the first time I've ever set foot in this apartment complex, and it's definitely the first time I've ever laid eyes on this man.

"Yes, sir," I say cautiously. "Do you work here?"

"I do indeed."

He nods his head toward the elevator, and my eyes move to the illuminated numbers overhead. Eleven floors to go before it arrives. I pray it gets here quickly.

"I push the button for the elevator," he says. "I don't think there's an official title for my position, but I like to refer to myself as a flight captain, considering I do send people as high as twenty stories up in the air."

I smile at his words, since my brother and father are both pilots. "How long have you been flight captain of this elevator?" I ask as I wait. I swear this is the slowest damn elevator I've ever encountered.

"Since I got too old to do maintenance on this building. Worked here thirty-two years before I became captain. Been sending people on flights now for more than fifteen years, I think. Owner gave me a pity job to keep me busy till I died." He smiles to himself. "What he didn't realize is that God gave me a lot of great things to accomplish in my life, and right now, I'm so far behind I ain't *ever* gonna die."

I find myself laughing when the elevator doors finally open. I reach down to grab the handle of my suitcase and turn to him one more time before I step inside. "What's your name?"

"Samuel, but call me Cap," he says. "Everybody else does."

"You got any birthmarks, Cap?"

He grins. "As a matter of fact, I do. Seems in my past life, I was shot right in the ass. Must have bled out."

I smile and bring my hand to my forehead, giving him a proper captain's salute. I step into the elevator and turn around to face the open doors, admiring the extravagance of the lobby. This place seems more like a historic hotel than an apartment complex, with its expansive columns and marble floors.

When Corbin said I could stay with him until I found a job, I had no idea he lived like an actual adult. I thought it would be similar to the last time I visited him, right after I graduated from high school, back when he had first started working toward his pilot's license. That was four years and a two-story sketchy complex ago. That's kind of what I was expecting.

I certainly wasn't anticipating a high-rise smack dab in the middle of downtown San Francisco.

I find the panel and press the button for the eighteenth floor, then look up at the mirrored wall of the elevator. I spent all day yesterday and most of this morning packing up everything I own from my apartment back in San Diego. Luckily, I don't own much. But after making the solo five-hundred-mile drive today, my exhaustion is pretty evident in my reflection. My hair is in a loose knot on top of my head, secured with a pencil, since I couldn't find a hair tie while I was driving. My eyes are usually as brown as my hazelnut hair, but right now, they look ten shades darker, thanks to the bags under them.

I reach into my purse to find a tube of ChapStick, hoping to salvage my lips before they end up as weary-looking as the rest of me. As soon as the elevator doors begin to close, they open again. A guy is rushing toward the elevators, preparing to walk on as he acknowledges the old man. "Thanks, Cap," he says.

I can't see Cap from inside the elevator, but I hear him grunt something in return. He doesn't sound nearly as eager to make small talk with this guy as he was with me. This man looks to be in his late twenties at most. He grins at me, and I know exactly what's going through his mind, considering he just slid his left hand into his pocket.

The hand with the wedding ring on it.

"Floor ten," he says without looking away from me. His eyes fall to what little cleavage is peeking out of my shirt, and then he looks at the suitcase by my side. I press the button for floor ten. *I should have worn a sweater.*

"Moving in?" he asks, blatantly staring at my shirt again.

I nod, although I doubt he notices, considering his gaze isn't planted anywhere near my face.

"What floor?"

Oh, no, you don't. I reach beside me and cover all the buttons on the panel with my hands to hide the illuminated eighteenth-floor button, and then I press every single button between floors ten and eighteen. He glances at the panel, confused.

"None of your business," I say.

He laughs.

He thinks I'm kidding.

He arches his dark, thick eyebrow. It's a nice eyebrow. It's attached to a nice face, which is attached to a nice head, which is attached to a nice body.

A *married* body.

Asshole.

He grins seductively after seeing me check him out—only I wasn't checking him out the way he thinks I was. In my mind, I was wondering how many times that body has been pressed against a girl who wasn't his wife.

I feel sorry for his wife.

He's looking at my cleavage again when we reach floor ten. "I can help you with that," he says, nodding toward my suitcase.

His voice is nice. I wonder how many girls have fallen for that married voice. He walks toward me and reaches to the panel, bravely pressing the button that closes the doors.

I hold his stare and press the button to open the doors. "I've got it."

He nods as if he understands, but there's still a wicked gleam in his eyes that reaffirms my immediate dislike of him. He steps out of the elevator and turns to face me before walking away.

"Catch you later, Tate," he says, just as the doors close.

I frown, not comfortable with the fact that the only two people I've interacted with since walking into this apartment building already know who I am.

I remain alone on the elevator as it stops on every single floor until it reaches the eighteenth. I step off, pull my phone out of my pocket, and open up my messages to Corbin. I can't remember which apartment number he said was his. It's either 1816 or 1814.

Maybe it's 1826?

I come to a stop at 1814, because there's a guy passed out on the floor of the hallway, leaning against the door to 1816.

Please don't let it be 1816.

I find the message on my phone and cringe. It's 1816.

Of course it is.

I walk slowly to the door, hoping I don't wake up the guy. His legs are sprawled out in front of him, and he's leaning with his back propped up against Corbin's door. His chin is tucked to his chest, and he's snoring.

"Excuse me," I say, my voice just above a whisper.

He doesn't move.

I lift my leg and poke his shoulder with my foot. "I need to get into this apartment."

He rustles and then slowly opens his eyes and stares straight ahead at my legs.

His eyes meet my knees, and his eyebrows furrow as he slowly leans forward with a deep scowl on his face. He lifts a hand and pokes my knee with his finger, almost as if he's never seen a knee before. He drops his hand, closes his eyes, and falls back asleep against the door.

Great.

Corbin won't be back until tomorrow, so I dial his number to see if this guy is someone I should be concerned about.

"Tate?" he asks, answering his phone without a hello.

"Yep," I reply. "Made it safe, but I can't get in because there's a drunk guy passed out at your front door. Suggestions?"

"Eighteen sixteen?" he asks. "You sure you're at the right apartment?"

"Positive."

"Are you sure he's drunk?"

"Positive."

"Weird," he says. "What's he wearing?"

"Why do you want to know what he's wearing?"

"If he's wearing a pilot's uniform, he probably lives in the building. The complex contracts with our airline."

This guy isn't wearing any type of uniform, but I can't help but notice that his jeans and black T-shirt do fit him very nicely.

"No uniform," I say.

"Can you get past him without waking him up?"

"I'd have to move him. He'll fall inside if I open the door."

He's quiet for a few seconds while he thinks. "Go downstairs and ask for Cap," he says. "I told him you were coming tonight. He can wait with you until you're inside the apartment."

I sigh, because I've been driving for six hours, and going all the way back downstairs is not something I feel like doing right

now. I also sigh because Cap is the last person who could probably help in this situation.

"Just stay on the phone with me until I'm inside your apartment."

I like my plan a lot better. I balance my phone against my ear with my shoulder and dig inside my purse for the key Corbin sent me. I insert it into the lock and begin to open the door, but the drunk guy begins to fall backward with every inch the door opens. He groans, but his eyes don't open again.

"It's too bad he's wasted," I tell Corbin. "He's not bad-looking."

"Tate, just get your ass inside and lock the door so I can hang up."

I roll my eyes. He's still the same bossy brother he always was. I knew that moving in with him would not be good for our relationship, considering how fatherly he acted toward me when we were younger. However, I had no time to find a job, get my own apartment, and get settled before my new classes started, so it left me with little choice.

I'm hoping things will be different between us now, though. Corbin is twenty-five, and I'm twenty-three, so if we can't get along better than we did as kids, we've got a lot of growing up left to do.

I guess that mostly depends on Corbin and whether he's changed since we last lived together. He had an issue with anyone I dated, all of my friends, every choice I made—even what college I wanted to attend. Not that I ever paid any attention to his opinion, though. The distance and time apart has seemed to get him off my back for the last few years, but moving in with him will be the ultimate test of our patience.

I wrap my purse around my shoulder, but it gets caught on my suitcase handle, so I just let it fall to the floor. I keep my left

hand wrapped tightly around the doorknob and hold the door shut so the guy won't fall completely into the apartment. I take my foot and press it against his shoulder, pushing him from the center of the doorway.

He doesn't budge.

"Corbin, he's too heavy. I'm gonna have to hang up so I can use both hands."

"No, don't hang up. Just put the phone in your pocket, but don't hang up."

I look down at the oversized shirt and leggings I have on. "No pockets. You're going in the bra."

Corbin makes a gagging sound as I pull the phone from my ear and shove it inside my bra. I remove the key from the lock and drop it toward my purse, but it misses and falls to the floor. I reach down to grab the drunk guy so I can move him out of the way.

"All right, buddy," I say, struggling to pull him away from the center of the doorway. "Sorry to interrupt your nap, but I need inside this apartment."

I somehow manage to prop him up against the doorframe to prevent him from falling into the apartment, and then I push the door open farther and turn to get my things.

Something warm wraps around my ankle.

I freeze.

I look down.

"Let go of me!" I yell, kicking at the hand that's gripping my ankle so tightly I'm pretty sure it might bruise. The drunk guy is looking up at me now, and his grip sends me falling backward into the apartment when I try to pull away from him.

"I need to get in there," he mutters, just as my butt meets the floor. He makes an attempt to push the apartment door open with his other hand, and this immediately sends me into panic mode. I pull my legs the rest of the way inside, and his hand

comes with me. I use my free leg to kick the door shut, slamming it directly onto his wrist.

"Shit!" he yells. He's trying to pull his hand back into the hallway with him, but my foot is still pressing against the door. I release enough pressure for him to have his hand back, and then I immediately kick the door all the way shut. I pull myself up and lock the door, the dead bolt, and the chain lock as quickly as I can.

As soon as my heart rate begins to calm down, it starts to scream at me.

My heart is actually screaming at me.

In a deep male voice.

It sounds like it's yelling, "Tate! Tate!"

Corbin.

I immediately look down at my chest and pull my phone out of my bra, then bring it up to my ear.

"Tate! Answer me!"

I wince, then pull the phone several inches from my ear. "I'm fine," I say, out of breath. "I'm inside. I locked the door."

"Jesus Christ!" he says, relieved. "You scared me to death. What the hell happened?"

"He was trying to get inside. I locked the door, though." I flip on the living-room light and take no more than three steps inside before I come to a halt.

Good going, Tate.

I slowly turn back toward the door after realizing what I've done.

"Um. Corbin?" I pause. "I might have left a few things outside that I need. I would just grab them, but the drunk guy thinks he needs to get inside your apartment for some reason, so there's no way I'm opening that door again. Any suggestions?"

He's silent for a few seconds. "What did you leave in the hallway?"

I don't want to answer him, but I do. "My suitcase."

"Christ, Tate," he mutters.

"And . . . my purse."

"Why the hell is your *purse* outside?"

"I might have also left the key to your apartment on the hallway floor."

He doesn't even respond to that one. He just groans. "I'll call Miles and see if he's home yet. Give me two minutes."

"Wait. Who's Miles?"

"He lives across the hall. Whatever you do, don't open the door again until I call you back."

Corbin hangs up, and I lean against his front door.

I've lived in San Francisco all of thirty minutes, and I'm already being a pain in his ass. Figures. I'll be lucky if he lets me stay here until I find a job. I hope that doesn't take long, considering I applied for three RN positions at the closest hospital. It might mean working nights, weekends, or both, but I'll take what I can get if it prevents me from having to dip into savings while I'm back in school.

My phone rings. I slide my thumb across the screen and answer it. "Hey."

"Tate?"

"Yep," I reply, wondering why he always double-checks to see if it's me. *He* called *me*, so who else would be answering it who sounds exactly like me?

"I got hold of Miles."

"Good. Is he gonna help me get my stuff?"

"Not exactly," Corbin says. "I kind of need you to do me a huge favor."

My head falls against the door again. I have a feeling the next few months are going to be full of inconvenient favors, since he knows he's doing me a huge one by letting me stay here. Dishes?

Check. Corbin's laundry? Check. Corbin's grocery shopping? Check.

"What do you need?" I ask him.

"Miles kind of needs your help."

"The neighbor?" I pause as soon as it clicks, and I close my eyes. "Corbin, please don't tell me the guy you called to protect me from the drunk guy *is* the drunk guy."

Corbin sighs. "I need you to unlock the door and let him in. Let him crash on the couch. I'll be there first thing in the morning. When he sobers up, he'll know where he is, and he'll go straight home."

I shake my head. "What kind of apartment complex are you living in? Do I need to prepare to be groped by drunk people every time I come home?"

Long pause. "He groped you?"

"'Grope' might be a bit strong. He did grab my ankle, though."

Corbin lets out a sigh. "Just do this for me, Tate. Call me back when you've got him and all your stuff inside."

"Fine." I groan, recognizing the worry in his voice.

I hang up with Corbin and open the door. The drunk guy falls onto his shoulder, and his cell phone slips from his hand and lands on the floor next to his head. I flip him onto his back and look down at him. He cracks his eyes open and attempts to look up at me, but his eyelids fall shut again.

"You're not Corbin," he mutters.

"No. I'm not. But I am your new neighbor, and from the looks of it, you're about to owe me at least fifty cups of sugar."

I lift him by his shoulders and try to get him to sit up, but he doesn't. I don't think he can, actually. How does a person even get this drunk?

I grab his hands and pull him inch by inch into the apartment, stopping when he's just far enough inside for me to be able to close the door. I retrieve all of my things from outside the apartment, then shut and lock the front door. I grab a throw pillow from the couch, prop his head up, and roll him onto his side in case he pukes in his sleep.

And that's all the help he's getting from me.

When he's comfortably asleep in the middle of the living-room floor, I leave him there while I look around the apartment.

The living room alone could fit three of the living rooms from Corbin's last apartment. The dining area is open to the living room, but the kitchen is separated from the living room by a half-wall. There are several modern paintings throughout the room, and the thick, plush sofas are a light tan, offsetting the vibrant paintings. The last time I stayed with him, he had a futon, a beanbag chair, and posters of models on the walls.

I think my brother might finally be growing up.

"Very impressive, Corbin," I say out loud as I walk from room to room and flip on all the lights, inspecting what has just become my temporary home. I kind of hate that it's so nice. It'll make it harder to want to find my own place once I get enough money saved up.

I walk into the kitchen and open the refrigerator. There's a row of condiments in the door, a box of leftover pizza on the middle shelf, and a completely empty gallon of milk still sitting on the top shelf.

Of course he doesn't have groceries. I can't have expected him to change *completely*.

I grab a bottled water and exit the kitchen to go search for the room I'll be living in for the next few months. There are two bedrooms, so I take the one that isn't Corbin's and set my suitcase on top of the bed. I have about three more suitcases and at least six boxes down in the car, not to mention all my clothes on hangers, but I'm not about to attempt those tonight. Corbin said he'd be back in the morning, so I'll leave that to him.

I change into a pair of sweats and a tank top, then brush my teeth and get ready for bed. Normally, I would be nervous about the fact that there's a stranger in the same apartment I'm in, but I have a feeling I don't need to worry. Corbin would never ask me to help someone he felt might be a threat to me in any way. Which confuses me, because if this is common behavior for Miles, I'm surprised Corbin asked me to bring him inside.

Corbin has never trusted guys with me, and I blame Blake for that. He was my first serious boyfriend when I was fifteen, and he was Corbin's best friend. Blake was seventeen, and I had a huge crush on him for months. Of course, my friends and I had huge crushes on most of Corbin's friends, simply because they were older than we were.

Blake would come over most weekends to stay the night with Corbin, and we always seemed to find a way to spend time together when Corbin wasn't paying attention. One thing led to another, and after several weekends of sneaking around, Blake told me he wanted to make our relationship official. The problem Blake didn't foresee was how Corbin would react once Blake broke my heart.

And boy, did he break it. As much as a fifteen-year-old heart can be broken after the span of a two-week secret relationship. Turned out he was officially dating quite a few girls during the two weeks he was with me. Once Corbin found out, their friendship was over, and all of Corbin's friends were warned not to come near me. I found it almost impossible to date in high school until after Corbin finally moved away. Even then, though, the guys had heard horror stories and tended to steer clear of Corbin's little sister.

As much as I hated it then, I would more than welcome it now. I've had my fair share of relationships go wrong since high school. I lived with my most recent boyfriend for more than a year before we realized we wanted two separate things out of life. He wanted me home. I wanted a career.

So now I'm here. Pursuing my master's degree in nursing and doing whatever I can to avoid relationships. Maybe living with Corbin won't be such a bad thing after all.

I head back to the living room to turn out the lights, but when I've rounded the corner, I come to an immediate halt.

Not only is Miles up off the floor, but he's in the kitchen, with his head pressed against his arms and his arms folded on top of the kitchen counter. He's seated on the edge of a bar stool, and he looks as if he's about to fall off it any second. I can't tell if he's sleeping again or just attempting to recover.

"Miles?"

He doesn't move when I call his name, so I walk toward him and gently lay my hand on his shoulder to shake him awake. The second my fingers squeeze his shoulder, he gasps and sits up straight as if I just woke him from the middle of a dream.

Or a nightmare.

Immediately, he slides off the stool and onto very unstable legs. He begins to sway, so I throw his arm over my shoulder and try to walk him out of the kitchen.

"Let's go to the couch, buddy."

He drops his forehead to the side of my head and stumbles along with me, making it even harder to hold him up. "My name isn't Buddy," he slurs. "It's Miles."

We make it to the front of the couch, and I start to peel him off me. "Okay, Miles. Whoever you are. Just go to sleep."

He falls onto the couch, but he doesn't let go of my shoulders. I fall with him and immediately attempt to pull away.

"Rachel, don't," he begs, grabbing me by the arm, trying to pull me to the couch with him.

"My name isn't Rachel," I say, freeing myself from his iron grip. "It's Tate." I don't know why I clarify what my name is, because it's not likely he'll remember this conversation tomorrow. I walk to where the throw pillow is and pick it up off the floor.

I pause before handing it back to him, because he's on his side now, and his face is pressed into the couch cushion. He's gripping the couch so tightly his knuckles are white. At first, I think he's about to get sick, but then I realize how incredibly wrong I am.

He's not *sick*.

He's *crying*.

Hard.

So hard he isn't even making a sound.

I don't even know the guy, but the obvious devastation he's experiencing is difficult to witness. I look down the hallway and back to him, wondering if I should leave him alone in order to give him privacy. The last thing I want to do is get tangled up in someone's issues. I've successfully avoided most forms of drama in my circle of friends up to this point, and I sure as hell don't want to start now. My first instinct is to walk away, but for some reason, I find myself oddly sympathetic toward him. His pain actually appears genuine and not just the result of an overconsumption of alcohol.

I lower myself to my knees in front of him and touch his shoulder. "Miles?"

He inhales a huge breath, slowly lifting his face to look at me. His eyes are mere slits and bloodshot red. I'm not sure if that's a result of the crying or the alcohol. "I'm so sorry, Rachel," he says, lifting a hand out toward me. He wraps it around the back of my neck and pulls me forward toward him, burying his face in the crevice between my neck and shoulder. "I'm so sorry."

I have no idea who Rachel is or what he did to her, but if he's hurting this bad, I shudder to think what *she's* feeling. I'm tempted to find his phone and search for her name and call her so she can come rectify this. Instead, I gently push him back into the couch. I lay his pillow down and urge him onto it. "Go to sleep, Miles," I say gently.

His eyes are so full of hurt when he drops to the pillow. "You hate me so much," he says as he grabs my hand. His eyes fall shut again, and he releases a heavy sigh.

I stare at him silently, allowing him to keep hold of my hand until he's quiet and still and there aren't any more tears. I pull my hand away from his, but I stay by his side for a few minutes longer.

Even though he's asleep, he somehow still looks as if he's in a world of pain. His eyebrows are furrowed, and his breathing is sporadic, failing to fall into a peaceful pattern.

For the first time, I notice a faint, jagged scar, about four inches long, that runs smoothly across the entire right side of his jaw. It stops just two inches shy of his lips. I have the strange urge to touch it and run my finger down the length of it, but instead, my hand reaches up to his hair. It's short on the sides, a little longer on the top, and just the perfect blend of brown and blond. I stroke his hair, comforting him, even though he may not deserve it.

This guy may deserve every single bit of the remorse he's feeling for whatever he did to Rachel, but at least he's feeling it. I have to give him that much.

Whatever he did to Rachel, at least he loves her enough to regret it.

chapter two

MILES

Six years earlier

I open the door to the administration office and walk the roll sheet to the secretary's desk. Before I turn and head back to class, she stops me with a question. "You're in Mr. Clayton's senior English class, aren't you, Miles?"

"Yep," I reply to Mrs. Borden. "Need me to take something to him?"

The phone on her desk rings, and she nods, picking up the receiver. She covers it with her hand. "Wait around another minute or two," she says, nodding her head in the direction of the principal's office. "We've got a new student who just enrolled, and she also has Mr. Clayton this period. I need you to show her to the classroom."

I agree and plop down into one of the chairs next to the door. I look around the administration office and realize this is the first time in the four years I've been in high school that I've ever sat in one of these seats. Which means I've successfully made it four years without being sent to the office.

My mother would have been proud to know that, although it leaves me kind of disappointed in myself. Detention is something every male in high school should accomplish at least once. I have the rest of my senior year to achieve it, though, so there's that to look forward to.

I retrieve my phone from my pocket, secretly hoping Mrs. Borden sees me with it and decides to slap me with a detention slip. When I look up at her, she's still on the phone, but she makes eye contact with me. She simply smiles and goes about her secretarial duties.

I shake my head in disappointment and open up a text to Ian. It doesn't take much to excite people around here. Nothing new ever happens.

> **Me:** New girl enrolled today. Senior.
>
> **Ian:** Is she hot?
>
> **Me:** Haven't seen her yet. About to walk her to class.
>
> **Ian:** Take a picture if she's hot.
>
> **Me:** Will do. BTW, how many times have you had detention this year?
>
> **Ian:** Twice. Why? What'd you do?

Twice? Yeah, I need to rebel it up a little before graduation. I should definitely turn in some homework late this year.

I'm pathetic.

The door to the principal's office opens, so I close my phone. I slide it into my pocket and look up.

I never want to look down again.

"Miles is going to show you the way to Mr. Clayton's class,

Rachel." Mrs. Borden points Rachel in my direction, and she begins to walk toward me.

I instantly become aware of my legs and their inability to stand.

My mouth forgets how to speak.

My arms forget how to reach out to introduce the person they're attached to.

My heart forgets to wait and get to know a girl before it starts to claw its way out of my chest to get to her.

Rachel.

Rachel.

Rachel, Rachel, Rachel.

She's like poetry.

Like prose and love letters and lyrics, cascading down

the

center

of

a

page.

Rachel, Rachel, Rachel.

I say her name over and over in my head, because I'm positive it's the name of the next girl I'll fall in love with.

I'm suddenly standing. Walking toward her. I might be smiling, pretending I'm not affected by those green eyes that I hope will one day be smiling just for me. Or that red-as-my-heart hair that doesn't look like it's been tampered with since God created it specifically with her in mind.

I'm talking to her.

I tell her my name is Miles.

I tell her she can follow me and I'll show her the way to Mr. Clayton's class.

I'm staring at her because she hasn't spoken yet, but her nod is
the nicest thing a girl has ever said to me.
I ask her where she's from, and she tells me Arizona. "Phoenix,"
she specifies.
I don't ask her what brought her to California, but I do tell her
my father does business in Phoenix a lot because he owns a few
buildings there.
She smiles.
I tell her I've never been there but I'd like to go one day.
She smiles again.
I think she says it's a nice town, but it's hard to understand her
words when all I hear in my head is her name.
Rachel.
I'm gonna fall in love with you, Rachel.
Her smile makes me want to keep talking, so I ask her another
question as we pass Mr. Clayton's room.
We keep walking.
She keeps talking, because I keep asking her questions.
She nods some.
She answers some.
She sings some.
Or it sounds that way.
We get to the end of the hallway, right when she says
something about how she hopes she likes this school because
she wasn't ready to move away from Phoenix.
She doesn't look happy about the move.
She doesn't know how happy I am about the move.
"Where's Mr. Clayton's classroom?" she asks.
I stare at the mouth that just delivered that question. Her
lips aren't symmetrical. Her top lip is slightly thinner than
her bottom lip, but you can't tell until she talks. When
words come out of her mouth, it makes me wonder why

words are so much better coming from her mouth than any other mouth.

And her *eyes*. There's no way her eyes aren't seeing a prettier, more peaceful world than all the other eyes.

I stare at her for a few more seconds; then I point behind me and tell her we passed Mr. Clayton's classroom.

Her cheeks grow a shade pinker, like my confession affected her in the same way she's affecting me.

I smile again.

I nod my head toward Mr. Clayton's class.

We walk in that direction.

Rachel.

You're gonna fall in love with me, Rachel.

I open the door for her and let Mr. Clayton know that Rachel is new here. I also want to add, for the sake of all the other guys in the classroom, that Rachel is not theirs.

She's mine.

But I don't say anything.

I don't have to, because the only one who needs to be aware that I want Rachel is *Rachel.*

She looks at me and smiles again, taking the only empty seat, all the way across the room.

Her eyes tell me she already knows she's mine.

It's just a matter of time.

I want to text Ian and tell her she isn't hot. I want to tell him she's volcanic, but he would laugh at that.

Instead, I discreetly take a picture of her from where I'm seated.

I send the picture in a message to Ian that says, "She's gonna have all my babies."

Mr. Clayton begins class.

Miles Archer becomes obsessed.

• • •

I met Rachel on Monday.

It's Friday.

I've said nothing to her since the day we met. I don't know why. We have three classes together. Every time I see her, she smiles at me like she wants me to talk to her. Every time I work up the courage, I talk myself down.

I used to be confident.

Then Rachel happened.

I gave myself until today. If I didn't work up the courage by today, I'd be giving up my only shot with her. Girls like Rachel aren't available for long.

If she's even available.

I don't know her story or if she's wrapped up in a guy back in Phoenix, but there's only one way to find out.

I'm standing next to her locker, waiting for her. She exits the classroom and smiles at me. I say "Hi" when she walks up to her locker. I notice that same subtle change in her skin color. I like that.

I ask how her first week was. She tells me it was fine. I ask her if she's made any friends, and she shrugs as she says, "A few."

I smell her, subtly.

She notices anyway.

I tell her she smells good.

She says, "Thank you."

I push through the sound of my heart pounding in my ears. I push past the sheen of moisture developing on my palms. I drown out her name, which I keep wanting to repeat out loud, over and over. I push it all down and hold her stare while I ask her if she'd like to do something later.

I keep it all pushed away and make room for her response,
because it's the only thing I want.

I want that nod, actually. The one that doesn't require words?
Just a smile?

I don't get her nod.

She has plans tonight.

It all comes back tenfold, spilling over like a flood and I'm the
dam. The pounding, the sweaty palms, her name, a newfound
insecurity I never knew existed, burying itself in my chest. All
of it takes over and feels like it's building a wall around her.

"I'm not busy tomorrow, though," she says, obliterating the
wall with her words.

I make room for those words. Lots of room. I let them invade
me. I soak those words up like a sponge. I pluck them out of
the air and swallow them.

"Tomorrow works for me," I say. I pull my phone out of my
pocket, not even bothering to hide my smile. "What's your
number? I'll call you."

She tells me her number.

She's excited.

She's excited.

I save her contact in my phone, knowing it'll be there for a
long, long time.

And I'm gonna use it.

A lot.

chapter three

TATE

Normally, if I were to wake up, open my eyes, and see an angry man staring me down from a bedroom doorway, I might scream. I might throw things. I might run to the bathroom and lock myself inside.

I don't do any of these things, though.

I stare back, because I'm confused about how this is the same guy who was passed out drunk in the hallway. How is this the same guy who cried himself to sleep last night?

This guy is intimidating. This guy is angry. This guy is watching me like I should be giving him an apology or explaining myself.

It is the same guy, though, because he's wearing the same pair of jeans and the same black T-shirt he fell asleep in last night. The only difference in his appearance between last night and this morning is that he's now able to stand up without assistance.

"What happened to my hand, Tate?"

He knows my name. Does he know it because Corbin told him I was moving in or because he actually remembers my telling him last night? I'm hoping Corbin told him, because I don't really want him to remember last night. I suddenly feel embarrassed that he might recall my consoling him while he cried himself to sleep.

He apparently doesn't have a clue what happened to his hand, though, so I hope that means he has no recollection of anything beyond that.

He's leaning against my bedroom door with his arms folded across his chest. He looks defensive, like I'm the one responsible for his bad night. I roll over, still not quite finished with sleeping, even though he thinks I owe him some sort of explanation. I pull the covers over my head.

"Lock the front door on your way out," I say, hoping he'll take the hint that he is more than welcome to go back to his place now.

"Where's my phone?"

I squeeze my eyes shut and try to drown out the smooth sound of his voice as it slides into my ears and makes its way through every nerve in my body, warming me in places this flimsy blanket failed to do all night.

I remind myself that the person that sultry voice belongs to is now standing in the doorway, rudely demanding things without even acknowledging the fact that I helped him last night. I'd like to know where my *Thank you* is. Or my *Hey, I'm Miles. Nice to meet you.*

I get none of that from this guy. He's too worried about his hand. And his phone, apparently. Too worried about himself to be concerned about how many people his carelessness might have inconvenienced last night. If this guy and his attitude are going to be my neighbors for the next few months, I'd better set him straight now.

I toss the covers off and stand up, then walk to the door and meet his gaze. "Do me a favor and take a step back."

Surprisingly, he does. I keep my eyes locked with his until the bedroom door slams in his face and I'm looking at the back of the door. I smile and walk back to my bed. I lie down and pull the covers over my head.

I win.

Have I mentioned I'm not much of a morning person?

The door opens again.

Flies open.

"What the hell is wrong with you?" he yells.

I groan, then sit up on the bed and look at him. He's standing in the doorway once again, still looking at me like I owe him something.

"You!" I yell back.

He looks genuinely shocked at my harsh response, which kind of makes me feel bad. But *he's* the one being the jerk!

I think.

He started it.

I think.

He eyes me hard for a few seconds, then tilts his head slightly forward and arches an eyebrow.

"Did we . . ." He motions his finger back and forth between us. "Did we hook up last night? Is that why you're pissed?"

I laugh when my initial thoughts are confirmed.

He's being the jerk.

And this is great. I'm neighbors with a guy who gets shit-faced on weeknights and obviously brings home so many girls in the process that he can't even remember which ones he messed around with.

I open my mouth to respond but am cut off by the sound of the apartment door closing and Corbin's voice yelling out.

"Tate?"

I immediately jump up and rush to the door, but Miles is still blocking the doorway, glaring at me, expecting a response to his question. I look him straight in the eyes to give him an answer, but his eyes catch me off guard for a short moment.

They are the clearest blue eyes I've ever seen. Not at all the heavy-lidded, bloodshot eyes from last night. His eyes are so light blue they're almost colorless. I continue to stare at them, half expecting to see waves if I look closely enough. I'd say they were as clear blue as the waters of the Caribbean, but I've never actually been to the Caribbean, so I wouldn't know.

He blinks, and it immediately pulls me away from the Caribbean and back to San Francisco. Back to this bedroom. Back to the last question he asked before Corbin walked through the front door.

"Not sure if you can call what we did *hooking up*," I whisper.

I stare at him, waiting for him to move out of my way.

He stands taller, putting up an invisible wall of armor with his posture and his rigid body language.

Apparently, he doesn't like to envision the two of us making out, based on the unyielding look he's giving me. It almost seems like he's looking at me in disgust, which makes me dislike him that much more.

I don't back down, and neither of us breaks eye contact when he steps out of my way and allows me to pass him. Corbin is rounding the hallway when I exit my room. He glances back and forth between me and Miles, so I quickly shoot him a look to let him know that's not even remotely a possibility.

"Hey, Sis," he says, pulling me in for a hug.

I haven't seen him in almost six months. Sometimes it's easy to forget how much you miss people until you see them again. That's not the case with Corbin. I always miss him. As much as his protectiveness can get old at times, it's also a testament to how close we are.

Corbin releases me and pulls at a lock of my hair. "It's longer," he says. "I like it."

This may be the longest we've gone without seeing each other. I reach up and flick the hair hanging across his forehead. "So is yours," I say. "And I *don't* like it."

I smile to let him know I'm kidding. I actually like the shaggier look on him. People have always said we look a lot alike, but I don't see it. His skin is a lot darker than mine, which I've always envied. Our hair is the same rich hue of brown, but our facial features are nothing alike, specifically our eyes. Mom used to tell us that if we put our eyes together, they would look just like a tree. His were as green as the leaves, and mine were as brown as the trunk.

I always envied that he got to be the leaves of the tree, because green was my favorite color growing up.

Corbin acknowledges Miles with a nod of his head. "Hey, man. Rough night?" He asks the question with a laugh, as he knows exactly what kind of night Miles had last night.

Miles walks past both of us. "I don't know," he says in response. "I don't remember it." He walks into the kitchen and opens a cabinet, retrieving a cup like he's comfortable enough here to do so.

I don't like that.

I don't like comfortable Miles.

Comfortable Miles opens another cabinet and takes out a bottle of aspirin, fills his cup with water, and pops two of the aspirin into his mouth.

"Did you get all your stuff brought up?" Corbin asks me.

"Nope," I say, glancing at Miles when I respond. "I was kind of preoccupied with your neighbor most of the night."

Miles nervously clears his throat as he washes the glass and places it back in the cabinet. His discomfort with his lapse in memory makes me laugh. I like that he has no idea what happened last night. I even kind of like that the thought of being with me seems to unnerve him. I might keep this façade going for a while for my own sick enjoyment.

Corbin looks at me as if he knows what I'm trying to pull. Miles steps out of the kitchen and glances my way, then looks back to Corbin.

"I would have gone back to my place by now, but I can't find my keys. You have my spare set?"

Corbin nods and walks to a drawer in the kitchen. He opens it, grabs a key, and tosses it to Miles, who catches it in midair. "Can you come back in an hour and help me unload Tate's car? I want to shower first."

Miles nods, but his eyes cut briefly to mine as Corbin starts walking to his bedroom.

"We'll catch up when it's not too morning," Corbin tells me.

It may have been seven years since we've lived together, but he apparently remembers I'm not much of a talker in the morning. Too bad Miles doesn't know this about me.

After Corbin disappears into his bedroom, I turn and face Miles again. He's already looking at me expectantly, like he's still waiting for me to answer whatever questions he asked me earlier. I just want him to leave, so I answer them all at once.

"You were passed out in the hallway last night when I got here. I didn't know who you were, so when you tried to get inside the apartment, I might have slammed the door on your hand. It's not broken. I checked it out, and it's bruised at best. Just put some ice on it and wrap it for a few hours. And no, we didn't hook up. I helped you into the apartment, and then I went to bed. Your phone is on the floor by the front door where you dropped it last night because you were too shit-faced to walk."

I turn to head to my room, just wanting to get away from the intensity in his eyes.

I spin around when I reach my bedroom door. "When you come back in an hour and I've had a chance to wake up, we can try this again."

His jaw is firm. "Try *what* again?" he asks.

"Getting off on the right foot."

I close my bedroom door, putting up a barrier between me and that voice.

That *stare*.

• • •

"How many boxes do you have?" Corbin asks. He's slipping on his shoes by the door. I grab my keys off the bar.

"Six, plus three suitcases and all my clothes on hangers."

Corbin walks to the door directly across the hall and bangs on it, then turns and heads toward the elevators. He pushes the down button. "Did you tell Mom you made it?"

"Yeah, I texted her last night."

I hear his apartment door open just as the elevator arrives, but I don't turn to watch him walk out of it. I step in, and Corbin holds the elevator for Miles.

As soon as he comes into view, I lose the war. The war I didn't even know I was fighting. It doesn't happen often, but when I do find a guy attractive, it's better when it happens with a person I *want* it to happen with.

Miles is not the person I want to be feeling this for. I don't want to be attracted to a guy who drinks himself into oblivion, cries over other girls, and can't even remember if he screwed you the night before. But it's hard not to notice his presence when his presence becomes everything.

"Should just be two trips," Corbin says to Miles as he presses the button for the ground floor.

Miles is staring at me, and I can't quite judge his demeanor, because he still looks pissed. I stare back, because no matter how good-looking he may be with that attitude, I'm still waiting for the *thank you* I never got.

"Hi," Miles finally says. He steps forward and completely ignores unspoken elevator etiquette by stepping too close and holding out his hand. "Miles Archer. I live across the hall from you."

And I'm confused.

"I think we've established that," I say, looking down at his outstretched hand.

"Starting over," he says, arching a brow. "On the right foot?"

Ah. Yes. I did tell him that.

I take his hand and shake it. "Tate Collins. I'm Corbin's sister."

The way he steps back and keeps his eyes locked with mine makes me a little uncomfortable, since Corbin is standing only a foot away. Corbin doesn't seem to care, though. He's ignoring both of us, preoccupied with his phone.

Miles finally breaks his stare and pulls his phone out of his pocket. I take the opportunity to study him while his attention is off of me.

I come to the conclusion that his appearance is completely contradictory. It's as if two different creators were at war when he was envisioned. The strength in his bone structure contrasts with the soft, inviting appeal of his lips. They seem harmless and welcoming compared with the harshness in his features and the jagged scar that runs the length of the right side of his jaw.

His hair can't decide if it wants to be brown or blond or wavy or straight. His personality flips between inviting and callously indifferent, muddling my ability to discern hot from cold. His casual posture is at war with the fierceness I've seen in his eyes. His composure this morning contradicts his inebriated state from last night. His eyes can't decide if they want to look at his phone or at me, because they waver back and forth several times before the elevator doors open.

I stop staring and step off the elevator first. Cap is seated in his chair, ever so vigilant. He glances at the three of us exiting the elevator and pushes up on the arms of his chair, coming to a slow, shaky stand. Corbin and Miles both nod at him and continue walking.

"How was your first night, Tate?" he asks with a smile, stopping me midstride. The fact that he already knows my name doesn't surprise me, since he knew what floor I was going to last night.

I look at the back of Miles's head as they continue without me. "Kind of eventful, actually. I think my brother might have made a poor choice in the company he keeps."

I look at Cap, and he's staring at Miles now, too. His wrinkle-lined lips purse into a thin line, and he gives a slight shake of his head. "Ah, that boy probably can't help it none," he says, dismissing my comment.

I'm not sure if he's referring to Corbin or Miles when he says "that boy," but I don't ask.

Cap turns away from me and begins shuffling in the direction of the lobby restrooms. "I think I just pissed on myself," he mutters.

I watch him disappear through the restroom door, wondering at what point in a person's life he becomes old enough to lose his filter. Although Cap doesn't seem like the type of man who ever even *had* a filter. I kind of like that about him.

"Tate, let's go!" Corbin yells from the far end of the lobby. I catch up with them to show them the way to my car.

It takes three trips to get all my things up, not two.

Three entire trips where Miles doesn't speak another word to me.

chapter four

MILES

Six years earlier

Dad: "Where are you?"

Me: "Ian's house."

Dad: "We need to talk."

Me: "Can it wait until tomorrow? I'll be home late."

Dad: "No. I need you home now. I've been waiting for you
since school let out."

Me: "Fine. On my way."

That was the conversation that led to this moment. Me,
sitting in front of my dad on the couch. My dad, telling me
something I don't care to hear.

"I would have told you sooner, Miles. I just—"

"Felt guilty?" I interrupt. "Like you're doing something
wrong?"

34

His eyes meet mine, and I begin to feel bad for saying what I said, but I push the feeling down and keep going.

"She's been dead less than a year."

As soon as the words leave my mouth, I want to throw up.

He doesn't like being judged, especially by me. He's used to my supporting his decisions. Hell, *I'm* used to supporting his decisions. Until now, I always thought he made good ones.

"Look, I know this is hard for you to accept, but I need your support. You have no idea how hard it's been for me to move on since she died."

"Hard?" I'm standing. I'm raising my voice. I'm acting like I give a shit for some reason, when I really don't. I could care less that he's already dating again. He can see whoever he wants. He can screw whoever he wants.

I think the only reason I'm reacting this way is because she can't. It's hard to defend your marriage when you're dead. That's why I'm doing it for her.

"It's obviously not very hard for you at all, Dad."

I walk to the opposite end of the living room.

I walk back.

The house is too damn small to fit all of my frustration and disappointment.

I look at him again, recognizing that it's not so much the fact that he's seeing someone already. It's the look he gets in his eyes when he talks about her that I hate. I never saw him look at my mother that way, so whoever she is, I know it's not a casual thing. She's about to seep into our lives, intertwining around and through and between my relationship with my father like she's poison ivy. It'll no longer be just my father and me. It'll be me, my father, and *Lisa*. It doesn't feel right, considering my mother's presence is still everywhere in this house.

He's sitting with his hands folded in front of him, clasped together. He's looking down at the floor.

"I don't know if this will go anywhere, but I want to give it a shot. Lisa makes me happy. Sometimes moving on is . . . the only way to move on."

I open my mouth to respond to him, but my words are cut off by the doorbell. He looks up at me, hesitantly coming to a stand. He seems smaller. Less heroic.

"I'm not asking you to like her. I'm not asking you to spend time with her. I just want you to be nice to her." His eyes are pleading with me, and it makes me feel guilty for being so resistant.

I nod. "I will, Dad. You know I will."

He hugs me, and it feels good *and* bad. It doesn't feel like I just hugged the man I've had on a pedestal for seventeen years. It feels as though I just hugged my peer.

He asks me to get the door while he heads back to the kitchen to finish dinner, so I do. I close my eyes and let my mom know that I'm going to be nice to Lisa, but she'll always just be *Lisa* to me, no matter what happens between her and Dad. I open the door.

"Miles?"

I look at her face, and it's completely opposite from my mother's face. This makes me feel good. She's a lot shorter than my mother. She's not as pretty as my mother, either. There's nothing about her that can be compared to my mother, so I don't even try. I accept her for what she is: our dinner guest.

I nod and open the door wider to let her in. "You must be Lisa. Good to meet you." I point behind me. "My father is in the kitchen."

Lisa leans forward and gives me a hug—one that I successfully make awkward after it takes me several seconds to hug her back.

My eyes meet the eyes of the girl standing behind her.
The eyes of the girl standing behind her meet mine.

You're

    gonna

        fall

      in

          love

            with

            me,

             Rachel.

"Miles?" she says in a broken whisper.

Rachel sounds a little bit like her mother, but sadder.

Lisa looks back and forth between us. "You know each other?"

Rachel doesn't nod.

Neither do I.

Our disappointment melts to the floor and combines in a puddle of premature tears at our feet.

"He, um, . . . he . . ."

Rachel is stuttering, so I help her finish her words. "I go to school with Rachel," I blurt out. I regret saying that, because what I really want to say is, *Rachel is the next girl I'm gonna fall in love with.*

I can't say that, though, because it's obvious what's bound to happen. Rachel isn't the next girl I'll fall in love with, because Rachel is the girl who will more than likely become my new stepsister.

For the second time tonight, I feel sick.

Lisa smiles and clasps her hands together. "That's great," she says. "I'm so relieved."

My father walks into the room. He hugs Lisa. He says hi to Rachel and tells her it's good to see her again.

My father already knows Rachel.

Rachel already knows my father.

My father is Lisa's new boyfriend.

My father visits Phoenix a lot.

My father has been visiting Phoenix a lot since before my mother died.

My father is a bastard.

"Rachel and Miles already know each other," Lisa says to my father.

He smiles, and relief floods his face. "Good. Good," he says, repeating the word twice as if it could make things better.

No.

Bad. Bad.

"That'll make tonight a lot less awkward," he says with a laugh.

I look back at Rachel.

Rachel looks at me.

I can't fall in love with you, Rachel.

Her eyes are sad.

My thoughts are sadder.

And you can't fall in love with me.

She slowly walks inside, avoiding my gaze as she watches her feet with each step. They're the saddest steps I've ever seen taken.

I close the door.

It's the saddest door I've ever had to close.

chapter five

TATE

"Are you off for Thanksgiving?" my mother asks.

I switch my cell to my other ear and pull the apartment key out of my purse. "Yeah, but not Christmas. I only work weekends for now."

"Good. Tell Corbin we're not dead yet if he ever gets the urge to call us."

I laugh. "I'll tell him. Love you."

I hang up and put my cell phone into the pocket of my scrub top. It's only a part-time job, but it gets my foot in the door. Tonight was my last night of training before I start weekend rotations tomorrow night.

I like the job so far, and I was honestly shocked to land it after my first interview. It works out with my school schedule, too. I'm in school every weekday, doing either clinical or classroom hours, then I work second shift on the weekends over at the hospital. It's been a seamless transition up to this point.

I also like San Francisco. I know it's only been two weeks, but I could see myself staying here after graduation next spring rather than going back to San Diego.

Corbin and I have even been getting along, although he's gone more than he's home, so I'm sure that has everything to do with it.

I smile, finally feeling like I've found my place, and I open the door to the apartment. My smile fades as soon as it meets the eyes of three other guys—only two of whom I recognize. Miles is standing in the kitchen, and the married asshole from the elevator is sitting on the couch.

Why the hell is Miles here?

Why the hell are *any* of them here?

I glare at Miles as I kick off my shoes and drop my purse on the counter. Corbin isn't due back for two more days, and I was looking forward to the peace and quiet tonight so I could get some studying done.

"It's Thursday," Miles says when he sees the scowl on my face, like the day of the week is supposed to be some sort of explanation. He's watching me from his position in the kitchen. He can see I'm not happy.

"So it is," I reply. "And tomorrow is Friday." I turn to the other two guys sitting on Corbin's couch. "Why are you all in my apartment?"

The blond, lanky guy immediately stands up and walks over to me. He extends his hand. "Tate?" he asks. "I'm Ian. I grew up with Miles. I'm a friend of your brother's." He points to the elevator guy, who is still seated on the couch. "This is Dillon."

Dillon gives me a nod but doesn't bother speaking. He doesn't have to. His shit-eating grin says enough about what he's thinking right now.

Miles walks back into the living room and points to the television. "This is kind of a thing we do some Thursdays if either of us is home. Game night."

I don't care if it's their *thing*. I have homework.

"Corbin isn't even home tonight. Can't you do this at your apartment? I need to study."

Miles hands Dillon a beer and then looks back at me. "I don't have cable." *Of course you don't.* "And Dillon's wife doesn't let us use his place." *Of course she doesn't.*

I roll my eyes and walk to my bedroom, slamming the door unintentionally.

I change out of my scrubs and pull on a pair of jeans. I grab the shirt I slept in last night and just get it over my head when someone knocks on the door. I swing it open almost as dramatically as I slammed it earlier.

He's so *tall*.

I didn't realize how tall he was, but now that he's standing in my doorway—filling it—he seems really tall. If he were to wrap his arms around me right now, my ear would press against his heart. Then his cheek would rest comfortably on top of my head.

If he were to kiss me, I'd have to tilt my face up to meet his, but it would be nice, because he would probably wrap his arms around my lower back and pull me to him so that our mouths would come together like two pieces of a puzzle. Only they wouldn't fit very well, because they are most definitely not two pieces from the *same* puzzle.

Something strange is going on in my chest. A *flutter, flutter* kind of thing. I hate it, because I know what it means. It means my body is really starting to like Miles.

I just hope my brain never catches up.

"If you need quiet, you can go to my place," he says.

I cringe at the way his offer works knots into my stomach.

I shouldn't be excited about the possibility of being inside his apartment, but I am.

"We'll probably be here another two hours," he adds.

There's regret in his voice somewhere. It would more than likely take a search party to locate it, but it's buried there somewhere, beneath all the sultriness.

I expel a quick, relinquishing breath. I'm being a bitch. This isn't even my apartment. This is their *thing* that they obviously do on a regular basis, and who am I to think I can just move in and put a stop to it?

"I'm just tired," I say to him. "It's fine. I'm sorry if I was rude to your friends."

"*Friend*," he says as clarification. "Dillon is *not* my friend."

I don't ask him what he means by that. He glances into the living room, then looks back at me. He leans against the frame of the door, an indication that my relinquishing the apartment for their game wasn't the end of our conversation. He swings his eyes to the scrubs strewn across my mattress. "You got a job?"

"Yeah," I say, wondering why he's suddenly up for conversation. "Registered nurse in an ER."

A crease appears on his forehead, and I can't tell if it's a result of confusion or fascination. "Aren't you still in nursing school? How can you already work as an RN?"

"I'm getting my master's in nursing so I can work as a CRNA. I already have my RN license."

His expression is obstinate, so I clarify.

"It allows me to administer anesthesia."

He stares at me for a few seconds before standing up straight and pushing off the doorframe. "Good for you," he says.

There's no smile, though.

Why doesn't he ever smile?

He walks back to the living room. I step out of the doorway

and watch him. Miles takes his seat on the couch and gives the
TV his full attention.

Dillon is giving *me* his full attention, but I look away and
head to the kitchen to find something to eat. There isn't much,
considering I haven't cooked all week, so I grab all the stuff I
need from the refrigerator in order to make a sandwich. When
I turn around, Dillon is still staring. Only now he's staring from
about a foot away, instead of all the way from the living room.

He smiles, then steps forward and reaches into the refrigerator, coming inches from my face. "So you're Corbin's little sis?"

I think I'm with Miles on this one. I don't much like Dillon, either.

Dillon's eyes aren't anything like Miles's eyes. When Miles
looks at me, his eyes hide everything. Dillon's eyes don't hide
anything, and right now, they're clearly undressing me.

"Yes," I say simply as I make my way around him. I walk to
the pantry and open it to look for the bread. Once I find it, I
set it on the bar and begin making my sandwich. I lay out bread
for an extra sandwich to take to Cap. He's kind of grown on
me in the little time I've lived here. I found out he works up to
fourteen hours a day sometimes but only because he lives in the
building alone and doesn't have anything better to do. He seems
to appreciate my company and especially gifts in the form of
food, so until I make more friends here, I guess I'll be spending
my downtime with an eighty-year-old.

Dillon casually leans against the counter. "You a nurse or
something?" He opens his beer and brings it to his mouth but
pauses before taking a drink. He wants me to answer him first.

"Yep," I say with a clipped voice.

He smiles and takes a swig of his beer. I continue making my
sandwiches, intentionally trying to appear closed off, but Dillon
doesn't seem to take the hint. He just continues to stare at me
until my sandwiches are made.

I'm not offering to make him a damn sandwich if that's why he's still here.

"I'm a pilot," he says. He doesn't say it in a smug way, but when no one's asking you what your occupation is, voluntarily contributing it to the conversation naturally comes off as smug. "I work at the same airline as Corbin."

He's staring at me, waiting for me to be impressed by the fact that he's a pilot. What he doesn't realize is that all the men in my life are pilots. My grandfather was a pilot. My father was a pilot until he retired a few months ago. My brother is a pilot.

"Dillon, if you're trying to impress me, you're going about it the wrong way. I much prefer a guy with a little more modesty and a lot less *wife*." My eyes flash down to the wedding ring on his left hand.

"Game just started," Miles says, walking into the kitchen, directing his words toward Dillon. His words might be innocuous, but his eyes are definitely telling Dillon that he needs to return to the living room.

Dillon sighs as if Miles just stripped away all his fun. "It's good to see you again, Tate," he says, acting as if the conversation would have come to an end whether Miles decided it should or not. "You should join us in the living room." His eyes scroll over Miles, even though he's speaking to me. "Apparently, the game just started." Dillon straightens up and shoulders past Miles, heading back into the living room.

Miles ignores Dillon's display of annoyance and slides his hand into his back pocket, pulling out a key. He hands it to me. "Go study at my place."

It's not a request.

It's a demand.

"I'm fine studying here." I set the key on the counter and put the lid back on the mayonnaise, refusing to be displaced from my own apartment by three boys. I wrap both sandwiches in a paper towel. "The TV isn't even that loud."

He takes a step forward until he's close enough to whisper. I'm pretty sure I'm leaving finger indentations on the bread, considering every single part of me, right down to my toes, just tensed.

"*I'm* not fine with you studying here. Not until everyone leaves. Go. Take your sandwiches with you."

I look down at my sandwiches. I don't know why I feel like he just insulted them. "They aren't both for me," I say defensively. "I'm taking one to Cap."

I look back up at him, and he's doing that unfathomable staring thing again. With eyes like his, that should be illegal. I raise my eyebrows expectantly, because he's making me feel really awkward. I'm not an exhibit, yet the way he watches me makes me feel like one.

"You made a sandwich for Cap?"

I nod. "Food makes him happy," I say with a shrug.

He studies the exhibit a little longer before leaning into me again. He grabs the key off the bar behind me and slides it into my front pocket.

I'm not even sure if his fingers touched my jeans, but I inhale sharply and look down at my pocket as his hand pulls away, because *holy hell*, I wasn't expecting that.

I'm frozen while he's casually making his way back into the living room, unaffected. It feels like my pocket is on fire.

I persuade my feet to move, needing some time to process all of that. After delivering Cap's sandwich, I do as Miles says and head over to his apartment. I go on my own accord, not because he wants me over there and not because I really *do* have a lot of homework but because the thought of being inside his apartment without him there is sadistically exciting to me. I feel like I've just been handed a free pass to all his secrets.

. . .

I should have known better than to think his apartment would give me any sort of glimpse into who he is. Not even his eyes can do that.

Sure, it really is a lot quieter over here, and yeah, I've finished two solid hours of homework, but that's only because there aren't any distractions.

At *all*.

No paintings on the sterile white walls. No decorations. No color whatsoever. Even the solid oak table dividing the kitchen from the living room is undecorated. It's so unlike the home I grew up in, where the kitchen table was the focal point of my mother's entire house, complete with a table runner, an elaborate overhead chandelier, and plates to match whatever the current season was.

Miles doesn't even have a fruit bowl.

The only impressive thing about this apartment is the bookshelf in the living room. It's lined with dozens of books, which is more of a turn-on to me than anything else that could potentially line his barren walls. I walk over to the bookshelf to inspect his selection, hoping to get a glimpse of him based on his choice of literature.

Row after row of aeronautical themed books is all I find.

I'm a little disappointed that after a free inspection of his apartment, the best I can conclude is that he might be a workaholic with little to no taste in décor.

I give up on the living room and walk into the kitchen. I open the refrigerator, but there's hardly anything in it. There are a few takeout boxes. Condiments. Orange juice. It resembles Corbin's refrigerator—empty and sad and so very bachelor.

I open a cabinet, grab a cup, then pour myself some juice. I drink it and rinse the cup out in the sink. There are a few other dishes piled up on the left side of the sink, so I begin washing those, too. Even his plates and cups lack personality—plain and white and sad.

I have the sudden urge to take my credit card straight to the store and buy him some curtains, a new set of vibrant dishes, a few paintings, and maybe even a plant or two. This place needs a little life.

I wonder what his story is. I don't think he has a girlfriend. I've yet to see him with one up to this point, and the apartment and obvious lack of a female's touch make it a likely assumption. I don't think a girl could walk into this apartment without decorating it at least a little bit before she left, so I'm assuming girls just never walk into this apartment.

It makes me wonder about Corbin, too. All our years growing up together, he's never been open about his relationships, but I'm pretty sure that's because he's never been *in* a relationship. Every time I've ever been introduced to a girl in his past, she never seems to make it through an entire week with him. I don't know if that's because he doesn't like keeping someone around or if it's a sign that he's too difficult to *be* around. I'm sure it's the former, based on the number of random phone calls he receives from women.

Considering his abundance of one-night stands and lack of commitment, it confuses me how he could be so protective of me growing up. I guess he just knew himself too well. He didn't want me dating guys like him.

I wonder if Miles is a guy like Corbin.

"Are you washing my dishes?"

His voice catches me completely off guard, making me jump in my skin. I spin around and catch sight of a looming Miles, almost dropping the glass in my hands in the process. It slips, but I somehow manage to catch it before it crashes to the floor. I take a calming breath and set it down gently in the sink.

"Finished my homework," I say, swallowing the thickness that just swelled in my throat. I look at the dishes that are now in the strainer. "They were dirty."

He smiles.

I *think*.

Just as soon as his lips start to curl up, they mash back into a straight line. *False alarm*.

"Everyone's gone," Miles says, giving me the all clear to vacate his premises. He notices the orange juice still out on the counter, so he picks it up and puts it back in the refrigerator.

"Sorry," I mutter. "I was thirsty."

He turns to face me and leans his shoulder into the refrigerator, folding his arms over his chest. "I don't care if you drink my juice, Tate."

Oh, *wow*.

That was an oddly sexy sentence. So was his presence in delivering it.

Still no smile, though. *Jesus Christ*, this man. Does he not realize that facial expressions are supposed to accompany speech?

I don't want him to see my disappointment, so I turn back toward the sink. I use the sprayer to wash the remaining suds down the drain. I find it quite fitting, considering the weird vibes floating around his kitchen. "How long have you lived here?" I ask, attempting to alleviate the awkward silence as I turn and face him again.

"Four years."

I don't know why I laugh, but I do. He raises an eyebrow, confused about why his answer caused me to laugh.

"It's just that your apartment . . ." I glance toward the living room, then back to him. "It's kind of bland. I thought maybe you just moved in and haven't had a chance to decorate."

I didn't mean for that to come out like an insult, but that's exactly how it sounded. I'm just trying to make conversation, but I think I'm only making this awkwardness worse.

His eyes move slowly around his apartment as he processes my comment. I wish I could take it back, but I don't even try. I'd probably just make it worse.

"I work a lot," he says. "I never have company, so I guess it just hasn't been a priority."

I want to ask him why he never has company, but certain questions seem off limits to him. "Speaking of company, what's up with Dillon?"

Miles shrugs his shoulders, leaning his back completely against the refrigerator. "Dillon's an asshole who has no respect for his wife," he says flatly. He turns around completely and walks out of the kitchen, heading toward his bedroom. He pushes his bedroom door closed but leaves it open just enough so that I can still hear him speak. "Thought I'd warn you before you fell for his act."

"I don't fall for acts," I say. "Especially acts like Dillon's."

"Good," he says.

Good? Ha. Miles doesn't want me to like Dillon. I love that Miles doesn't want me to like Dillon.

"Corbin wouldn't like it if you started something up with him. He hates Dillon."

Oh. He doesn't want me to like Dillon for *Corbin's* sake. Why did that just disappoint me?

He walks back out of his bedroom, and he's no longer in his jeans and T-shirt. He's in a familiar pair of slacks and a crisp, white shirt, unbuttoned and open.

He's putting on a pilot's uniform.

"You're a pilot?" I ask, somewhat perplexed. My voice makes me sound oddly impressed.

He nods and walks into the laundry room adjacent to the kitchen. "That's how I know Corbin," he says. "We were in flight school together." He walks back into his kitchen with a laundry basket and sets it on the counter. "He's a good guy."

His shirt isn't buttoned.

I'm staring at his stomach.

Stop staring at his stomach.

Oh my word, he has *the V.* Those beautiful indentations on men that run the length of their outer abdominal muscles, disappearing beneath their jeans as if the indentations are pointing to a secret bull's-eye.

Jesus Christ, Tate, you're staring at his damn crotch!

He's buttoning his shirt now, so I somehow gain superhuman strength and force my eyes to look back up at his face.

Thoughts. I should have some of those, but I can't find them. Maybe it's because I just found out he's an airline pilot.

But why would that impress me?

It doesn't impress me that Dillon's a pilot. But then again, I didn't find out Dillon was a pilot while he was doing laundry and flaunting his abs. A guy folding laundry while flaunting his abs and being a pilot is seriously impressive.

Miles is fully dressed now. He's putting on his shoes, and I'm watching him like I'm in a theater and he's the main attraction.

"Is that safe?" I ask, finding a coherent thought somehow. "You've been drinking with the guys, and now you're about to be at the controls of a commercial jet?"

Miles zips his jacket, then picks up an already packed duffel bag from the floor. "I've only had water tonight," he says, right before exiting the kitchen. "I'm not much of a drinker. And I definitely don't drink on work nights."

I laugh and follow him toward the living room. I walk to the table to grab my things. "I think you're forgetting how we met," I say. "Move-in day? Someone-passed-out-drunk-in-the-hallway day?"

He opens the front door to let me out. "I have no idea what you're talking about, Tate," he says. "We met on an elevator. Remember?"

I can't tell if he's kidding, because there's no smile or gleam in his eyes.

He closes the door behind us. I hand him back his apartment key, and he locks his door. I walk to mine and open it.

"Tate?"

I almost pretend I don't hear him just so he'll have to say my name again. Instead, I turn around and face him, pretending to be completely unaffected by this man.

"That night you found me in the hallway? That was an exception. A very *rare* exception."

There's something unspoken in his eyes and maybe even in his voice.

He stands paused at his front door, poised to walk toward the elevators. He's waiting to see if I have anything to say in response. I should tell him good-bye. Maybe I should tell him to have a safe flight. That could be considered bad luck, though. I should just say good night.

"Was the exception because of what happened with Rachel?"

Yes. I really just chose to say that instead.

WHY did I just say that?

His posture changes. His expression freezes, as if my words jolted him with a bolt of lightning. He's more than likely confused that I said that, because he obviously doesn't remember anything about that night.

Quick, Tate. Recover.

"You thought I was someone named Rachel," I blurt out, explaining away the awkwardness as best I can. "I just thought maybe something happened between the two of you and that's why . . . you know."

Miles inhales a deep breath, but he tries to hide it. I hit a nerve.

We don't talk about Rachel, apparently.

"Good night, Tate," he says, turning away.

I can't tell what just happened. Did I embarrass him? Piss him off? Make him sad?

Whatever I did, I hate this thing now. This awkwardness that's filling the space between my door and the elevator he's now standing in front of.

I walk inside my apartment and close my door, but the awkwardness is everywhere. It didn't remain out in the hallway.

chapter six

MILES

Six years earlier

We eat dinner, but it's awkward.
Lisa and Dad try to include us in the conversation, but neither
of us is in the mood to talk. We stare at our plates. We push
around the food with our forks.
We don't want to eat.
Dad asks Lisa if she wants to go sit out back.
Lisa says yes.
Lisa asks Rachel to help me clear the table.
Rachel says okay.
We take the plates to the kitchen.
We're quiet.
Rachel leans against the counter while I load the dishwasher.
She watches me do my best to ignore her. She doesn't realize

she's everywhere. She's in everything. Every single thing has just become Rachel.

It's consuming me.

My thoughts aren't thoughts anymore.

My thoughts are Rachel.

I can't fall in love with you, Rachel.

I look at the sink. *I want to look at Rachel.*

I breathe in air. *I want to breathe in Rachel.*

I close my eyes. *I only see Rachel.*

I wash my hands. *I want to touch Rachel.*

I dry my hands on a towel before turning around to face her. Her hands are gripping the counter behind her. Mine are folded across my chest.

"They're the worst parents in the world," she whispers.

Her voice cracks.

My heart cracks.

"Despicable," I say to her.

She laughs.

I'm not supposed to fall in love with your laugh, Rachel.

She sighs. I fall in love with that, too.

"How long have they been seeing each other?" I ask her.

She'll be honest.

She shrugs. "About a year. It's been long-distance until she moved us here to be closer to him."

I feel my mother's heart breaking.

We hate him.

"A year?" I ask. "Are you sure?"

She nods.

She doesn't know about my mother. I can tell.

"Rachel?"

I say her name out loud, just like I've wanted to do since the second I met her.

She continues to look directly at me. She swallows, then
breathes out a shallow "Yeah?"

I step toward her.

Her body reacts. She stands taller but not by much. She
breathes heavier but not by much. Her cheeks grow redder but
not by much.

It's all just enough.

My hand fits her waist. My eyes search hers.

They don't tell me no, so I do.

When my lips touch hers, it's so many things. It's good and bad
and right and wrong and

revenge.

She inhales, stealing some of my breaths. I breathe into her,
giving her more. Our tongues touch and our guilt intertwines
and my fingers slide through the hair God made specifically
for her.

My new favorite flavor is Rachel.

My new favorite thing is Rachel.

I want Rachel for my birthday. I want Rachel for Christmas. I
want Rachel for graduation.

Rachel, Rachel, Rachel.

I'm gonna fall in love with you anyway, Rachel.

The back door opens.

I release Rachel.

She releases me but only physically. I can still feel her in every
other way.

I look away from her, but everything is still Rachel.

Lisa walks into the kitchen. She looks happy.

She has a right to be happy. She's not the one who died.

Lisa tells Rachel it's time to go.

I tell them both good-bye, but my words are only for Rachel.

She knows this.

I finish the dishes.

I tell my father Lisa was nice.

I don't tell him I hate him yet. Maybe I never will. I don't know what good it would do to let him know that I don't see him the same way anymore.

Now he's just . . . *normal*. Human.

Maybe that's the rite of passage before you become a man—realizing your father doesn't have life figured out any more than you do.

I go to my room. I take out my phone, and I text Rachel.

Me: What do we do about tomorrow night?

Rachel: We lie to them?

Me: Can you meet me at seven?

Rachel: Yes.

Me: Rachel?

Rachel: Yeah?

Me: Good night.

Rachel: Good night, Miles.

I turn off my phone, because I want that to be the last text I receive for the night. I close my eyes.

I'm falling, Rachel.

chapter seven

TATE

It's been two weeks since I've seen Miles but only two seconds since the last time I've thought about him. He seems to work just as much as Corbin does, and while it's nice to have the place to myself occasionally, it's also nice when Corbin isn't working and there's actually someone to talk to. I would say it's nice when Corbin and Miles are *both* off work, but that hasn't happened since I've lived here.

Until now.

"His dad is working, and he's off until Monday," Corbin says. I had no idea he'd invited Miles to come back home with us for Thanksgiving until just now. He's knocking on Miles's apartment door. "He doesn't have anything else to do."

I'm pretty sure I nod after hearing those words, but I turn and walk straight toward the elevator. I'm afraid that when Miles opens his door, my excitement over the fact that he's coming with us will be transparent.

I'm on the elevator, at the far back wall, when they both step on. Miles finds me and nods, but that's all I get. The last time I spoke to him, I made things completely awkward between us, so I don't say a word. I also try not to stare at him, but it's extremely difficult to focus on anything else. He's casually dressed in a baseball cap, jeans, and a 49ers T-shirt. I think that's why I find him hard to look away from, though, because I've always found guys more attractive when they put less effort into trying to appear attractive.

My eyes leave his clothes and meet his concentrated stare. I don't know whether to smile in embarrassment or look away, so I just choose to copy his next move, waiting for him to look away first.

He doesn't. He continues to watch me in silence for the remainder of the elevator ride, and I stubbornly do the same. When we finally make it to the ground floor, I'm relieved he steps off first, because I have to inhale a pretty noticeable breath, considering I haven't inhaled in at least sixty seconds.

"Where you three headed?" Cap asks once we're all off the elevator.

"Home to San Diego," Corbin says. "You have any plans for Thanksgiving?"

"Gonna be a busy day for flights," Cap says. "Reckon I'll be here working." He winks in my direction, and I wink back before he shifts his attention toward Miles. "How about you, boy? You headed home yourself?"

Miles silently watches Cap in the same way he silently stared at me on the elevator. This disappoints me tremendously, because on the elevator, I had a small glimmer of hope that Miles was staring at me like he was because he feels the same pull to me that I feel when I'm around him. But now, watching his visual standoff with Cap, I'm almost certain it doesn't mean Miles is attracted to a person simply because he stares unabashedly. Miles apparently just looks at *everyone* this way. A very silent and awkward five seconds follows, with neither of them speaking. Maybe Miles doesn't like being referred to as "boy"?

"Have a good Thanksgiving, Cap," Miles finally utters, not even bothering to answer Cap's question. He turns and begins walking through the lobby with Corbin.

I look at Cap and shrug my shoulders. "Wish me luck," I say quietly. "Seems Mr. Archer might be having another bad day."

Cap smiles. "Nah," he says, backing up a step toward his chair. "Some people just don't like questions is all." He falls into his chair. He gives me a farewell salute, and I salute him back before walking toward the exit.

I can't tell if Cap excuses Miles's rude behavior because he likes Miles or if he just makes excuses for *everyone*.

"I'll drive there if you want," Miles says to Corbin when we all reach the car. "I know you haven't slept yet. You can drive back tomorrow."

Corbin agrees, and Miles opens the driver's-side door. I climb into the backseat and try to figure out where to sit. I don't know if I should sit directly behind Miles, in the middle, or behind Corbin. Anywhere I sit, I'll feel him. He's everywhere.

Everything is Miles.

That's how it is when a person develops an attraction toward someone. He's nowhere, then suddenly he's everywhere, whether you want him to be or not.

It makes me wonder if I'm anywhere to him, but the thought doesn't last long. I can tell when a guy is attracted to me, and Miles definitely does not fall into that category. Which is why I need to figure out how to stop whatever this is I feel when I'm around him. The last thing I want right now is a silly crush on a guy when I've barely got time to focus on both work and school.

I pull a paperback out of my purse and begin to read. Miles turns on the radio, and Corbin lays his seat back and kicks his feet up on the dash. "Don't wake me up until we're there," he says, pulling his cap over his eyes.

I glance at Miles, and he's adjusting his rearview mirror. He turns around and looks behind us to back out of the spot, and his eyes briefly meet mine.

"You comfortable?" he asks. He turns around before getting my answer and puts the car in drive, then glances at me in the rearview mirror.

"Yep," I say. I make sure to tack a smile onto the end of that word. I don't want him to think I'm upset that he came, but it's hard for me not to appear closed off when I'm around him, since I'm trying so hard to be.

He looks straight ahead, and I look back down at my book.

Thirty minutes pass, and the movement of the car accompanied by my attempt to read is making my head hurt. I set the book down beside me and readjust myself in the backseat. I lean my head back and prop my feet up on the console between Miles and Corbin. He glances at me in the rearview mirror, and his eyes feel like they're hands, running over every inch of me. He holds his stare for no longer than two seconds, then looks back at the road.

I hate this.

I have no idea what's going through his head. He never smiles. He never laughs. He doesn't flirt. His face appears as if he keeps a constant veil of armor between his expressions and the rest of the world.

I've always been a sucker for the quiet types of guys. Primarily because most guys talk too much, and it's painful having to suffer through every single thought that goes through their heads. Miles makes me wish he were the opposite of the quiet type, though. I want to know all the thoughts that pass through his head. Especially the one thought that's in there right now, hiding behind that unwavering, stoic expression.

I'm still staring at him in the rearview mirror, trying to figure him out, when he glances at me again. I look down at my phone, a little embarrassed that he caught me staring at him. But that mirror is like a magnet, and dammit if my eyes don't shoot back up to it.

The second I look into the mirror again, so does he.

I look back down.

Shit.

This drive is about to be the longest drive of my entire life.

I make it three minutes, then I look again.

Shit. So does he.

I smile, amused by whatever game this is we're playing.

He smiles, too.

He.

Smiles.

Too.

Miles looks back at the road, but his smile remains for several seconds. I know, because I can't stop staring at it. I want to take a picture of it before it disappears again, but that would be weird.

He lowers his arm to rest it on the console, but my feet are in his way. I push up on my hands. "Sorry," I say, as I begin to pull them back.

His fingers wrap around my bare foot, stopping me. "You're fine," he says.

His hand is still wrapped around my foot. I'm staring at it.

Holy hell, his thumb just moved. *Deliberately* moved, stroking the side of my foot. My thighs clench together and my breath halts in my lungs and my legs tense, because I'll be damned if his hand didn't just caress my foot before he pulled it away.

I have to chew on the inside of my cheek to keep from smiling.

I think you're attracted to me, Miles.

• • •

As soon as we arrive at my parents' place, my father puts Corbin and Miles to work hanging Christmas lights. I take our things into the house and give Corbin and Miles my room, since it's the only one with two beds. I take Corbin's old bedroom, then head to the kitchen to help my mom finish prepping dinner.

Thanksgiving has always been a small affair at our house. Mom and Dad didn't like having to choose between families, and my dad was hardly ever home, since a pilot's busiest times of year are the holidays. My mother decided Thanksgiving would be reserved for immediate family only, so every year on Thanksgiving Day, it's always just been me, Corbin, Mom, and Dad, when Dad is home. Last year, it was just Mom and me, since Dad and Corbin were both working.

This year, it's all of us.

And *Miles.*

It's strange, him being here like this. Mom seemed happy to meet him, so I guess she didn't mind too much. My dad loves everyone, and he's more than happy to have someone else helping with the Christmas lights, so I know the presence of a third person doesn't bother him in the least.

My mother passes me the pan of boiled eggs. I begin cracking them to prepare them for deviled eggs, and she leans across the kitchen island and rests her chin in her hands. "That Miles sure is a looker," she says with an arch of her eyebrow.

Let me explain something about my mother. She's a great mom. A really great mom. But I have never been comfortable talking to her about guys. It started when I was twelve and I got my first period. She was so excited she called three of her friends to tell them before she even explained what the hell was happening to me. I learned pretty early on that secrets aren't secrets once they reach her ears.

"He's not bad," I say, completely lying. I'm absolutely lying, because he *is* a looker. His golden-brown hair paired with those mesmerizing blue eyes, his broad shoulders, the scruff that lines his firm jaw when he's had a couple of days off work, the way he always smells so fantastically delicious, like he just stepped out of the shower and hasn't even towel-dried yet.

Oh, my God.

Who the hell am I right now?

"Does he have a girlfriend?"

I shrug. "I don't really know him, Mom." I take the pan to the sink and run water over the eggs to loosen the shells. "How is Dad liking retirement?" I ask, attempting to change the subject.

My mother grins. It's a knowing grin, and I absolutely hate it.

I guess I never have to tell her anything, because she's my mom. She already knows.

I blush, then turn around and finish cracking the damn eggs.

chapter eight

MILES

Six years earlier

"I'm going to Ian's tonight," I tell him.
My father doesn't care. He's going out with Lisa. His mind is
on Lisa.
His everything is Lisa.
His everything *used* to be Carol. Sometimes his everything was
Carol and Miles.
Now his everything is Lisa.
That's okay, because my everything used to be him and Carol.
Not anymore.
I text her to see if she can meet me somewhere. She says Lisa
just left to come to my house. She says I can come to her house
and pick her up.
When I get there, I don't know if I should get out of the car. I
don't know if she wants me to.

I do.

I walk to her door, and I knock. I'm not sure what to say when she opens the door. Part of me wants to tell her I'm sorry, that I shouldn't have kissed her.

Part of me wants to ask her a million questions until I know everything about her.

Most of me wants to kiss her again, especially now that the door is open and she's standing right in front of me.

"Want to come in for a little while?" she asks. "She won't be back for a few hours, at least."

I nod. I wonder if she loves my nod as much as I love hers.

She shuts the door behind me, and I look around. Their apartment is small. I've never lived in a place this small. I think I like it. The smaller the house, the more a family is forced to love one another. They have no extra space *not* to. It makes me wish my dad and I would get a smaller place. A place where we'd be forced to interact. A place where we'd stop having to pretend that my mother didn't leave way too much space in our house after she died.

Rachel walks to the kitchen. She asks me if I want something to drink.

I follow her and ask her what she has. She tells me she has pretty much everything except milk, tea, soda, coffee, juice, and alcohol. "I hope you like water," she says. She laughs at herself. I laugh with her. "Water is perfect. Would have been my first choice."

She gets us each a glass of water. We lean against opposite counters.

We stare at each other.

I shouldn't have kissed her last night.

"I shouldn't have kissed you, Rachel."

"I shouldn't have let you," she tells me.

We stare at each other some more. I'm wondering if she would
let me kiss her again. I'm wondering if I should leave.

"It'll be easy to stop this," I say.

I'm lying.

"No, it won't," she says.

She's telling the truth.

"You think they'll get married?"

She nods. For some reason, I don't love this nod as much. I
don't love the question it's answering.

"Miles?"

She looks down at her feet. She says my name like it's a gun
and she's firing a warning shot and I'm supposed to run.

I sprint. "What?"

"We only rented the apartment for a month. I overheard her
on the phone with him yesterday." She looks back up at me.
"We're moving in with you in two weeks."

I trip over the hurdle.

She's moving in with me.

She'll be living in my house.

Her mother is going to fill all my mother's empty spaces.

I close my eyes. *I still see Rachel.*

I open my eyes. *I stare at Rachel.*

I turn around and grip the counter. I let my head fall between
my shoulders. I don't know what to do. I don't want to like her.

I don't want to fall in love with you, Rachel.

I'm not stupid. I know how lust works.

Lust wants what lust can't have.

Lust wants me to have Rachel.

Reasoning wants Rachel to go away.

I take Reasoning's side, and I turn to face Rachel again. "This
won't go anywhere," I tell her. "This thing with us. It won't end
well."

"I know," she whispers.

"How do we stop it?" I ask her.

She looks at me, hoping I'll answer my own question.

I can't.

Silence.

Silence.

Silence.

LOUD, DEAFENING SILENCE.

I want to cover my ears with my hands.

I want to cover my heart with armor.

I don't even know you, Rachel.

"I should leave," I say.

She tells me okay.

"I can't," I whisper.

She tells me okay.

We stare at each other.

Maybe if I stare at her enough, I'll get tired of staring at her.

I want to taste her again.

Maybe if I taste her enough, I'll get tired of tasting her.

She doesn't wait for me to reach her. She meets me halfway.
I grab her face and she grabs my arms, and our guilt collides
when our mouths collide. We lie to ourselves about the truth.
We tell ourselves we've got this . . . when we don't have it at
all.

My skin feels better with her touching it. My hair feels better
with her hands in it. My mouth feels better with her tongue
inside of it.

I wish we could breathe like this.

Live like this.

Life would feel better with her like this.

Her back is against the refrigerator now. My hands are beside
her head. I pull away and look at her.

"I want to ask you a million questions," I say to her.

She smiles. "I guess you'd better get started."

"Where are you going to college?"

"Michigan," she says. "What about you?"

"Staying here to get my bachelor's, and then my best friend, Ian, and I are going to flight school. I want to be a pilot. What do you want to be?"

"Happy," she says with a smile.

That's the perfect answer.

"When's your birthday?" I ask her.

"January third," she says. "I'll be eighteen. When's yours?"

"Tomorrow," I tell her. "I'll be eighteen."

She doesn't believe that my birthday is tomorrow. I show her my ID. She tells me happy early birthday. She kisses me again.

"What happens if they get married?" I ask her.

"They'll never approve of us being together, even if they don't get married."

She's right. It would be hard to explain to their friends. Hard to explain to the rest of the family.

"So what's the point of continuing this if we know it won't end well?" I ask her.

"Because we don't know how to stop."

She's right.

"You're going to Michigan in seven months, and I'll be here in San Francisco. Maybe that's our answer."

She nods. "Seven months?"

I nod. I touch her lips with my finger, because her lips are the kind of lips that need appreciating, even when they aren't being kissed. "We do this for seven months. We don't tell anyone. Then . . ." I stop talking, because I don't know how to say the words *We stop*.

"Then we stop," she whispers.

"Then we stop," I agree.

She nods, and I can actually hear our countdown begin.

I kiss her, and it feels even better now that we have a plan.

"We've got this, Rachel."

She smiles in agreement. "We've got this, Miles."

I give her mouth the appreciation it deserves.

I'm gonna love you for seven months, Rachel.

chapter nine

TATE

"Nurse!" Corbin yells. He walks into the kitchen, and Miles is following behind him. Corbin steps aside and points toward Miles. His hand is covered in blood. It's dripping. Miles is looking at me like I'm supposed to know what to do. This isn't an ER. This is my mom's kitchen.

"A little help here?" Miles says, gripping his wrist tightly. His blood is dripping all over the floor.

"Mom!" I yell. "Where's your first-aid kit?" I'm opening cabinets, trying to find it.

"Downstairs bathroom! Under the sink!" she yells.

I point toward the bathroom, and Miles follows me. I open the cabinet and pull out the kit. Closing the lid on the toilet, I direct Miles to take a seat, then I sit on the edge of the tub and pull his hand to me. "What'd you do?" I begin to clean it and inspect the cut. It's deep, right across the center of his palm.

"Grabbed the ladder. It was falling."

I shake my head. "You should have just let it fall."

"I couldn't," he says. "Corbin was on it."

I look up at him, and he's watching me with those contrastingly intense blue eyes of his. I look back down at his hand. "You need stitches."

"You sure?"

"Yeah," I say. "I can drive you to the ER."

"Can't you just stitch it up here?"

I shake my head. "I don't have the right supplies. I need sutures. It's pretty deep."

He uses his other hand to rifle through the first-aid kit. He pulls out a spool of thread and hands it to me. "Do your best."

"It's not like I'm sewing on a damn button, Miles."

"I'm not spending the whole day in an emergency room for a cut. Just do what you can. I'll be fine."

I don't want him to spend the day in an emergency room, either. That means he wouldn't be *here*. "If your hand gets infected and you die, I'm denying any part in this."

"If my hand gets infected and I die, I'd be too dead to blame you."

"Good point," I say. I clean his wound again, then take the supplies I'll need and lay them out on the counter. I can't get a good angle with how we're positioned, so I stand up and prop my leg on the edge of the tub. I put his hand on my leg.

I put his hand on my leg.

Oh, hell.

This isn't gonna work with his arm draped across my leg like this. If I want my hands to remain calm and not shake, I'm going to need to reposition us.

"This won't work," I say, turning to face him. I take his hand and rest it on the counter, then stand directly in front of him. The other way worked better, but I can't have him touching my leg while I do this.

"It's gonna hurt," I warn.

He laughs as though he knows pain and to him, this isn't pain.

I pierce his skin with the needle, and he doesn't even flinch. He doesn't make a sound.

He watches me work quietly. Every now and then, he looks up from my hand and watches my face. We don't speak, like always.

I try to ignore him. I try to focus on his hand and his wound and how it desperately needs to be closed, but our faces are so close, and I can feel his breath on my cheek every time he exhales. And he begins to exhale a lot.

"You'll have a scar," I say in a quiet whisper.

I wonder where the rest of my voice went.

I push the needle in for the fourth time. I know it hurts, but he doesn't let it show. Every time it pierces his skin, I have to stop myself from wincing for him.

I should be focusing on his injury, but the only thing I can sense is the fact that our knees are touching. The hand of his that I'm not stitching is resting on top of his knee. One of the tips of his fingers is touching my knee.

I have no idea how so much can be going on right now, but all I can focus on is the tip of that finger. It feels as hot against my jeans as a branding iron. Here he is with a serious gash, blood soaking into the towel beneath his hand, my needle piercing his skin, and all I can focus on is that tiny little contact between my knee and his finger.

It makes me wonder what that touch would feel like if there wasn't a layer of material between us.

Our eyes lock for two seconds, and then I quickly look back down at his hand. He's not looking at his hand at all now. He stares at me, and I do my best to ignore the way he's breathing.

I can't tell if his breathing has sped up because of how close I'm standing to him or because I'm hurting him.

Two of the tips of his fingers are touching my knee.

Three.

I inhale again and try to focus on finishing his stitches.

I *can't.*

This is deliberate. This touch isn't an accidental graze. He's touching me because he *wants* to be touching me. His fingers trail around my knee, and his hand slips to the back of my leg. He lays his forehead against my shoulder with a sigh, and he squeezes my leg with his hand.

I have no idea how I'm still standing.

"Tate," he whispers. He says my name painfully, so I pause what I'm doing and wait for him to tell me it hurts. I wait for him to ask me to give him a minute. That's why he's touching me, isn't it? Because I'm hurting him?

He doesn't speak again, so I finish the last stitch and knot the thread.

"It's over," I say, replacing the items on the counter. He doesn't release me, so I don't back away from him.

His hand slowly begins to slide up the back of my leg, all the way up my thigh, around to my hip and up to my waist.

Breathe, Tate.

His fingers grip my waist, and he pulls me closer, still with his head pressed against me. My hands find his shoulders, because I have to grab onto something in order to steady myself. Every muscle in my body somehow just forgot how to do its job.

I'm still standing, and he's still sitting, but I'm positioned between his legs now that he's pulled me so close. He slowly begins to lift his face from my shoulder, and I have to close my eyes, because he's making me so nervous I can't look at him.

I feel him tilt his face up to look at me, but my eyes are still closed. I squeeze them a little tighter. I don't know why. I don't know anything right now. I just know Miles.

And right now, I think Miles wants to kiss me.

And right now, I'm pretty damn sure I want to kiss Miles.

His hand slowly trails all the way up my back until he's touching the back of my neck. I feel like his hand has left marks on every single part of me he's touched. His fingers are at the base of my neck, and his mouth is no more than half an inch from my jaw. So close I can't distinguish if it's his lips or his breaths that are feathering my skin.

I feel like I'm about to die, and there isn't a damn thing in that first-aid kit that could save me.

He tightens his grip on my neck . . . and then he kills me.

Or he kisses me. I can't tell which, since I'm pretty sure they would feel the same. His lips against mine feel like everything. Like living and dying and being reborn, all at the same time.

Good Lord. He's kissing me.

His tongue is already in my mouth, gently caressing mine, and I don't even remember how that happened. I'm okay with it, though. I'm okay with this.

He begins to stand, but his mouth remains on mine. He walks me a few feet until the wall behind me replaces the hand that was on the back of my head. Now he's touching my waist.

Oh, my God, his mouth is so possessive.

His fingers are splayed out again, digging into my hip.

Holy hell, he just groaned.

His hand moves from my waist and glides down to my leg.

Kill me now. Just kill me now.

He lifts my leg and wraps it around him, then presses against me so beautifully I moan into his mouth. The kiss comes to an abrupt halt.

Why is he pulling away? Don't stop, Miles.

He drops my leg, and his palm hits the wall beside my head as if he needs the support to continue standing.

No, no, no. Keep going. Put your mouth back on mine.

I try to look at his eyes again, but they're shut.

They're regretting this.

Don't open them, Miles. I don't want to see you regret this.

He presses his forehead against the wall beside my head, still leaning against me as we both stand quietly, attempting to return air to our lungs. After several deep breaths, he pushes off the wall, turns around, and walks to the counter. Luckily, I didn't see his eyes before he opened them, and now his back is to me, so I can't see the regret he obviously feels. He picks up a pair of medical scissors and cuts through a roll of gauze.

I'm stuck to the wall. I think I'll be here forever.

I'm wallpaper now. That's it. That's all I am.

"I shouldn't have done that," he says. His voice is firm. Hard. Like metal. Like a sword.

"I didn't mind," I say. My voice isn't firm. It's like liquid. It evaporates.

He wraps his wounded hand, then turns around and faces me.

His eyes are firm like his voice was. They're also hard, like metal. Like swords, slicing through the ropes that held what little dangling hope I had for him and me and that kiss.

"Don't let me do that again," he says.

I want him to do that again more than I want Thanksgiving dinner, but I don't tell him that. I can't speak, because his regret is caught in my throat.

He opens the bathroom door and leaves.

I'm still stuck to the wall.

What.

The.

Hell?

• • •

I'm no longer stuck to the bathroom wall.

Now I'm stuck to my chair, conveniently seated at the dinner table next to Miles.

Miles, whom I haven't spoken to since he referred to himself or us or our kiss as "that."

Don't let me do "that" again.

I couldn't stop him if I wanted to. I want "that" so much I don't even want to eat, and he probably doesn't realize how much I love Thanksgiving dinner. Which means I want "that" a lot, and "that" isn't referring to the plate of food in front of me. "That" is Miles. Us. Me kissing Miles. Miles kissing me.

I'm suddenly very thirsty. I grab my glass and down half of my water in three huge gulps.

"Do you have a girlfriend, Miles?" my mother asks.

Yes, Mom. Keep asking him questions like that, since I'm too scared to do it myself.

Miles clears his throat. "No, ma'am," he says.

Corbin laughs under his breath, which stirs up a cloud of disappointment in my chest. Apparently, Miles has the same view on relationships as Corbin does, and Corbin finds it amusing that my mother would assume he's capable of commitment.

I suddenly find the kiss we shared earlier a lot less impactful.

"Well, aren't you quite the catch, then," she says. "Airline pilot, single, handsome, polite."

Miles doesn't respond. He smiles faintly and shovels a bite of potatoes into his mouth. He doesn't want to talk about himself.

That's too bad.

"Miles hasn't had a girlfriend in a long time, Mom," Corbin says, confirming my suspicion. "Doesn't mean he's single, though."

My mom tilts her head in confusion. So do I. So does Miles.

"What do you mean?" she says. Her eyes immediately grow wide, though. "Oh! I'm so sorry. That's what I get for being nosy." She says the last part of her sentence like she just came to some realization that I still haven't come to.

She's apologizing to Miles now. She's embarrassed.

Still confused.

"Am I missing something?" my dad asks.

My mother points her fork at Miles. "He's gay, honey," she says.

Um . . .

"Is not," my dad says firmly, laughing at her assumption.

I'm shaking my head. *Don't shake your head, Tate.*

"Miles isn't gay," I say defensively, looking at my mother.

Why did I say that out loud?

Now Corbin looks confused. He looks at Miles. A spoonful of potatoes is paused in midair in front of Miles, and his eyebrow is cocked. He's staring at Corbin.

"Oh, shit," Corbin says. "I didn't know it was a secret. Dude, I'm so sorry."

Miles lowers his spoonful of mashed potatoes to his plate, still eyeing Corbin with a perplexed look about him. "I'm not gay."

Corbin nods. He holds up his palms and mouths, "I'm sorry," like he didn't mean to reveal such a big secret.

Miles shakes his head. "Corbin. I'm not gay. Never have been and pretty sure I never will be. What the *hell*, man?"

Corbin and Miles are staring at each other, and everyone else is watching Miles.

"B-but," Corbin stutters. "You said . . . one time you told me . . ."

Miles drops his spoon and covers his mouth with his hand, stifling his loud laughter.

Oh, my God, Miles. Laugh.

Laugh, laugh, laugh. Please think this is the funniest thing that's ever happened, because your laugh is also so much better than Thanksgiving dinner.

"What did I say to you that made you think I was gay?"

Corbin sits back in his chair. "I don't remember, exactly. You said something about not being with a girl in more than three years. I just thought that was your way of telling me you were gay."

Everyone is laughing now. Even me.

"That was more than three years ago! This whole time, you've thought I was gay?"

Corbin is still confused. "But . . ."

Tears. Miles has tears he's laughing so hard.

It's beautiful.

I feel bad for Corbin. He's kind of embarrassed. I do like how Miles thinks it's funny, though. I like that it didn't embarrass him.

"Three years?" my dad says, still stuck on the same thought I'm still kind of stuck on.

"That was three years ago," Corbin says, finally laughing along with Miles. "It's probably been six by now."

The table slowly grows quiet. *This* embarrasses Miles.

I keep thinking about that kiss in the bathroom earlier and how I know for a fact it hasn't been six years since he's been with a girl. A guy with a mouth as possessive as that one knows how to use it, and I'm sure it gets used a lot.

I don't want to think about it.

I don't want my *family* thinking about it.

"You're bleeding again," I say, looking down at the blood-soaked gauze that's still wrapped around his hand. I turn to my mother. "Do you have any liquid bandage?"

"No," she says. "That stuff scares me."

I look at Miles. "After we eat, I'll check it," I say.

Miles nods but never looks at me. My mother asks me about work, and Miles is no longer the center of attention. I think he's relieved about that.

• • •

I turn off my light and crawl into bed, not sure what to make of today. We never spoke again after dinner, even though I spent a good ten minutes redressing his wound in the living room.

We didn't speak through the entire process. Our legs didn't touch. His finger didn't touch my knee. He didn't even look up at me. He just watched his hand the entire time, focused on it like it would fall off if he looked away.

I don't know what to think about Miles or that kiss. He's obviously attracted to me, or he wouldn't have kissed me. Sadly, that's enough for me. I don't even care if he *likes* me. I just want him to be attracted to me, because the liking can come later.

I close my eyes and try to fall asleep for the fifth time, but it's pointless. I roll onto my side and face the door just in time to see the shadow of someone's feet approach it. I watch the door, waiting for it to open, but the shadows disappear, and footsteps continue down the hall. I'm almost positive that was Miles but only because he's the only person on my mind right now. I release a few controlled breaths in order to calm myself down enough to decide whether I want to follow him. I'm only on the third breath when I hop out of bed.

I debate brushing my teeth again, but it's only been twenty minutes since I last brushed them.

I check my hair in the mirror, then open my bedroom door and walk as quietly as I can into the kitchen.

When I round the corner, I see him. All of him. He's leaning against the bar, facing me, almost like he was expecting me.

God, I hate that.

I pretend it's just a coincidence that we ended up here at the same time, even though it's midnight. "Can't sleep?" I walk past him to the refrigerator and reach for the orange juice. I take it out, pour myself a glass, then lean against the counter across from him. He's watching me, but he doesn't answer my question.

"Are you sleepwalking?"

He smiles, soaking me up from head to toe with his eyes like a sponge. "You really love orange juice," he says, amused.

I look down at my glass, then back up to him, and shrug. He takes a step toward me and motions for the glass. I hand it to him, and he brings it to his lips, takes a slow sip, and hands it back to me. All these movements are completed without his ever breaking eye contact with me.

Well, I definitely love orange juice *now*.

"I love it, too," he says, even though I never answered him.

I set the glass down beside me, grip the edges of the counter, and push myself up until I'm seated on it. I pretend he isn't invading my entire being, but he's still everywhere. Filling the kitchen.

The entire *house*.

It's way too quiet. I decide to make the first move.

"Has it really been six years since you've had a girlfriend?"

He nods without hesitation, and I'm both shocked and extremely pleased by that answer. I'm not sure why I like it. I guess it's just so much better than what I was imagining his life was like.

"Wow. Have you at least . . ." I don't know how to finish this sentence.

"Had sex?" he interjects.

I'm glad the only light on is the one over the kitchen stove, because I'm absolutely blushing right now.

"Not everyone wants the same things out of life," he says. His voice is soft, like a down comforter. I want to roll around in it, wrap myself up in that voice.

"Everyone wants love," I say. "Or at least sex. It's human nature."

I can't believe we're having this conversation.

He folds his arms across his chest. His feet cross at the ankles. I've noticed this is his form of personal armor. He's putting up his invisible shield again, guarding himself from giving too much away.

"Most people can't have one without the other," he says. "So I find it easier to just give up both." He's studying me, gauging my reaction to his words. I do my best not to give him one.

"So which of the two do you not want, Miles?" My voice is embarrassingly weak. "Love or sex?"

His eyes remain the same, but his mouth changes. His lips curl up into a barely there smile. "I think you already know the answer to that, Tate."

Wow.

I blow out a controlled breath, not even caring if he knows those words affected me like they did. The way he says my name makes me feel just as flustered as his kiss did. I cross my legs at the knees, hoping he doesn't notice it's my own personal armor.

His eyes drop to my legs, and I watch him softly inhale.

Six years. Unbelievable.

I look down at my legs, too. I want to ask him another question, but I can't look at him when I ask it. "How long has it been since you kissed a girl?"

"Eight hours," he replies without hesitation. I raise my eyes to his, and he grins, because he knows what I'm asking him. "The same," he utters quietly. "Six years."

I don't know what happens to me, but something changes. Something melts. Something hard or cold or covered in my own personal armor is turning to liquid now that I'm realizing what that kiss really meant. I feel like I'm nothing but liquid, and liquid doesn't do a good job of standing or walking away, so I don't move.

"Are you kidding me?" I ask, disbelievingly.

I think he's the one blushing now.

I'm so confused. I don't understand how I've pegged him so wrong or how what he's saying is even possible. He's good-looking. He has a great job. He definitely knows how to kiss, so why hasn't he been doing it?

"What's your deal, then?" I ask him. "You have STDs?" It's the nurse in me. I have no medical filter.

He laughs. "Pretty damn clean," he says. He still doesn't explain himself, though.

"If it's been six years since you kissed a girl, then why did you kiss me? I was under the impression you didn't even really like me. You're really hard to read."

He doesn't ask me why I'm under the impression that he doesn't like me.

I think if it's obvious to me that he's different when he's around me, it's been intentional on his part.

"It's not that I don't like you, Tate." He sighs heavily and runs his hands through his hair, gripping the back of his neck. "I just don't *want* to like you. I don't want to like *anyone*. I don't want to *date* anyone. I don't want to *love* anyone. I just . . ." He folds his arms back across his chest and looks down at the floor.

"You just what?" I ask, urging him to finish that sentence. His eyes slowly lift back to mine, and it takes all I have to stay seated on this counter with the way he's looking at me right now—like I'm Thanksgiving dinner.

"I'm attracted to you, Tate," he says, his voice low. "I want you, but I want you without any of that other stuff."

I have no thoughts left.

Brain = Liquid.

Heart = Butter.

I can still sigh, though, so I do.

I wait until I can think again. Then I think a *lot*.

He just admitted that he wants to have sex with me; he just doesn't want it to lead to anything. I don't know why this flatters me. It should make me want to punch him, but the fact that he chose to kiss me after not having kissed anyone for six straight years makes this new confession seem like I just won a Pulitzer.

We're staring at each other again, and he looks a little bit nervous. I'm sure he's wondering if he just pissed me off. I don't want him to think that, because, honestly, I want to yell "I won!" at the top of my lungs.

I have no idea what to say. We've had the strangest and most awkward conversations since I met him, and this one definitely takes the cake.

"Our conversations are so weird," I say.

He laughs with relief. "Yes."

The word *yes* is so much more beautiful coming from his mouth, laced with that voice. He could probably make any word beautiful. I try to think of a word I hate. I kind of hate the word *ox*. It's an ugly word. Too short and clipped. I wonder if his voice could make me love that word.

"Say the word *ox*."

His eyebrow rises, like he's wondering if he heard me right. He thinks I'm weird.

I don't care.

"Just say it," I tell him.

"Ox," he says, with slight hesitation.

I smile. *I love the word* ox. *It's my new favorite word.*

"You're so weird," he says, amused.

I uncross my legs. He notices. "So, Miles," I say. "Let me see if I've got this straight. You haven't had sex in six years. You haven't had a girlfriend in six years. You haven't kissed a girl in eight hours. You don't like relationships, obviously. *Or* love. But you're a guy. Guys have needs."

He's watching me, still amused. "Go on," he says with that unintentionally sexy smirk.

"You don't want to be attracted to me, but you are. You want to have sex with me, but you don't want to date me. You also don't want to *love* me. You also don't want *me* to want to love *you*."

I'm still amusing him. He's still smiling. "I didn't realize I was so transparent."

You're not, Miles. Believe me.

"If we do this, I think we should take it slow," I say teasingly. "I don't want to pressure you into anything you aren't ready for. You're practically a virgin."

He loses his smile and takes three deliberately slow steps toward me. I stop smiling, because he is seriously intimidating. When he reaches me, he places his hands on either side of me, then leans in close to my neck. "It's been six years, Tate. Believe me when I tell you . . . I'm ready."

Those all just became my new favorite words, too. *Believe* and *me* and *when* and *I* and *tell* and *you* and *I'm* and *ready*.

Favorites. All of them.

He pulls back and can more than likely tell I'm not breathing at the moment. He steps back to his spot opposite from me. He's shaking his head like he can't believe what just happened. "I can't believe I just asked you for sex. What kind of guy does that?"

I swallow. "Pretty much all of them."

He laughs, but I can tell he feels guilty. Maybe he's afraid I can't handle this. He might be right, but I'm not about to let him know that. If he thinks I can't handle this, he'll retract everything he's saying. If he retracts everything he's saying, that means I don't get to experience another kiss like the one he gave me earlier.

I'd agree to anything if it means I get to be kissed by him again. Especially if it means I get to experience *more* than just his kiss.

Simply thinking about it makes my throat dry. I pick up my glass and take another slow sip of my juice while I silently work this out in my head.

He wants me for sex.

I kind of miss sex. It's been a while.

I know I'm definitely attracted to him and can't think of anyone else in my life I'd rather have casual, meaningless sex with than my airline pilot, laundry-folding neighbor.

I set the cup of juice back down, then press my palms into the counter and lean slightly forward. "Listen to me, Miles. You're single. I'm single. You work way too much, and I'm focused on my career in an almost unhealthy way. Even if we wanted a relationship out of this, it would never work. Our lives wouldn't fit one. We also aren't really friends, so we don't have to worry about our friendship being ruined. You want to have sex with me? I'll totally let you. A lot."

He's watching my mouth like all my words just became his new favorite words. "A lot?" he asks.

I nod. "Yes. A lot."

He looks me in the eyes with a challenging stare. "Okay," he says, almost like it's a dare.

"Okay."

We're still several feet apart. I just told this guy I would have sex with him without any expectations, and he's still way over there, and I'm way over here, and it's becoming clear that I definitely had him pegged wrong. He's more nervous than I am. Although I think our nerves stem from two different places. He's nervous because he doesn't want this to turn into anything.

I'm nervous because I'm not so sure that *just sex* with him is possible. Based on the way I'm drawn to him, I have a pretty good feeling sex will be the least of our problems. Yet here I sit, pretending to be fine with *just sex*. Maybe if it starts out this way, it'll eventually end up being something more.

"Well, we can't have sex right now," he says.

Dammit.

"Why not?"

"The only condom I have in my wallet has probably disintegrated by now."

I laugh. I love his self-deprecating humor.

"I do want to kiss you again, though," he says with a hopeful smile.

I'm actually surprised he *isn't* kissing me. "Sure."

He slowly walks back to where I'm seated, until my knees are on either side of his waist. I'm watching his eyes, because they're looking at me like he's waiting for me to change my mind. I'm not changing my mind. I probably want this more than he wants this.

He brings his hands up and slides them through my hair, brushing his thumbs across my cheeks. He inhales a shaky breath while looking down at my mouth. "You make it so hard to breathe."

He punctuates his sentence with his kiss, bringing his lips over mine. Every remaining part of me that had yet to melt in his presence is now liquefied like the rest of me. I try to recall a time when a man's mouth felt this good against mine. His tongue slides across my lips, then dips inside, tasting me, filling me, claiming me.

Oh . . . my.

I.

Love.

His.

Mouth.

I tilt my head so I can taste more of it. He tilts his to taste more of mine. His tongue has a great memory, because it knows exactly how to do this. He drops his injured hand and rests it on my thigh, while his other hand grips the back of my head, crushing our lips together. My hands no longer have hold of his shirt. They're exploring his arms, his neck, his back, his hair.

I moan softly, and the sound causes him to press into me, pulling me several inches closer to the edge of the bar.

"Well, you're definitely not gay," someone says from behind us.

Oh, my God.

Dad.

Dad!

Shit.

Miles. Pulling away.

Me. Jumping off the bar.

Dad. Walking past us.

He opens the refrigerator and grabs a bottle of water, like he walks in on his daughter being felt up by his houseguest every single night. He turns around and faces us, then takes a long drink. When he's finished, he puts the lid back on the bottle of water and puts it back in the fridge. He closes the refrigerator and walks toward us, passing between us, putting even more space there.

"Go to bed, Tate," he says as he exits the kitchen.

I cover my mouth with my hand. Miles covers his face with his. We're both completely mortified. He more so than I, I'm sure.

"We should go to sleep," he says.

I agree with him.

We walk out of the kitchen without touching. We reach my bedroom door first, so I pause and turn around and face him. He pauses, too.

He looks to his left, then briefly to his right, to make sure we're alone in the hallway. He takes a step forward and steals another kiss. My back meets my bedroom door, but he's somehow able to pull his mouth away.

"You sure this is okay?" he asks, searching my eyes for doubt.

I don't know if this is okay. It feels good, and he tastes good, and I can't think of anything I want more than being with him. However, the reasons behind his six years of abstinence are what I'm concerned about.

"You worry too much," I say with a forced smile. "Would it help if we had rules?"

He studies me quietly before taking a step back. "It might," he says. "I can only think of two right now."

"What are they?"

His eyes focus on mine for several seconds. "Don't ask about my past," he says firmly. "And never expect a future."

I absolutely don't like either of those rules. They both make me want to change my mind about this arrangement and turn and run away, but instead, I'm nodding. I'm nodding because I'll take what I can get. I'm not Tate when I'm near Miles. I'm liquid, and liquid doesn't know how to be firm or stand up for itself. Liquid flows. That's all I want to do with Miles.

Flow.

"Well, I only have one rule," I say quietly. He waits for my rule. I can't think of a rule. I don't have any rules. Why don't I have rules? He's still waiting. "I don't know what it is yet. But when I think of it, you have to follow it."

Miles laughs. He leans forward and kisses me on the forehead, then walks toward his room. He opens the door but glances back at me for a brief second before disappearing into the room.

I'm not positive, but I'm pretty sure the expression I just saw on his face was fear. I just wish I knew what he was scared of, because Lord knows I know exactly what I'm afraid of.

I'm afraid of how this is going to end.

Six years earlier

Ian knows.
I had to tell him. After the first week of school, he knew
everything became Rachel.
Rachel knows Ian knows. Rachel knows he won't say
anything.
I give Rachel my room when she moves in, and I take the
spare bedroom. My room is the only spare bedroom with its
own bathroom. I want Rachel to have the better room.
"Do you want this box in here?" Ian asks Rachel. Rachel asks
what it is, and he tells her it's all her bras and underwear. "I
thought maybe I should just go ahead and put it in Miles's
room."
Rachel rolls her eyes at Ian. "Hush," she tells him. He laughs.

He likes that he's in on such a private thing. That's why he would never tell. He knows the power of secrets.

Ian leaves after all the boxes are unloaded. My father passes me in the hallway and pauses. His pause means I should pause, too.

"Thank you, Miles."

He thinks I'm okay with this. With the fact that he's allowing another woman to push out the last reminders of my mother.

I'm not okay with it.

I'm just pretending to be okay with it, because none of it matters. Rachel matters.

Not him.

"No problem," I say.

He begins walking, then pauses again. He tells me he appreciates that I'm being nice to Rachel. He says he wishes he and Mom could have given me a sibling when I was younger.

He says I make a good brother.

Words are awful when they come out of his mouth.

I walk back to Rachel's room. I close the door.

It's just the two of us.

We smile.

I walk to her and wrap my arms around her, then I kiss her neck. It's been three weeks since the first night I kissed her.

I can count the times I've kissed her since then. We can't interact like this at school. We can't interact like this in public. We can't interact like this in front of our parents. I can only touch her when we're alone, and we haven't been able to be alone much in the last three weeks.

Now?

Now I kiss her.

"We need a few guidelines so we don't get ourselves in

trouble," she says. She separates herself from me. She sits at my desk, and I sit on my bed.

Well . . . she sits at *her* desk, and I sit on *her* bed.

"First," she says, "no making out when they're home. It's too risky."

I don't want to agree to that rule, but I'm nodding my head.

"Second, no sex."

I'm not nodding anymore.

"Ever?" I ask her.

She's nodding. Oh, I *really* hate that nod.

"Why?"

She sighs heavily. "Sex will make it that much harder when our time is up. You know that."

She's right. She's also completely wrong, but I have a feeling she'll figure that out later.

"Can I ask what rule number three is before I agree to rule number two?"

She grins. "There is no rule number three."

I grin. "So sex is the only thing off limits? And we're talking penetration, right? Not oral?"

She covers her face with her hands. "Oh, my God, do you have to get so specific?"

She's cute when she's embarrassed. "Just clarifying. I have a lifetime of things I want to do to you and only six months left to do them all."

"Let's leave the specifics up to the situation," she says.

"Fair enough," I say, admiring the blush in her cheeks. "Rachel? Are you a virgin?"

Her cheeks grow even redder. She shakes her head and tells me no. She asks if that bothers me.

"Not at all," I say, being honest.

She asks if I'm a virgin, but her voice is timid when she asks it.

"No," I say. "But now that I've met you, I kind of wish I was."

She likes that I said this to her.

I stand up and prepare to head to my new bedroom to begin rearranging. Before I walk out, I lock her bedroom door from the inside, and then I turn around and smile at her.

I slowly walk to her.

I take her by the hands and pull her up. I wrap my arm around her lower back and pull her against me.

I kiss her.

chapter eleven

TATE

"I have to pee."

Corbin groans. "Again?"

"I haven't been in two hours," I say defensively.

I really don't have to use the bathroom, but I do need to get out of this car. After the conversation I had with Miles last night, the car feels different with him in it. It feels like there's more of him, and every minute that passes and he's not talking, I'm wondering what's going through his head. I'm wondering if he regrets our conversation. I'm wondering if he's going to pretend it never happened.

I wish my dad would have pretended it never happened. Before we left this morning, I was seated at the kitchen table with him when Miles walked in.

"Sleep well, Miles?" he asked as Miles took a seat at the table.

I thought he was going to flush with embarrassment, but

instead, he regarded my dad with a shake of his head. "Not too well," Miles replied. "Your son talks in his sleep."

My father picked up his glass and lifted it in Miles's direction. "Good to know you were in the room with Corbin last night."

Luckily, Corbin had yet to sit down and hear that comment from my father. Miles was quiet through the rest of breakfast, and the only time I noticed him speaking after that was when Corbin and I were both in the car. Miles stepped over to my father and shook his hand, saying something that only my father could hear. I tried to read my father's expression, but he kept a tight lid on it. My father is almost as good at hiding his thoughts as Miles is.

I really want to know what Miles said to my father this morning before we left.

I also want to know about a dozen other answers to questions I have about Miles.

When we were younger, Corbin and I always agreed that if we could have any superpower, it would be the ability to fly. Now that I know Miles, I've changed my mind. If I had a superpower, it would be infiltration. I would infiltrate his mind so I could see every single one of his thoughts.

I would infiltrate his heart and spread myself around like a virus.

I would call myself the Infiltrator.

Yeah. That has a nice ring to it.

"Go *pee*," Corbin says with agitation as he puts the car in park.

I wish I were in high school again so I could call him a butthole. Adults don't call their brothers buttholes, though.

I get out of the car and feel a little more like I can breathe again, until Miles opens his door and steps out of the car and into the world. Now Miles seems even bigger, and my lungs seem smaller. We walk together into the gas station, but we don't speak.

It's funny how that works. Sometimes not speaking says more than all the words in the world. Sometimes my silence is saying, *I don't know how to speak to you. I don't know what you're thinking. Talk to me. Tell me everything you've ever said. All the words. Starting from your very first one.*

I wonder what his silence is saying.

Once we're inside, he spots the sign for the bathrooms first, so he nods his head and steps in front of me. He leads. I let him. Because he's a solid and I'm a liquid, and right now, I'm just his wake.

When we reach the bathrooms, he walks into the men's restroom without pause. He doesn't turn and look at me. He doesn't wait for me to walk into the women's first. I push the door open, but I don't need to use the restroom. I just wanted to breathe, but he's not letting me. He's invading. I don't think he means to. He's just invading my thoughts and my stomach and my lungs and my world.

That's his superpower. Invasion.

The Invader and the Infiltrator. They pretty much have the same meaning, so I guess we make one screwed-up team.

I wash my hands and waste enough time to make it seem like I actually needed Corbin to stop here. I open the door to the bathroom, and he's invading again. He's in my way, standing in front of the doorway that I'm trying to exit.

He doesn't move, even though he's invading. I don't really want him to, though, so I let him stay.

"You want something to drink?" he asks.

I shake my head. "I have water in the car."

"Hungry?"

I tell him I'm not. He seems slightly disappointed that I don't want anything. Maybe he doesn't want to go back to the car yet.

"I might want some candy, though," I say.

One of his rare and treasured smiles slowly appears. "I'll buy you some candy, then."

He turns and walks toward the candy aisle. I stop next to him and look at my options. We stare at the candy for way too long. I don't even really want any, but we both stare at it anyway and pretend we do.

"This is weird," I whisper.

"What's weird?" he asks. "Picking out candy or having to pretend we don't both want to be in the backseat right now?"

Wow. I feel like I really did infiltrate his thoughts somehow. Only they were words that he willingly spoke. Words that made me feel really good.

"Both," I say steadily. I turn to face him. "Do you smoke?"

He gives me the look again. The look that tells me I'm weird. I don't care.

"Nope," he replies casually.

"Remember those candy cigarettes they sold when we were kids?"

"Yeah," he says. "Kind of morbid, if you think about it."

I nod. "Corbin and I used to get those all the time. There's no way in hell I'd let my child buy those things."

"I doubt they make them anymore," Miles says.

We face the candy again.

"Do you?" he asks.

"Do I what?"

"Smoke."

I shake my head. "Nope."

"Good," he says. We stare at the candy a little bit longer. He turns to face me, and I glance up at him. "Do you even want any candy, Tate?"

"Nope."

He laughs. "Then I guess we should get back to the car."

I agree with him, but neither of us moves.

He reaches down to my hand and touches it so softly it's as if he's aware he's made of lava and I'm not. He grips two of my fingers, not even coming close to holding my entire hand, and gives them a soft tug.

"Wait," I say to him, tugging back on his hand. He glances at me over his shoulder and then turns to face me completely. "What did you say to my father this morning? Before we left?"

His fingers tighten around mine, and his expression doesn't deviate from the poignant look he's perfected. "I apologized to him."

He turns toward the door once again, and I follow him this time. He doesn't release my hand until we're close to the exit. When he finally does let my hand fall, I evaporate again.

I follow him toward the car and hope I don't really believe I'm capable of infiltration. I remind myself he's made of armor. He's impenetrable.

I don't know if I can do this, Miles. I don't know if I can follow rule number two, because I suddenly want to climb into your future more than I want to climb into the backseat with you.

"Long line," Miles says to Corbin once we're both inside the car. Corbin puts the car in drive and changes the radio station. He doesn't care how long the line was. He wasn't suspicious, or he would have said something. Besides, there's nothing to be suspicious of yet.

We drive for a good fifteen minutes before I realize I'm not thinking about Miles anymore. For the last fifteen minutes of the drive, my thoughts have just been memories.

"Remember when we were kids and we wished our super-power could be to fly?"

"Yeah, I remember," Corbin says.

"You have your superpower now. You can fly."

Corbin smiles at me in the rearview mirror. "Yeah," he says. "I guess that makes me a superhero."

I lean back in the seat and stare out the window, a little envious of both of them. Envious of the things they've seen. The places they've traveled. "What's it like, watching the sunrise from up in the air?"

Corbin shrugs. "I don't really look at it," he says. "I'm too busy working when I'm up there."

This makes me sad. *Don't take it for granted, Corbin.*

"*I* look," Miles says. He's staring out his window, and his voice is so quiet I almost don't hear it. "Every time I'm up there, I watch it."

He doesn't say what it's like, though. His voice is distant, like he wants to keep that feeling to himself. I let him.

"You bend the laws of the universe when you fly," I say. "It's impressive. Defying gravity? Watching sunrises and sunsets from places Mother Nature didn't intend for you to watch them from? You really are superheroes, if you think about it."

Corbin glances at me in the rearview mirror and laughs. *Don't take it for granted, Corbin.* Miles isn't laughing, though. He's still staring out his window.

"You save lives," Miles says to me. "That's way more impressive."

My heart absorbs those words on impact.

Rule number two is not looking good from back here.

chapter twelve

MILES

Six years earlier

Rule number one of no fooling around while our parents are home has been amended.
It now consists of making out but only when we're behind a locked door.
Rule number two stands firm, unfortunately. Still no sex.
And a rule number three was recently added: no sneaking around at night. Lisa still checks on Rachel in the middle of the night sometimes, only because Lisa is the mother of a teenage daughter and it's the right thing to do.
But I hate that she does it.
We've made it an entire month in the same house. We don't talk about the fact that there are just a little more than five months left. We don't talk about what will happen when my father marries her mother. We don't talk about the fact that

when this happens, we'll be connected for much longer than
five months.

Holidays.

Weekend visits.

Reunions.

We'll both have to attend every function, but we'll be
attending as family.

We don't talk about that, because it makes us feel like what
we're doing is wrong.

We also don't talk about it because it's hard. When I think
about the day she moves to Michigan and I stay in San
Francisco, I can't see beyond that. I can't see anything where
she won't be my everything.

"We'll be back Sunday," he says.

"You'll have the house to yourself. Rachel is staying with a
friend. You should invite Ian over."

"I did," I lie.

Rachel lied, too. Rachel will be here all weekend. We
don't want to give them any reason to suspect us. It's
hard enough trying to ignore her in front of them. It's
hard pretending I have nothing in common with her,
when I want to laugh at everything she says. I want to
high-five everything she does. I want to brag to my father
about her intelligence, her good grades, her kindness,
her quick-wittedness. I want to tell him I have this really
amazing girlfriend whom I want him to meet because he
would absolutely love her.

He does love her. Just not in the way I wish he loved her.

I want him to love her for *me.*

We tell our parents good-bye. Lisa tells Rachel to behave, but
Lisa isn't really worried. As far as Lisa knows, Rachel is good.

Rachel behaves. Rachel doesn't break rules.

Except rule number three. Rachel is definitely breaking rule number three this weekend.

We play house.

We pretend it's ours. We pretend it's our kitchen, and she cooks for me. I pretend she's mine, and I follow her around while she cooks, holding on to her. Touching her. Kissing her neck. Pulling her away from the tasks she's trying to complete so I can feel her against me. She likes it, but she pretends not to. When we're finished eating, she sits with me on the couch. We put on a movie, but it doesn't get watched at all. We can't stop kissing. We kiss so much our lips hurt. Our hands hurt. Our stomachs hurt, because our bodies want to break rule number two so, so bad.

It's gonna be a long weekend.

I decide I need a shower, or I'll be begging for an amendment to rule number two.

I take a shower in her bathroom. I like this shower. I like it more than I liked it back when it was just my shower. I like seeing her things in here. I like looking at her razor and imagining what she looks like when she uses it. I like looking at her shampoo bottles and thinking about her with her head tilted back beneath the stream of water as she rinses it out of her hair.

I love that my shower is her shower, too.

"Miles?" she says. She's knocking, but she's already inside the bathroom. The water is hot on my skin, but her voice just made it even hotter. I open the shower curtain. Maybe I open it too far because I want her to *want* to break rule number two.

She inhales a soft breath, but her eyes fall where I want them to.

"Rachel," I say, grinning at the embarrassed look on her face. She looks me in the eyes.

She wants to take a shower with me. She's just too shy to ask.

"Get in," I say.

My voice is hoarse, like I've been screaming.

My voice was fine five seconds ago.

I close the shower curtain to hide what she's doing to me but also to give her privacy while she undresses. I haven't seen her without her clothes on. I've felt what's underneath them.

I'm suddenly nervous.

She turns the light off.

"Is that fine?" she asks timidly. I say it is, but I wish she were more confident. I need to make her more confident.

She opens the shower curtain, and I see one of her legs make its way in first. I swallow when the rest of her body follows. Luckily, there's just enough light from the night-light to cast a faint glow over her.

I can see her enough.

I can see her perfectly.

Her eyes lock with mine again. She steps closer to me. I wonder if she's ever shared a shower with anyone before, but I don't ask her. I take a step toward her this time, because she seems scared. I don't want her to be scared.

I'm scared.

I touch her shoulders and guide her so that she's standing under the water. I don't press myself against her, even though I need to. I keep distance between us.

I have to.

The only things that connect are our mouths. I kiss her softly, barely touching her lips, but it hurts so bad. It hurts worse than any other kiss we've shared. Kisses where our mouths collide. Our teeth collide. Frantic kisses that are so rushed they're sloppy. Kisses that end with me biting her lip or her biting mine.

None of those kisses hurt like this one does, and I can't tell why this one is hurting so much.

I have to pull back. I tell her to give me a minute, and she nods, then rests her cheek against my chest. I lean back against the wall and pull her with me while I keep my eyes closed tightly.

The words are once again attempting to break the barrier I've built up around them. Every time I'm with her, they want to come out, but I work and work to cement the wall that surrounds them. She doesn't need to hear them.

I don't need to say them.

But they're pounding on the walls. They always pound so hard until all our kisses end up like this. Me needing a minute and her giving me one. They need out now worse than ever before. They need air. They're demanding to be heard.

There's only so much pounding I can take before the walls collapse.

There are only so many times my lips can touch hers without the words spilling over the walls, breaking through the cracks, traveling up my chest until I'm holding her face, looking into her eyes, allowing them to tear down all the barriers that stand between us and the inevitable heartbreak.

The words come anyway.

"I can't see anything," I tell her.

I know she doesn't know what I'm talking about. I don't want to elaborate, but *the words come anyway*. They've taken over. "When you move to Michigan and I stay in San Fran? I don't see anything after that. I used to see whatever future I wanted, but now I don't see anything."

I kiss the tear that's running down her cheek.

"I can't do this," I tell her. "The only thing I want to see is you, and if I can't have that . . . nothing else is even worth it. You make it better, Rachel. Everything." I kiss her hard on the mouth, and it doesn't hurt at all this time, now that the words are free. "I love you," I tell her, freeing myself completely.

I kiss her again, not even giving her the chance to respond. I don't need to hear her say the words to me until she's ready, and I don't want to hear her tell me that the way I feel is wrong.

Her hands are on my back, tugging, pulling me closer. Her legs are wrapping around mine like she's trying to embed herself inside me.

She already has.

It's frantic again. Teeth-crashing, lip-biting, hurried, rushed, panting, touching.

She's moaning, and I can feel her trying to pull from my mouth, but my hand is wrapped in her hair, and I'm covering her mouth desperately, hoping she'll never break for breath.

She makes me release her.

I drop my forehead to hers, gasping in an effort to keep my emotions from spilling over the edge.

"Miles," she says breathlessly. "Miles, I love you. I'm so scared. I don't want us to end."

You love me, Rachel.

I pull back and look her in the eyes.

She's crying.

I don't want her to be scared. I tell her it'll be okay. I tell her we'll wait until we graduate, then we'll tell them. I tell her they'll have to be okay with it. Once we're out of the house, everything will be different. Everything will be good. They'll have to understand.

I tell her we've got this.

She nods feverishly.

"We've got this," she responds back, agreeing with me.

I press my forehead to hers. "We've got this, Rachel," I tell her.

"I can't quit you now. No way."

She takes my face between her palms, and she kisses me.

You fell in love with me, Rachel.

Her kiss removes a weight from my chest that is so heavy I feel
like I'm floating. I feel like she's floating with me.

I turn her until her back is against the wall.

I bring her arms above her head and link my fingers through
hers, pressing her hands into the tile wall behind her.

We look into each other's eyes . . . and we completely shatter
rule number two.

chapter thirteen

TATE

"Thanks for making me go," Miles says to Corbin. "Aside from another hand injury and finding out you thought I was gay, I had a good time."

Corbin laughs and turns to unlock our door. "It's not exactly my fault I assumed you were gay. You never talk about girls, and you've apparently left sex off your schedule for six years straight."

Corbin gets the door open and walks inside, toward his bedroom. I stand in the doorway, facing Miles.

He's looking straight at me. Invading me. "It's on the agenda now," he says with a smile.

I'm an *agenda* now. I don't want to be an agenda. I want to be a plan. A map. I want to be on a map to his future.

But that breaks rule number two.

Miles backs into his apartment after opening his door, and he nods his head in the direction of his bedroom.

"After he goes to sleep?" he whispers.

Fine, Miles. You can stop begging. I'll be your agenda.

I nod before closing the door.

I shower and shave and brush my teeth and sing and put on just enough makeup to make it look like I didn't put on any makeup at all. And fix my hair to make it look like I didn't fix my hair at all. And put back on the same clothes I had on earlier so it doesn't look like I changed clothes at all. But really, I changed my bra and my underwear, because they didn't match before but now they do. And then I freak the hell out because Miles will see my bra and underwear tonight.

And possibly touch them.

If it's part of his agenda, he might even be the one to remove them.

My phone receives a text, and the sound startles me, because a text isn't on the agenda at eleven o'clock at night. The text is from an unrecognized number. All it says is:

Is he in his room yet?

Me: How do you have my number?

Miles: I stole it from Corbin's phone while we were driving.

There's a weird voice in my head, singing, "Na-na-na-na boo-boo. He stole my number."

I'm such a child.

Me: No, he's watching TV.

Miles: Good. I have to run an errand. I'll be back in twenty minutes. Leaving the apartment unlocked in case he goes to bed before then.

Who runs errands at eleven o'clock at night?

Me: See ya.

I stare at my last text to him and cringe. It sounds way too casual. I'm giving him the impression that I do this all the time. He probably thinks all my days go something like this:

Random guy: Tate, you want to have sex?

Me: Sure. Let me finish up with these two guys, and I'll be right over. By the way, I don't have any rules, so anything goes.

Random guy: Awesome.

Fifteen minutes pass, and the television finally switches off. As soon as the door to Corbin's bedroom closes, mine opens. I'm across the living room and slipping out the front door and then bumping into Miles, who is standing in the hallway.

"Good timing," he says.

He's holding a bag. He moves it to his other hand so it's not as visible to me.

"After you, Tate," he says, pushing open his door.

No, Miles. I follow. That's how it is with us. You're solid, I'm liquid. You part the waters, I'm your wake.

"You thirsty?" He walks toward his kitchen, but I'm not sure if I can follow him this time. I don't know how to do this, and I'm scared he'll notice that I've never had a rule number one or two before. If the past and the future are off limits, that only leaves the present, and I have no idea what to do in the present.

I walk to the kitchen in the present. "What do you have?" I ask him.

The bag is on the counter now, and he sees me eyeing it, so he pushes it aside, out of my view.

"Tell me what you want, and I'll see if I have it," he says.

"Orange juice."

He grins, then reaches toward the bag. He pulls out a container of orange juice, and the simple fact that he even thought about it is testament to his generosity. It's also testament that it doesn't take much to make me melt. I should tell him my one rule has just become *Stop doing things that make me want to break your rules.*

I take the orange juice from him with a smile. "What else is in the bag?"

He shrugs. "Stuff."

He watches me open the juice. He watches me take a drink of the juice. He watches me put the lid back on the juice. He watches me set the juice on his kitchen counter, but he doesn't watch me closely enough to notice how fast I can lunge for the bag.

I grab it right before his arms wrap around my waist.

He's laughing. "Put it back, Tate."

I open it and look inside.

Condoms.

I laugh and toss it back onto the counter. When I turn around, his arms don't leave me. "I really want to say something inappropriate or embarrassing, but I can't think of anything. Just pretend I did and laugh anyway."

He doesn't laugh, but his arms are still around me. "You're so weird," he says.

"I don't care."

He smiles. "This whole thing is weird."

He's telling me how weird this is, but it feels pretty damn good to me. I'm not sure if weird feels good or bad to him. "Is weird good or bad?"

"Both," he says. "Neither."

"You're weird," I tell him.

He grins. "I don't care."

He moves his hands up my back, to my shoulders, and slowly down my arms until his hands are touching mine.

That reminds me.

I pull his hand between us. "How's your hand?"

"Fine," he says.

"I should probably check it out tomorrow," I say.

"I won't be here tomorrow. I leave in a few hours."

Two thoughts cross my mind. One, *I'm very disappointed he's leaving tonight.* Two, *Why am I here if he's leaving tonight?*

"Shouldn't you be asleep?"

He shakes his head. "I can't sleep now."

"You didn't even try," I say. "You can't fly a plane on no sleep, Miles."

"The first flight is short. Besides, I'm copilot. I'll sleep on the plane."

Sleep isn't on his agenda. *Tate* is.

Tate overrules sleep on his agenda.

I wonder what else Tate overrules?

"So," I whisper as I drop his hand. I pause, because I don't have anything to follow the *So.* Nothing. Not even a *la-ti-do.*

It's quiet.

It's getting awkward.

"So," he says. His fingers move through mine and spread them apart. My fingers like his fingers.

"Do you want to know how long it's been for me, since I know such an intimate detail about you?" I ask him.

It's only fair, considering my entire family knows how long it's been for him.

"No," he says simply. "But I do want to kiss you."

Hmm. Not sure how to take that, but I'm not about to analyze his *no* when it's followed up with a statement like that.

"Then kiss me," I say.

His fingers leave mine and move to the sides of my head, and he holds me still. "I hope you taste like orange juice again."

One, two, three, four, five, six, seven, eight.

I count the words in that last sentence, then search around in my head for a place to store those eight words forever. I want to hide them in a mind drawer and label it *Things to pull out and read when his stupid rule number two becomes a sad and lonely present.*

Miles is in my mouth. He's invading me again. I shut the mind drawer and get out of my head and come back to him.

Invade me, invade me, invade me.

I must taste like orange juice, because he's certainly acting as though he's enjoying the taste. I must enjoy tasting him, too, because I'm pulling him to me, kissing him, doing my best to infiltrate him with nothing but Tate.

He pulls away to catch his breath and speak. "I forgot how good this feels."

He's comparing me. I don't like that he's comparing me to whoever else once made him feel this good.

"Want to know something?" he says.

I do. I want to know everything, but for some reason, I pick this moment to get revenge on that one word he spoke to me.

"No." I pull him back to my mouth. He doesn't kiss me back right away, because he doesn't know what to think about what just happened. His mouth catches up pretty quickly, though. I think he hated my clipped response as much as I hated his, and now he's using his hands to get his own revenge. I can't tell where he's touching me, because as soon as he touches me in one spot, his hands move to another. He's touching me everywhere, nowhere, not at all, all at once.

My favorite part about kissing Miles is the sound. The sound of his lips when they close over mine. The sound of our breaths

UGLY LOVE | 113

being swallowed by each other. I love the way he groans when our bodies join together. Guys usually tend to hold back their sounds more than girls do.

Not Miles. Miles wants me, and he wants me to know it, and I love that.

God, I love that.

"Tate," he mutters against my mouth. "Let's go to my bedroom."

I nod, so he pulls away from my mouth. He reaches across the bar to get the box of condoms. He begins walking with me to his bedroom, but he quickly walks back into the kitchen and grabs the orange juice. When he shoulders past me to lead the way to his bedroom, he winks.

The way that one little wink makes me feel leaves me terrified about what it'll feel like once he's inside me. I don't know if I can survive it.

Once we're in his bedroom, I begin to grow apprehensive. Mostly because this is his place, and this whole situation is pretty much on his terms, and I feel a little bit at a disadvantage.

"What's wrong?" he asks. He's slipping off his shoes. He walks to the bathroom and flips off the light, then closes the door.

"I just got kind of nervous," I whisper. I'm standing in the middle of his bedroom, knowing exactly what's about to happen. Usually, these things aren't discussed and prearranged like this. They're spontaneous and heated, and neither party knows what's happening until it happens.

But Miles and I both know what's about to happen.

He walks to the bed and sits on the edge of it. "Come here," he says. I smile, then walk a few feet to where he's seated. He cups the backs of my thighs, then presses his lips to the T-shirt covering my stomach. My hands fall to his shoulders, and I look down at him. He's looking up at me, and the calmness in his eyes is contagious.

"We can go slow," he says. "It doesn't have to be tonight. That wasn't one of the rules."

I laugh, but I also shake my head. "No, it's fine. You're leaving in a few hours and won't be back for, what, five days?"

"Nine this time," he says.

I hate that number.

"I don't want to make you wait nine days after getting your hopes up," I say.

His hands slide up the backs of my thighs and come around to the front of my jeans. He flicks the button open effortlessly.

"Being able to imagine doing this with you is in no way torture for me," he says as his fingers touch my zipper. He begins to pull it down, and my heart is hammering away in my chest so hard it feels like it's building something. Maybe my heart is building a stairway for himself all the way to heaven, since he knows he'll explode and die the second these jeans slide off.

"It'll for sure be torture for me," I whisper.

My zipper is undone, and his hand is sliding inside my jeans. He pushes his hand around to my hip, then begins to tug them off.

I close my eyes and try not to sway, but his other hand has lifted up my shirt just enough for his lips to press against my stomach. It's overwhelming.

Both his hands slip inside my jeans now, around to my backside. He pushes my jeans down slowly until they're around my knees. His tongue meets my stomach, and my hands get lost in his hair.

When my jeans are finally around my ankles, I step out of both them and my shoes at the same time. His hands slide back up my thighs and to my waist. He pulls me to him so that I'm straddling him. He adjusts my legs on either side of him, then cups my rear and pulls me flush against him. I gasp.

I don't know why it seems like I'm the inexperienced one here. I certainly expected him to be a little less take-charge, but I'm not complaining.

Not at all.

I lift my arms for him when he attempts to pull off my shirt. He throws it to the floor behind me, and his lips reconnect with mine as his hands work the clasp of my bra.

It's not fair. I'm about to be left with one article of clothing, and he hasn't removed anything yet.

"You're so beautiful," he whispers, pulling back to slide off my bra. His fingers slip beneath the straps, and he begins to slide them down my arms. I'm holding my breath, waiting for him to take it off. I want his mouth on me so bad I can't think straight. When the bra lowers, revealing all of me, he exhales. "Wow," he says with shaky breath.

He tosses the bra onto the floor and looks back up at me. He smiles and briefly presses his lips to mine, kissing them softly. When he pulls back, he brings his hands up to my cheeks and looks me in the eyes. "You having fun?"

I bite my bottom lip to keep from smiling as much as I want to smile right now. He leans forward and takes my lip into his mouth, pulling it away from my teeth. He kisses it for a few seconds, then releases it. "Don't bite that again," he says. "I like seeing you smile."

Of course, I smile again.

My hands are on his shoulders, so I slide them lower on his back and begin to tug on his shirt. He releases my face and lifts his arms so I can take it off of him. I lean back and take him in, just as he's taking me in right now. I run my hands over his chest, touching every contour of every muscle. "You're beautiful, too."

He presses his palms into my back, urging me to sit up straight. As soon as I do, he lowers his mouth to my breast and softly glides his tongue across my nipple. I moan, and he covers it with his mouth completely.

One of his hands moves to my hip and slides beneath the hem of my underwear. "I want you on your back," he whispers. He keeps one hand on my back as he seamlessly switches positions, pulling me from his lap to his bed. He's bent over me now, pulling on my underwear as his tongue dips inside my mouth. My hands immediately fall to the button on his jeans, and I unbutton them, but he pulls away quickly. "I wouldn't do that yet," he warns. "Otherwise this will be over faster than it started."

I kind of don't care how long it lasts. I just really want his clothes off of him.

He begins to slide my underwear off of me. He bends one of my legs and slips it off my foot, then does the same to the other. He's definitely not looking me in the eyes anymore.

He allows my legs to fall back to the bed as he stands up straight and backs two feet away from me.

"Wow," he whispers, staring down on me. He's just standing here, staring at me as I lie naked on his bed, while he's still in the comfort of his jeans.

"This feels a little unfair," I say.

He shakes his head and pulls his fist against his mouth, biting his knuckles. He turns around until his back is to me and takes a long, deep breath. He faces me again, scrolling up the length of my body until he meets my eyes. "It's too much, Tate."

I feel the disappointment seep in with his words. He's still shaking his head, but he's walking to the nightstand. He picks up the box of condoms and opens it, then pulls one out and puts it between his teeth, ripping it open.

"I'm sorry," he says, frantically stepping out of his jeans. "I wanted this to be good for you. I wanted it to be memorable, at least." He's out of his jeans now. He's looking me in the eyes, but I'm finding it hard to keep eye contact with him, because now his boxers are off. "But if I'm not inside you in two seconds, this is going to be really embarrassing for me."

He walks swiftly to me and somehow slides the condom on at the same time as he's pushing my knees apart with his other hand. "I'll make it up to you in a few minutes. Promise," he says, pausing between my legs, waiting for my approval.

"Miles," I say, "I don't care about any of that. I just want you inside me."

"Thank God." He sighs. He takes my leg behind the knee with his right hand, and then his lips meet mine. He thrusts himself inside me so unexpectedly hard and fast I practically scream into his mouth. He doesn't stop to ask me if it hurts. He doesn't slow down. He pushes harder and deeper until there isn't any way we could possibly get any closer.

It does hurt but in the best possible way.

I'm moaning into his mouth, and he's groaning against my neck, and his lips are everywhere, along with his hands. It's rough. It's carnal and heavy and hot, and it's not quiet at all. It's fast, and I can tell by the tensing of his back beneath my hands that he was right. This won't take him long.

"Tate," he breathes. "*God*, Tate."

The muscles in his legs become tight, and he begins to shake. "*Fuck*," he groans. His lips press to mine, hard, and he holds himself still, despite the tremors moving throughout his legs and his back. He pulls his lips from mine and exhales a huge breath, dropping his forehead to the side of my head. "Jesus fucking *Christ*," he says, still tense. Still shaking. Still pressed deep inside me.

The second he pulls out of me, his lips are on my neck, moving down until they meet my breasts. He kisses them but only briefly before he's back at my mouth again. "I want to taste you," he says. "Is that okay?"

I nod.

I nod vigorously.

He pulls away from the bed, disposes of the condom, and returns to his spot next to me. I watch him the entire time, because—as much as he didn't want to know how long it's been since I've been with a guy—it's been almost a year. That's not anywhere near the six years he's waited, but it's been long enough that I don't want to miss this by keeping my eyes closed. Especially now that I get to stare freely at that *V* and not have to be embarrassed by the fact that I can't take my eyes off of him.

He's watching my body now with the same fascination as his hand glides across my stomach, then moves down until he reaches my thighs. He pushes my legs apart as he watches what he's doing to me with so much enthrallment I have to keep my eyes open so I can watch him watch me. Seeing what I do to him is enough of a turn-on without him even touching me.

Two of his fingers slide into me, and I suddenly find it a lot more difficult to continue watching him. His thumb remains outside me, teasing every spot it can touch. I moan and let my hands fall to the bed above my head as my eyes close.

I pray he doesn't stop. I don't want him to stop.

His mouth meets mine, and he kisses me softly, his lips a stark contrast to the pressure of his hand. His mouth slowly begins to explore its way down my chin until it's on my neck, the dip in my throat, trailing down my chest, covering my nipple, down my stomach, down, down, *holy shit*, down.

He settles himself between my legs, leaving his fingers inside me as his tongue meets my skin, separating me, causing my back to arch and my mind to let go.

I just let go.

I don't care that I'm moaning so loudly I probably just woke up the entire floor.

I don't care that I'm digging my heels into the mattress, trying to pull away from him because it's too much.

I don't care that his fingers leave me in order to grip my hips and hold me against his mouth, refusing to let me climb away from him, *thank God.*

I don't care that I'm more than likely hurting him, pulling his hair, pushing him into me, doing whatever I can to reach a point so high I'm almost positive I've never been there before.

My legs begin to shake, and his fingers find their way back inside me, and I'm pretty sure I'm trying to smother myself with his pillow, because I don't want to get him kicked out of this apartment building by screaming as loudly as I need to scream right now.

All of a sudden, I feel as if I'm up in the air, flying. I feel like I could look down and there would be a sunrise below me. I feel like I'm soaring.

I'm . . .

Oh, God.

I'm . . .

Jesus Christ.

I'm . . . this . . . *him.*

I'm falling.

I'm floating.

Wow.

Wow, wow, wow.

I never want to touch the ground again.

When I've completely melted to the bed, he hungrily works his mouth back up my body. He takes the pillow off my face and tosses it aside, then kisses me briefly.

"One more time," he says. He's off the bed and back on it in a matter of seconds, and then he's inside me again, but I don't even try to open my eyes this time. My arms are splayed out above my head, and his fingers are entwined with mine, and he's pushing, thrusting, living inside me. Our cheeks are pressed together, and his forehead is against my pillow, and neither of us has the energy left to even make a sound this time.

He tilts his head until his lips meet my ear, and then he slows down to a gentle rhythm, pushing into me, then pulling completely out. He holds himself still, then pushes into me again, then pulls all the way out. He does this several more times, and all I can do is lie here and feel him.

"Tate," he whispers, his lips close to my ear. He pulls out of me and stills himself again. "I can already say this with one hundred percent certainty."

He thrusts back inside me.

"The."

He pulls out, then repeats his movement again.

"Best."

Again.

"Thing."

Again.

"I've."

Again.

"Ever."

Again

"Felt."

He holds himself still, breathing heavily against my ear, gripping my hands so hard they hurt; but he doesn't make a single sound while he releases for the second time.

We don't move.

We don't move for a long time.

I can't wipe the exhausted smile off my face. I'm pretty sure it's there permanently now.

Miles pulls back and looks down on me. He smiles when he sees my face, and looking at him brings it to my attention that he never once made eye contact either time he was inside me. It makes me wonder if this was intentional or if it was just a coincidence.

"Comments?" he asks teasingly. "Suggestions?"

I laugh. "I'm sorry. I'm just . . . I can't . . . words . . ." I shake my head, letting him know I still need a little time before I can speak.

"Speechless," he says. "Even better."

He kisses me on the cheek, then stands up and walks to his bathroom. I close my eyes and wonder how in the hell this whole thing between us will ever end well.

It can't.

I can already tell because I never want to do this with anyone else ever again.

Only Miles.

He walks back into the bedroom and bends down to pick up his boxer shorts. He picks up my underwear and jeans in the process and lays them on the bed beside me.

I'm guessing that's his hint that he wants me to get dressed?

I sit up and watch as he picks up my bra and shirt and hands them to me. Every time his eyes meet mine, he smiles, but I'm finding it hard to smile back.

Once I'm dressed, he pulls me up and kisses me, then wraps his arms around me. "I changed my mind," he says. "After this, I'm pretty sure the next nine days are going to be pure torture."

I bite my smile, but he doesn't notice, because I'm still wrapped in his arms. "Yep."

He kisses me on the forehead. "Can you lock the door on your way out?"

I swallow my disappointment and somehow find the strength to smile at him when he releases me. "Sure." I walk toward his bedroom door and hear him fall onto his bed.

I leave, not knowing what to feel. He didn't promise me anything more than what just happened between us. We did what I willingly agreed to, which was have sex.

I just wasn't expecting this overwhelming feeling of embarrassment. Not because of the way he dismissed me immediately after we had sex but rather for the way that dismissal made me feel. I thought I would want this to be strictly sex between us just as much as he does, but based on the beating my heart took in the last two minutes, I'm not so sure I'm capable of anything simple with him.

There's a small voice in the back of my head, warning me to pull away from this situation before things become too complicated with him. Unfortunately, there's a much louder voice urging me to just go for it—telling me I deserve a little fun in my life with all the work I've got going on.

Just thinking about how much I enjoyed tonight is enough to make me accept and even embrace his casualness afterward. Maybe with a little more practice, I can even learn how to enforce it myself.

I walk to my apartment door but pause when I hear someone speaking. I press my ear to the door and listen. Corbin is having a one-sided conversation in the living room, presumably with someone on the other end of his cell phone.

I can't walk in now. He thinks I'm in bed.

I look back at Miles's apartment door, but I'm not about to knock on it. Not only would that be awkward, but it would also mean he'd get even less sleep than he's already about to get.

I walk to the elevator and decide to sit out the next half hour in the lobby, hoping Corbin will go back to his bedroom soon.

It's ridiculous that I even feel I have to hide this from Corbin, but the last thing I want is for him to be upset with Miles. And that's exactly what would happen.

I make it to the lobby and step off the elevator, not quite sure what I'm even doing. I guess I could go wait it out in my car.

"You lost?"

I glance over to Cap, and he's seated in his usual spot, despite the fact that it's almost midnight. He pats the empty chair next to him. "Have a seat."

I walk past him to the empty chair. "I didn't bring any food this time," I say. "Sorry."

He shakes his head. "I don't like you for your food, Tate. You're not that good of a cook."

I laugh, and it feels good to laugh. Things have just felt so intense for the past two days.

"How was Thanksgiving?" he asks. "Did the boy have a good time?"

I look at him and tilt my head in confusion. "The boy?"

He nods. "Mr. Archer. Didn't he spend the holiday with you and your brother?"

I nod, understanding his question now. "Yes," I say. I want to add that I'm pretty sure Mr. Archer just had the best Thanksgiving he's had in more than six years, but I don't. "Mr. Archer had a great time, I think."

"And what's the smile for?"

I immediately wipe away the grin I didn't realize was plastered on my face. I scrunch up my nose. "What smile?"

Cap laughs. "Oh, hell," he says. "You and the boy? Are you fallin' in love, Tate?"

I shake my head. "No," I say immediately. "It's not like that."

"How so, then?"

I quickly look away as soon as I feel the blush creep up my

neck. Cap laughs when he sees my cheeks turn as red as the chairs we're seated on.

"I may be old, but that don't mean I can't read body language," he says. "Does this mean you and the boy are . . . what's the term they use now? Hookin' up? Bumpin' uglies?"

I lean forward and bury my face in my hands. I can't believe I'm having this conversation with an eighty-year-old man.

I quickly shake my head. "I'm not answering that."

"I see," Cap says with a nod. We're both quiet for a moment while we process what I more or less just told him. "Well, good," he says. "Maybe that boy will actually smile every now and then."

I nod in complete agreement. I could definitely use more of his smile. "Can we change the subject now?"

Cap slowly turns his head toward me and arches his bushy gray eyebrow. "I ever tell you about the time I found a dead body on the third floor?"

I shake my head, relieved that he changed the subject but confused that the subject of a dead body has somehow helped me find relief.

I'm just as morbid as Cap.

chapter fourteen

MILES

Six years earlier

"Do you think the fact that we shouldn't be doing this is why
we like doing it so much?" Rachel asks.

She's referring to kissing me.

We kiss a lot.

Every chance we get and even chances we don't get.

"When you say *shouldn't*, do you mean because our parents are
together?"

She says yes. Her voice is breathless, because I'm currently
kissing my way up her neck.

I like that I take her breath away.

"Remember the first time I saw you, Rachel?"

She moans a sound that means yes.

"And do you remember me walking you to Mr. Clayton's
class?"

She gives me another wordless yes.

"I wanted to kiss you that day." I work my way back up to her mouth and look her in the eyes. "Did you want to kiss me?"

She says yes, and I can see in her eyes that she's thinking back to that day.

To the day she

Became

My

Everything.

"We didn't know about our parents that day," I explain. "Yet we still wanted to be doing this. So no, I don't think that's why we like it now."

She smiles.

"See?" I whisper, brushing my lips softly across hers to show her how good it feels.

She lifts off her pillow and holds herself up on her elbow. "What if we just like kissing in general?" she asks. "What if it has nothing to do with me or you in particular?"

She always does this. I tell her she should be a lawyer, because she likes playing devil's advocate so much. But I love it when she does it, so I always go along with it.

"Good point," I tell her. "I do like kissing. I don't know of anyone who *doesn't* like it. But there's a difference between *this* and simply liking to kiss."

She looks at me curiously. "What's the difference?"

I lower my mouth to hers once more. "*You*," I whisper. "I like kissing *you*."

That answers her question, because she shuts up and brings her mouth back to mine.

I like that Rachel questions everything.

It makes me look at things in a different way.

I have always enjoyed kissing the girls I've kissed in the past but only because I was attracted to them. It didn't really have anything to do with them in particular.

When I kissed all the other girls, I felt pleasure. That's why people enjoy kissing, because it feels good.

But when you like to kiss someone because of who she is, the difference isn't found in the pleasure.

The difference is found in the pain you feel when you're *not* kissing her.

It doesn't hurt when I'm not kissing any of the other girls I've kissed.

It only hurts when I'm not kissing Rachel.

Maybe this explains why falling in love is so damn painful.

I like kissing you, Rachel.

chapter fifteen

TATE

Miles: Are you busy?
Me: Always busy. What's up?
Miles: I need your help. Won't take long.
Me: Be there in five.

I should have given myself ten minutes rather than five, because I haven't had a shower today. After a ten-hour shift last night, I'm sure I need one. If I knew he was home, a shower would have been my top priority, but I thought he wasn't due back until tomorrow.

I pull my hair up into a loose bun and change from my pajama bottoms into a pair of jeans. It's not quite noon yet, but I'm embarrassed to admit I was still in bed.

He yells for me to come in after I knock on his door, so I push it open. He's standing on a chair next to one of the living-room windows. He glances down at me, then nods his head toward a chair.

"Grab that chair and push it right there," he says, pointing to a spot a few feet away from him. "I'm trying to measure these, but I've never bought curtains before. I don't know if I'm supposed to measure the outside frame or the actual window itself."

Well, I'll be damned. He's buying curtains.

I scoot the chair to the other side of the window and climb up onto it. He hands me one end of the measuring tape and begins to pull.

"It all depends on what kind of curtains you want, so I'd get measurements for both," I suggest.

He's dressed casually again in a pair of jeans and a dark blue T-shirt. Somehow the dark blue in his shirt make his eyes look less blue. It makes them look clear. See-through, almost, but I know that's impossible. His eyes are anything but see-through with that wall he keeps up behind them.

He enters the measurement into his phone, and then we take a second measurement. Once he's got both entered into his phone, we step down and push the chairs back under the table.

"What about a rug?" he asks, staring at the floor beneath the table. "You think I should get a rug?"

I shrug. "Depends on what you like."

He nods his head slowly, still staring down at the bare floor.

"I don't know what I like anymore," he says quietly. He tosses the tape measure onto the couch and looks at me. "You want to come?"

I refrain from immediately nodding. "Where to?"

He brushes his hair off his forehead and reaches for his jacket tossed over the back of his couch. "Wherever people buy curtains."

I should say no. Picking out curtains is something couples do. Picking out curtains is something friends do. Picking out curtains is not something Miles and Tate should do if they want to stick to their rules, but I absolutely, positively, most definitely don't want to do anything else.

I shrug to make my answer appear much more casual than it is. "Sure. Let me lock my door."

• • •

"What's your favorite color?" I ask him once we're on the elevator. I'm trying to stay focused on the task at hand, but I can't deny the desire I have for him to reach out and touch me. A kiss, a hug . . . anything. We're standing on opposite sides of the elevator, though. We haven't touched since the night we first had sex. We haven't even spoken or texted since then, either.

"Black?" he says, unsure of his own answer. "I like black."

I shake my head. "You can't decorate with black curtains. You need color. Maybe something close to black but not black."

"Navy?" he asks. I notice his eyes aren't focused on mine anymore. His eyes are scrolling slowly from my neck all the way down to my feet. Everywhere his eyes focus, I can feel it.

"Navy might work," I say quietly. I'm pretty sure this conversation is only taking place for the sake of having conversation. I can see by the way he's looking at me that neither of us is thinking about colors or curtains or rugs right now.

"Do you have to work tonight, Tate?"

I nod. I like that he's thinking about tonight, and I love how he ends most of his questions with my name. I love how he says my name. I should require him to say my name every time he speaks to me. "I don't have to be in until ten."

The elevator reaches the bottom floor, and we both move to the doors at the same time. His hand connects with the small of my back, and the current that moves through me is undeniable. I've had crushes on guys before, hell, I've even been in *love* with guys before, but none of their touches have ever been able to make me respond the way his do.

As soon as I step off the elevator, his hand leaves my back. I'm more aware of the absence of his touch now than before he even touched me. Each little bit I get, I crave it that much more.

Cap isn't in his usual spot. That's not surprising, though, considering it's only noon. He's not much of a morning person. Maybe that's why we get along so well.

"You feel like walking?" Miles asks.

I tell him yes, despite the fact that it's cold out. I prefer walking, and we're near several stores that would work for what he's looking for. I suggest a store I passed a couple of weeks ago that's only two blocks from where we are.

"After you," he says, holding the door open for me. I step outside and pull my coat a little tighter around me. I highly doubt Miles is the type of guy who holds hands in public, so I don't even worry about making my hands available to him. I hug myself to keep warm, and we begin walking side-by-side.

We're quiet most of the way, but I'm fine with it. I'm not someone who feels the need for constant conversation, and I'm learning that he might be the same way.

"It's right up here," I say, pointing to the right when we reach a crosswalk. I glance down at an elderly man seated on the sidewalk, bundled up in a tattered, thin coat. His eyes are closed, and the gloves on his shivering hands are rifled with holes.

I've always been sympathetic to people who have nothing and nowhere to go. Corbin hates that I can never pass homeless people without giving them money or food. He says the majority of them are homeless because they have addictions and that when I give them money, it only feeds those addictions.

Honestly, I don't care if that's the case. If someone is homeless because he has a need for something that is stronger than his need for a home, it doesn't deter me in the least. Maybe it's because I'm a nurse, but I don't believe addiction is a choice. Addiction is an illness, and it pains me to see people forced to live this way because they're unable to help themselves.

I would give him money if I had brought my purse.

I realize I'm no longer walking when I feel Miles steal a glance back in my direction. He's watching me watch the old man, so I pick up my pace and catch back up with him. I don't say anything to defend the troubled expression on my face. It's pointless. I've been through it enough with Corbin to know that I don't have the desire to try to change all the opinions I disagree with.

"This is it," I say, coming to a pause in front of the store.

Miles stops walking and inspects the display inside the store window. "Do you like that?" he asks, pointing at the window. I take a step closer and look at it with him. It's a bedroom display, but there are elements in it that he's looking for. The rug on the floor is gray with several geometric shapes in various shades of blue and black. It actually looks like something that would fit his taste.

The curtains aren't navy, though. They're a slate gray, with one solid white line running vertically down the left side of the panel.

"I do like it," I reply.

He steps in front of me and opens the door to let me walk in first. A saleswoman is making her way toward the front before the door even closes behind us. She asks if she can help us find anything. Miles points to the window. "I want those curtains. Four of them. And the rug."

The saleswoman smiles and motions for us to follow her. "What width and height do you need?"

UGLY LOVE | 133

Miles pulls his phone out and reads off the measurements to her. She helps him pick out curtain rods and then tells us she'll be a few minutes. She heads to the back and leaves us alone at the register. I look around, suddenly developing the urge to pick out decorations for my own place. I plan on staying with Corbin for a couple more months, but it wouldn't hurt to have an idea of what I'll want for my own place when I do finally move out. I'm hoping it'll be just as easy to shop when that time comes as it was for Miles today.

"I've never seen anyone shop this fast," I tell him.

"Disappointed?"

I quickly shake my head. If there's one thing I don't do well as a girl, it's shop. I'm actually relieved it only took him a minute.

"You think I should look around longer?" he asks. He's leaning against the counter now, watching me. I like the way he looks at me—like I'm the most interesting thing in the store.

"If you like what you already picked out, I wouldn't keep looking. When you know, you know."

I meet his gaze, and the second I do, my mouth gets dry. He's concentrating on me, and the serious look on his face makes me feel uncomfortable and nervous and interesting, all at once. He pushes off the counter and takes a step toward me.

"Come here." His fingers reach down and wrap around mine, and he begins to pull me behind him.

My pulse is being ridiculous. It's sad, really.

They're just fingers, Tate. Don't let them affect you like this.

He continues walking until he reaches a wooden trifold screen, decorated with Asian writing on the outside. It's the kind of screen people place in the corners of bedrooms. I never understood them. My mother has one, and I doubt she's ever once stepped behind it to change clothes.

"What are you doing?" I ask him.

He turns and faces me, still holding on to my hand. He grins and steps behind the screen, pulling me with him so we're both shielded from the rest of the store. I can't help but laugh, because it feels like we're in high school, hiding from the teacher.

His finger meets my lips. "Shh," he whispers, smiling down at me while he stares at my mouth.

I immediately stop laughing but not because I don't find this amusing anymore. I stop laughing because as soon as his finger is pressed against my lips, I forget how to laugh.

I forget everything.

Right now, the only thing I can focus on is his finger as it slides softly down my mouth and chin. His eyes follow the tip of his finger as it keeps moving, trailing gently down my throat, all the way to my chest, down, down, down to my stomach.

That one finger feels as if it's touching me with the sensation of a thousand hands. My lungs and their inability to keep up are signs of that.

His eyes are still focused on his finger as it comes to a pause at the top of my jeans, right above the button. His finger isn't even making contact with my skin, but you wouldn't know that based on the rapid response of my pulse. His entire hand comes into play now as he lightly traces my stomach over the top of my shirt until his hand meets my waist. Both of his hands grip my hips and pull me forward, securing me against him.

His eyes close briefly, and when he opens them again, he's no longer looking down. He's looking straight at me.

"I've been wanting to kiss you since you walked through my front door today," he says.

His confession makes me smile. "You have incredible patience."

His right hand leaves my hip, and he brings it up to the side of my head, touching my hair as softly as possible. He begins to shake his head in slow disagreement. "If I had incredible patience, you wouldn't be with me right now."

I latch on to that sentence and immediately try to figure out the meaning behind it, but the second his lips touch mine, I'm no longer interested in the words that left his mouth. I'm only interested in his mouth and how it feels when it invades mine.

His kiss is slow and calm—the complete opposite of my pulse. His right hand moves to the back of my head, and his left hand slips around to my lower back. He explores my mouth patiently, as if he plans on keeping me behind this partition for the rest of the day.

I'm summoning every last bit of willpower I can find in order to keep myself from wrapping my arms and legs around him. I'm trying to find the patience he somehow shows, but it's hard when his fingers and hands and lips can pull these kinds of physical reactions out of me.

The door to the back room opens, and the click of the saleswoman's heels can be heard against the floor. He stops kissing me, and my heart cries out. Luckily, the cry can only be felt, not heard.

Rather than pulling away to walk back to the counter, he brings both his hands to my face and holds me still while he looks at me in silence for several seconds. His thumbs brush lightly across my jaw, and he releases a soft breath. His brows furrow, and his eyes close. He presses his forehead to mine, still holding on to my face, and I can feel his internal struggle.

"Tate."

He says my name so quietly I can feel his regret in the words he hasn't even spoken yet. "I like . . ." He opens his eyes and looks at me. "I like kissing you, Tate."

I don't know why that sentence seemed hard for him to say,

but his voice trailed off toward the end as though he was attempting to stop himself from finishing his words.

As soon as the sentence leaves his mouth, he releases me and quickly steps around the partition as if he's trying to escape from his own confession.

I like kissing you, Tate.

Despite the regret I think he feels for saying them, I'm pretty sure I'll be silently repeating those words for the rest of the day.

I spend a good ten minutes mindlessly browsing, running his compliment through my head over and over while I wait for him to finish his transaction. He's handing over his credit card when I reach the counter.

"We'll have these delivered within the hour," the saleswoman says. She hands him back his credit card and begins to take the bags off the counter to place them behind her. He takes one of the bags from her when she begins to lift it. "I'll take this one," he says.

He turns and faces me. "Ready?"

We make our way outside, and it somehow feels as if it dropped twenty degrees since we were last out here. That may just be because he made things seem a lot warmer *inside*.

We reach the corner, and I begin to head back in the direction of the apartment complex, but I notice he's stopped walking. I turn around, and he's pulling something out of the bag he's holding. He tears away a tag, and a blanket unfolds.

No, he didn't.

He holds the blanket out to the old man still there bundled up on the sidewalk. The man looks up at him and takes the blanket. Neither of them says a word.

Miles walks to a nearby trash can and tosses the empty bag into it, then heads back toward me while staring down at the ground. He doesn't even make eye contact with me when we

UGLY LOVE | 137

both begin walking in the direction of the apartment complex.

I want to tell him thank you, but I don't. If I tell him thank you, it would seem like I assume he did that for me.

I know he didn't do it for me.

He did it for the man who was cold.

• • •

Miles asked me to go home as soon as we returned. He said he didn't want me to see his apartment until he had everything decorated, which was good, because I had a lot of homework to catch up on anyway. I didn't really have time carved out of my schedule to hang up curtains, so I appreciated that he didn't expect my help.

He seemed a little bit excited about hanging up new curtains. As excited as Miles can seem, anyway.

It's been several hours now. I have to be at work in less than three hours, and as soon as I begin to wonder if he's even going to ask me to come back over, I receive a text from him.

Miles: Have you eaten yet?
Me: Yes.

I'm suddenly disappointed that I already ate dinner. But I got tired of waiting for him, and he never said anything about dinner plans.

Me: Corbin made meat loaf last night before he left. You want me to bring you a plate?
Miles: I'd love that. Starving. Come look now.

I make him a plate and wrap it in foil before heading across the hall. He's opening the door before I even knock. He takes the plate out of my hands. "Wait here," he says. He steps inside his apartment and returns seconds later without the plate. "Ready?"

I have no idea how I know he's excited, because he's not smiling. I can hear it in his voice, though. There's a subtle change, and it makes me smile, knowing something as simple as hanging up some curtains makes him feel good. I don't know why, but it seems as if there isn't a lot in his life that makes him feel good, so I like that this does.

He opens the door all the way, and I take a few steps into the apartment. The curtains are up, and even though it's a small change, it feels huge. Knowing he's lived here for four years and he's just now putting up curtains gives the whole apartment a different feel.

"You made a good choice," I tell him, admiring how well the curtains match what little I know about his personality.

I look down at the rug, and he can see the confusion as it crosses my face.

"I know it's supposed to go under the table," he says, looking down at it. "It will. Eventually."

It's positioned in an odd spot. It's not in the center of the room or even in front of the couch. I'm confused about why he placed it where he did if he knows where it would look the best.

"I left it there because I was hoping we could christen it first."

I look back up at him and see the adorably hopeful expression on his face. It makes me smile. "I like that idea," I say, looking back down at the rug.

A long silence passes between us. I'm not sure if he wants to christen the rug right this minute or if he wants to eat first. I'm fine with either. As long as his plan fits within my three-hour time frame.

We're both still staring at the rug when he speaks again. "I'll eat later," he says, answering the question that was silently running through my head.

He pulls off his shirt, and I kick off my shoes, and the rest of our clothes eventually end up together, next to the rug.

chapter sixteen

MILES

Six years earlier

Everything is better now that I have Rachel.

Falling asleep is better, knowing Rachel is falling asleep right across the hall.

Waking up every morning is so much better, knowing Rachel is waking up right across the hall.

Going to school is better, now that we go together.

"Let's skip today," I tell Rachel when we pull into the parking lot of the school.

I'm sure skipping school is even better with Rachel.

"What if we get caught?"

She doesn't sound like she really cares if we get caught.

"I *hope* we get caught," I tell her. "That means we'd be grounded. Together. In the same house."

My words make Rachel smile. She leans across the seat and

slides her hand around my neck. I love it when she does that. "Being grounded with you sounds really fun. Let's do it." She leans forward and gives me a simple, quick peck on the lips.

Simple kisses are better when they're from Rachel.

"You make everything better," I tell her. "My life. It's better with you in it."

My words make Rachel smile again. Rachel doesn't know this, but every word I speak is voiced for that sole reason. *To make her smile.*

I pull out of the parking lot and tell Rachel we're going to the beach. She says she wants her bathing suit, so we go to the house first and get our bathing suits. We also pack a lunch and a blanket.

We go to the beach.

Rachel wants to sunbathe while she reads.

I want to watch Rachel sunbathe while she reads.

She's lying on her stomach, propped up on her elbows. I lay my head on my arms and watch her.

My eyes follow the smooth curves of her shoulders . . . the sway in her back . . . the way her knees are bent and her legs are up in the air with her feet crossed at the ankles.

Rachel is happy.

I make Rachel happy.

I make Rachel's life better.

Her life is better with me in it.

"Rachel," I whisper.

She places her bookmark inside the book and closes it, but she doesn't look at me.

"I want you to know something."

She nods, but she closes her eyes as though she wants to focus on my voice and nothing else.

"When my mom died, I stopped believing in God."

She lays her head on her arms and keeps her eyes shut.

"I didn't think God would make someone go through that much physical pain. I didn't think God would make someone suffer like she suffered. I didn't think God was capable of making someone go through something so ugly."

A tear falls from Rachel's closed eyes.

"But then I met you, and every single day since then, I've wondered how someone could be so beautiful if there wasn't a God. I've wondered how someone could make me so incredibly happy if God didn't exist. And I realized . . . just now . . . that God gives us the ugliness so we don't take the beautiful things in life for granted."

My words don't make Rachel smile.

My words make Rachel frown.

My words make Rachel cry.

"Miles," she whispers.

She says my name so quietly it's as if she doesn't want me to hear it.

She looks at me, and I can see that this moment isn't one of the beautiful moments for her. Not like it is for me.

"Miles . . . I'm late."

chapter seventeen

TATE

Corbin: Want to grab dinner? What time do you get off
work?
Me: Ten minutes. Where at?
Corbin: We're nearby. We'll just meet you out front.

We?

I can't ignore the excitement that just flooded me with that text. Surely the *we* means him and Miles. I can't think of anyone else who would be coming with him, and I know Miles came home last night.

I finish up the last of my paperwork, then make a stop in the restroom to check my hair (I hate that I care) before heading outside to meet them.

The three of them are standing near the entrance when I walk outside. Ian and Miles are both with Corbin. Ian smiles when he sees me, since he's the only one facing me. Corbin spins around when I reach them.

"Ready? We're going to Jack's."

They're quite the team. All good-looking in their own ways but even more so when they're sporting their pilot jackets and walking in a group like this. I can't deny I feel somewhat under-dressed, walking next to them in my scrubs. "Let's do it," I say. "I'm starving."

I glance at Miles, and he gives me the slightest nod but no smile. His hands are planted firmly in the pockets of his jacket, and he looks away as we all begin walking. He stays a step ahead of me the entire time, so I walk next to Corbin.

"What's the occasion?" I ask as we head toward the restaurant. "Are we celebrating the fact that all three of you are off on the same night?"

A silent conversation passes around me. Ian looks at Miles. Corbin looks at Ian. Miles looks at no one. He keeps his eyes forward, focused on the sidewalk ahead of us.

"Remember when we were kids and Mom and Dad took us to La Caprese?" Corbin asks.

I remember that night. I've never seen my parents happier. I couldn't have been older than five or six, but it's one of the few memories I have from that young an age. It was the day my father made captain with his airline.

I stop in my tracks and immediately look at Corbin. "You made captain? You can't get captain. You're too young." I know for a fact how hard it is to make captain and how many hours a pilot has to put in to be considered. Most pilots in their twenties are copilots.

Corbin shakes his head. "I didn't get captain. I've changed airlines too much." He cuts his eyes to Miles. "But Mr. Sign Me Up for More Hours over here got a nice little promotion today. Broke the company record."

I look at Miles, and he's shaking his head at Corbin. I can tell he's embarrassed that Corbin just called him out, but his modesty is just one more thing I find appealing about him. I have a feeling that if their friend Dillon were ever to make captain, he'd be on top of a bar somewhere, announcing it to the entire world with a megaphone.

"It's not that big a deal," Miles says. "It's a regional airline. Not many people to promote."

Ian shakes his head. "*I* didn't get promoted. *Corbin* didn't get promoted. *Dillon* didn't get promoted. You've been at this a year less than any of us, not to mention the fact that you're only twenty-four." He spins around and walks backward, facing all three of us. "Abandon the modesty for once, man. Rub it in our faces a little. We'd do it to you if the roles were reversed."

I don't know how long they've been friends, but I like Ian. I can tell he and Miles are close, because Ian is genuinely proud of him and not at all jealous. I like that these are Corbin's friends. It makes me happy for Corbin that he has this support. I've always pictured him living here, working too much, spending all his time alone and away from home. I don't know why, though. Our father was a pilot, and he was home a fair amount of time, so I shouldn't have misconceptions when it comes to Corbin's life as a pilot.

I guess Corbin isn't the only one to worry unnecessarily about his sibling.

We reach the restaurant, and Corbin holds the door open for us. Ian walks in first, and Miles steps back, allowing me to walk in ahead of him.

"I'm going to the restroom," Ian says. "I'll find you guys."

Corbin walks to the hostess stand, and Miles and I are both behind him. I steal a glance in Miles's direction. "Congratulations, Captain."

I say it under my breath, but I don't know why. It's not as if

Corbin would become suspicious if he heard me congratulating Miles. I guess I feel if I say it in a tone only Miles can hear, there's more meaning behind it.

Miles cuts his eyes to mine and smiles, then glances at Corbin. When he sees Corbin's back is still to us, he leans over and plants a quick kiss on the side of my head.

I should be ashamed of my weakness. A man should not be allowed to make me feel the way that stolen kiss just made me feel. It's as if I'm suddenly floating or sinking or flying. Anything that doesn't require support from my legs, because they've just become useless to me.

"Thank you," he whispers, still sporting that gorgeous yet somehow modest grin. He nudges my shoulder with his and looks down at his feet. "You look pretty, Tate."

I want to plaster those four words on a billboard and require myself to pass it on my drive to work every day. I would never take another day off work again.

As much as I want to believe he's being sincere with his compliment, I frown down at the scrubs I've been wearing for twelve hours straight. "I'm wearing Minnie Mouse scrubs."

He leans into me again until our shoulders are touching. "I've kind of always had a thing for Minnie Mouse," he says quietly.

Corbin turns around, so I immediately wipe the grin off my face. "Booth or table?"

Miles and I both shrug. "Either," he says to Corbin.

Ian returns from the restroom just as the hostess begins to lead us to our seats. Corbin and Ian lead the way, and Miles follows close behind me. *Really* close. His hand grips my waist as he leans forward toward my ear from behind me. "Kind of have a thing for nurses, too," he whispers.

I raise my shoulder to rub the ear he just whispered his admission into, because my entire neck is now covered in chills. He releases my waist and puts distance between us when we reach the booth. Corbin and Ian scoot into each side of the booth. Miles sits next to Ian, so I sit next to Corbin, directly across from Miles.

Miles and I both order sodas, compared with Ian and Corbin's beer. His drink choice is just one more thing to mull over. Several weeks ago, he admitted he doesn't usually drink, but considering he was beyond wasted the first night I met him, I figured he would at least have one drink tonight. He certainly has reason to celebrate. When the drinks are brought to the table, Ian raises his glass. "To showing us up," he says.

"Again," Corbin adds.

"To working twice as many hours as either of you," Miles says in mock defensiveness.

"Corbin and I actually have sex lives that interfere with working overtime," Ian retorts.

Corbin shakes his head. "No discussing my sex life in front of my sister."

"Why not?" I pipe up. "It's not like I don't notice all the random nights you spend away from the apartment when you aren't working."

Corbin groans. "I'm serious. Change of subject."

I grant him his request gladly. "How long have the three of you known each other?" I ask the question to no one in particular, but I only care to hear the answers that involve Miles.

"Miles and I have known your brother since meeting him in flight school a few years back. I've known Miles since I was nine or ten," Ian says.

"We were both eleven," Miles corrects. "We met during fifth grade."

I have no idea if this conversation is breaking rule one of no asking about the past, but Miles doesn't seem uncomfortable talking about it.

The waitress brings us a complimentary basket of bread, but none of us has even opened a menu yet, so she tells us she'll be back to take our order.

"I still can't believe you're not gay," Corbin says to Miles, completely changing the subject again while he opens his menu.

Miles peers at him over his menu. "I thought we weren't discussing sex lives."

"No," Corbin says. "I said we weren't discussing *my* sex life. Besides, you don't even have one to discuss." Corbin lays his menu flat on the table and engages Miles directly. "Seriously, though. Why don't you ever date?"

Miles shrugs, more interested in the drink between his hands than in having a stare-down with my brother. "Relationships aren't worth the end result to me."

Something in my heart cracks, and I start to worry that one of the guys might actually hear it fragmenting over the silence. Corbin leans back in the seat.

"Damn. She must have been a serious bitch."

My eyes are suddenly glued to Miles, waiting for his reaction to a possible revelation about his past. He gives his head a slight shake, silently dismissing Corbin's assumption. Ian gently clears his throat, and his expression changes as he loses the smile normally affixed to his face. It's obvious by Ian's reaction that whatever issues Miles has from his past, Ian is definitely aware of them.

Ian sits up straight in his seat and raises his glass, pasting a forced grin onto his lips. "Miles doesn't have time for girls. He's too busy breaking company records by becoming the youngest captain our airline has ever seen."

We take Ian's interruption for what it is and raise our glasses. We clink them together, and everyone takes a drink.

The appreciative look Miles shoots in Ian's direction doesn't go unnoticed by me, although Corbin seems to be clueless. Now I'm even more curious about Miles. And equally concerned that I'm getting in over my head, because the more time I spend with him, the more I want to know everything there is to know about him.

"We should celebrate," Corbin says.

Miles moves his menu down. "I thought that's what we were doing."

"I mean *after* this. We're going out tonight. We need to find a girl to put an end to your dry spell," Corbin says.

I almost spit my drink out, but luckily, I'm able to contain my laugh. Miles notices my reaction and taps my ankle under the table with his foot. But he leaves his foot right next to mine.

"I'll be fine," Miles says. "Besides, the captain needs his rest."

All the letters on the menu begin to blur as my mind replaces them with words like *ending* and *dry spell* and *rest.*

Ian looks at Corbin and nods. "I'll go. Let the captain go back to his apartment and sleep off the effects of his cola."

Miles pegs me with his eyes and adjusts slightly in his seat so that our knees touch. He wraps his foot around the back of my ankle. "Sleep actually sounds really good," he says. He trades my stare for the menu in front of him. "Let's hurry up and order so I can go back to my apartment and sleep. It feels like I haven't slept in more than nine days, and it's all I've been able to think about."

My cheeks are on fire, along with several other areas of my body.

"In fact, I kind of have the urge to fall asleep right now,"

Miles says. He lifts his eyes to meet mine. "Right here at the table."

Now the temperature in the rest of my body matches the heat in my cheeks.

"God, you're lame," Corbin says, laughing. "We should have brought Dillon instead."

"No, we should *not* have," Ian immediately says with an exaggerated roll of his eyes.

"What's the deal with Dillon?" I ask. "Why do you all hate him so much?"

Corbin shrugs. "It's not that we hate him. We just can't stand him, and none of us realized it until after we had already invited him to our game nights. He's a prick." Corbin shoots me that all-too-familiar glare. "And I don't ever want you alone with him. Being married doesn't stop him from being an asshole."

And *there's* that possessive, brotherly love I've been missing all these years.

"Is he dangerous?"

"No," Corbin says. "I just know how he treats his marriage, and I don't want you getting involved with that. But I've already made it clear to him that you're off limits."

I laugh at his absurdity. "I'm twenty-three, Corbin. You can stop acting like Dad now."

His face pinches together, and for a second, he even starts resembling our dad. "The hell I will," Corbin growls. "You're my little sister. I have standards for you, and Dillon doesn't come close to meeting even one of them."

He hasn't changed a bit. As annoying as it was in high school, and still kind of is, I do love that he wants the best for me. I'm just afraid his version of what's best for me doesn't exist.

"Corbin, no guy will ever come close to the standards you've set for me."

He nods, getting all righteous. "Damn right."

If he warned Dillon to stay away from me, it makes me wonder if he warned Miles and Ian, too. Then again, he did think Miles was gay, so he probably didn't see a possibility there.

I wonder if Miles would meet Corbin's standards.

My eyes want to look at Miles so incredibly much right now, but I'm afraid I'd be too obvious. Instead, I force a smile and shake my head. "Why couldn't I have been born first?"

"Wouldn't have made a difference," Corbin replies.

• • •

Ian smiles at the waitress and motions for the check. "It's on me tonight." He lays down enough cash to cover the bill and tip, and we all stand and stretch.

"So who's going where?" Miles asks.

"Bar," Corbin replies immediately, blurting it out like he's calling dibs.

"I just got off a twelve-hour shift," I say. "I'm beat."

"Mind if I catch a ride with you?" Miles asks as we all make our way outside. "I don't feel like going out tonight. I just want *sleep*."

I like how he doesn't disguise the emphasis in front of Corbin when he says *sleep*. It's like he wants to ensure that I'm aware he has no intentions of actually sleeping.

"Yeah, my car is back at the hospital," I say, pointing in that general direction.

"All right, then," Corbin says, clasping his hands together. "You lame asses go sleep. Ian and I are going out." Corbin turns, and he and Ian waste no time heading in the other direction. Corbin spins around, walking backward in pace with Ian. "We'll drink a shot in your honor, El Capitán!"

Miles and I remain motionless, boxed into a circle of light

cascading down from a streetlamp as we watch them walk away. I look down at the sidewalk below us and scoot one of my shoes to the edge of the circle of light, watching as it disappears into the darkness. I look up at the streetlamp, wondering why it's shining down on us with the intensity of a spotlight.

"Feels like we're on a stage," I say, still looking up at the light.

He tilts his head back and joins my inspection of the odd lighting. "*The English Patient*," he says. I look at him questioningly. He gestures to the streetlamp above our heads. "If we were on a stage, it would probably be a production of *The English Patient*." He flicks his hand back and forth between us. "We're already dressed the part. A nurse and a pilot."

I mull over what he says, probably a little too much. I know he says he's the pilot, but if this really were a stage production of *The English Patient*, I think he would be the soldier rather than the pilot. The soldier is the character who is sexually involved with the nurse. Not the pilot.

But the pilot *is* the one with the secretive past . . .

"That movie is the reason I became a nurse," I say, looking at him with a straight face.

He returns his hands to his pockets, shifting his gaze from the light overhead back to me. "For real?"

My laugh escapes. "No."

Miles smiles.

That rhymes.

We both turn at the same time to head back toward the hospital. I find myself using the lull in our conversation to construct a really bad poem in my head.

Miles smiles
For no one else
Miles only smiles
For me.

"Why are you grinning?" he asks.

Because I'm reciting embarrassing third-grade-level rhymes about you.

I pin my lips together, forcing my smile away. When I know it's gone for good, I answer him. "Just thinking about how tired I am. Looking forward to a really good"—I cut my eyes to his—"*sleep* tonight."

He's the one smiling now. "I know what you mean. I don't think I've ever been this tired. I might even sleep as soon as we're inside your car."

That would be nice.

I smile but bow out of the metaphor-laden conversation. It's been a long day, and I actually really am tired. We walk in silence, and I can't help but notice that his hands are shoved firmly into his jacket pockets, as if he's protecting me from them. Or maybe he's protecting *them* from *me*.

We're only a block away from the parking lot when his footsteps slow, then stop completely. Naturally, I stop walking and turn around to see what caught his attention. He's looking up at the sky, and my eyes focus on the scar that runs the length of his jaw. I want to ask him about it. I want to ask him about everything. I want to ask him a million questions, starting with when his birthday is and then what his first kiss was like. After that, I want to ask him about his parents and his entire childhood and his first love.

I want to ask him about Rachel. I want to know what happened with them and why whatever happened caused him to want to avoid any form of intimacy for more than six years.

Most of all, I want to know what it was about me that finally put an end to it.

"Miles," I say, each question wanting to dive off the tip of my tongue.

"I felt a raindrop," he says.

Before the sentence leaves his mouth, I feel one, too. We're both looking up at the sky now, and I'm swallowing all the questions along with the lump in my throat. The drops begin to fall faster, but we continue to stand there with our faces tilted up toward the sky. The sporadic drops turn into sprinkles, which then turn into full-on rain, but neither of us has moved. Neither of us is making a mad dash for the car. The rain is sliding down my skin, down my neck, into my hair, and soaking my shirt. My face is still tilted toward the sky, but my eyes are closed now.

There's nothing in the world that compares to the feel and smell of brand-new rain.

As soon as that thought crosses my mind, warm hands meet my cheeks and slide to the nape of my neck, stealing the strength from my knees and the air from my lungs. His height is shielding me from most of the rain now, but I keep my eyes closed and tilted toward the sky. His lips come down gently over mine, and I find myself comparing the feel and smell of brand-new rain to his kiss.

His kiss is much, *much* better.

His lips are wet from the rain, and they're a little bit cold, but he counterbalances that with the warm caress of his tongue against mine. The falling rain, the darkness surrounding us, and being kissed like this make it feel like we really are on a stage and our story has just reached its climax. It feels as if my heart and my stomach and my soul are all scrambling to get out of me and into him. If all my twenty-three years were laid on a graph, this moment would be the crest in my bell curve.

I should probably be a little bit sad and disappointed about this realization. I've had a few serious relationships in my past, but I can't recall a single kiss with any of those guys where I felt this much. The fact that I'm not even in a relationship with

Miles and I feel this affected by him should tell me something, but I'm too invested in his mouth to scrutinize that thought.

The rain has turned into a downpour, but neither of us seems to be affected by it. His hands drop to my lower back, and I fist his shirt in my hands, pulling him closer. His mouth fits mine as if we're two pieces from the same puzzle.

The only thing that could possibly separate me from him right now would be a bolt of lightning.

Or the fact that it's raining so hard I can't breathe. My clothes are stuck to parts of me I didn't even know clothes could stick to. My hair is so saturated it can't absorb another drop of water.

I push against him until he releases my mouth from his, and then I bury my head under his chin and look down so I can take a breath without drowning. He wraps his arm around my shoulders and ushers me toward the parking lot, lifting his jacket over my head. He picks up his pace, and I match him step for step until we're both running.

We finally reach my car, and he approaches the driver's-side door with me, still shielding me from the rain. Once I'm inside the car, he rushes around to the passenger side. When both of our doors are shut, the silence inside the car magnifies the intensity of our heavy breathing. I reach my hands behind my head and gather my hair, then squeeze the excess water from it. It runs down my neck, my back, and my seat. It's the first time I'm relieved to have leather seats in California.

I drop my head back and sigh heavily, then steal a glance in his direction. "I don't think I've ever been this wet in my life."

I watch as a slow grin spreads across his face. His thoughts obviously plummet into the gutter with that statement.

"Pervert," I whisper playfully.

He cocks his eyebrow and smirks. "Your fault." He reaches

across the seat and wraps his fingers around my wrist, pulling me toward him. "Come here."

I make a quick inventory of our surroundings, but the rain is falling so hard I can't even see outside. Which means no one can see *in*.

I adjust myself on top of him and straddle his lap as he scoots the seat as far back as it goes. He doesn't kiss me, though. His hands slide down my arms and come to rest on my hips.

"I've never had sex in a car before," he says with a little bit of hope in his confession.

"I've never had sex with a *captain* before," I offer.

He runs his hands under my scrub top, sliding them up my stomach until they meet my bra. He cups both breasts, then leans forward and kisses me. His kiss doesn't last long, because he breaks it to speak again. "I've never had sex *as* a captain before."

I smile. "I've never had sex in scrubs before."

His hands slide around to my back, and he dips them inside my waistband. He pulls my hips toward him at the same time as he lifts himself ever so slightly, immediately causing my grip to tighten around his shoulders and a gasp to pass my lips. His mouth moves to my ear as his hands re-create the sensual rhythm between us by pulling my hips forward again. "As hot as you look in uniform, I'd much rather have sex with you in nothing at all."

I'm embarrassed at how easily his words alone can make me moan. I'm also embarrassed at how quickly his voice can undo me, to the point where I probably want my clothes to come off more than he does. "Please tell me you came prepared," I say, my voice already heavy with want.

He shakes his head. "Just because I knew I would see you tonight doesn't mean I came with expectations." I'm immediately filled with disappointment. He lifts himself off the seat and slides his hand into his back pocket. "I did, however, come with a hell of a lot of hope." He pulls the condom out of his wallet with a grin, and we both immediately begin to take action. My hands connect with the button on his jeans faster than our mouths connect. He slides his hands up the back of my top and begins to unclasp my bra, but I shake my head.

"Just leave it on," I say breathlessly. The less clothes we take off, the faster we'll be able to get dressed if we get caught.

He continues to unfasten it, despite my protest. "I don't want to be inside you unless I can feel you against me."

Wow. Okay, then.

When my bra is undone, he lifts my shirt over my head, and his fingers slide under the straps of my bra. He pulls them down my arms until the bra falls away. He tosses it into the backseat and then pulls his own shirt over his head. After his shirt joins my bra in the backseat, he wraps his arms around me and pulls me against him until our bare chests meet.

We both immediately inhale sharp breaths. The warmth of his body creates a sensation that I don't want to pull away from. He begins kissing his way down my neck, his breath coming in rough waves against my skin.

"You have no idea what you do to me," he whispers against my throat.

I smile, because that same exact thought just went through my own head. "Oh, I think I have an idea," I reply.

His left hand palms one of my breasts, and he groans as his right hand dips into my pants.

"Off," he says simply, tugging at the elastic band.

He doesn't have to ask twice. I scoot back to my empty seat and begin removing the rest of my clothes while I watch him unzip his jeans.

His eyes are all over me as he rips open the condom wrapper with his teeth. When the only article of clothing remaining between us is his unbuttoned pair of jeans, I scoot toward him.

I feel ridiculously self-conscious that I'm in my car in the parking lot of my workplace and I'm completely naked. I've never done anything like this before. I've never really *wanted* to do anything like this before. I love how desperate we are for each other right now, but I also know I've never felt this kind of chemistry with anyone before.

I place my hands on his shoulders and begin to straddle him while he slides on the condom.

"Keep it quiet," he says teasingly. "I'd hate to be the reason you get fired."

I glance at the window, still unable to see outside. "It's raining too hard for anyone to hear us," I say. "Besides, you were the louder one last time."

He dismisses that with a quick laugh and begins kissing me again. His hands grip my hips, and he pulls me to him, readying himself against me. This position would normally cause me to moan, but I'm suddenly feeling stubborn with my noises now that he's mentioned it.

"There's no way I was the louder one," he says with his lips still touching mine. "If anything, we tied."

I shake my head. "I don't believe in ending things with a tie. That's a copout for people who are too scared they might lose."

His hands meet my hips, and he's positioned against me in such a way all I would have to do to take him inside me would be to allow it to happen. However, I'm refusing to lower myself onto him simply because I like competition and I feel one about to begin.

He lifts his hips, obviously ready to get things going between us. My legs tense, and I pull away just enough.

He laughs at my resistance. "What's wrong, Tate? You scared

now? Afraid once I'm inside you, we'll both see who the loud one really is?"

There's a challenging gleam in his eyes. I don't verbally accept his challenge to see who can stay quieter. Instead, I keep my eyes locked with his while I slowly ease myself onto him. Both of us gasp simultaneously, but that's the only sound that passes between us.

As soon as he's all the way inside me, his hands meet my back, and he pulls me against him. The only sounds we make are heavy sighs and even heavier gasps. The rain slapping against the windows and the roof magnifies the silence we're experiencing inside the car.

The strength it takes to hold back is coupled with a need to hold on to each other with more desperation. His arms are around my waist, gripping me so tightly it makes it hard to move. My arms are wrapped around his neck, and my eyes are shut. We're barcly moving now because of the tight grips we have on each other, but I like it. I like how slow and steady our rhythm remains while we both focus on how to continue suppressing the moans caught in our throats.

For several minutes, we continue in the same manner, moving just enough but at the same time not *nearly* enough. I think we're both too afraid to make any sudden movements, or the intensity will cause one of us to lose.

One of his hands glides around to my lower back, and the other hand meets the back of my head. He takes a handful of my hair and gently tugs until my throat is exposed to his mouth. I wince the second his lips meet my neck, because staying quiet is a lot more challenging than I imagined it would be. Especially since he's at an advantage with the way we're positioned. His hands are free to roam anywhere they want, and that's exactly what they're doing right now.

Roaming, caressing, trailing down my stomach so that he can touch the one place that could make me cede victory.

I feel like he's cheating somehow.

As soon as his fingers find the exact spot that would normally make me scream his name, I tighten my hold around his shoulders and reposition my knees so that I have more control of my movements. I want to put him through just as much torture as he's putting me through right now.

As soon as I'm repositioned and able to ease myself further onto him, the slow-and-steady disappears. His mouth meets mine in a frantic kiss—one with more need and more force than any kiss before it. It's as if we're attempting to kiss away our natural desire to verbalize just how good this feels.

I'm suddenly hit with a sensation that ripples through my entire body, and I have to lift myself off of him and hold still before I lose. Despite my need to slow things down, he does the opposite and applies more pressure to me with his hand. I bury my face against his neck and bite down gently on his shoulder in order to stop myself from moaning his name.

The second my teeth meet his skin, I hear the hitch in his breath and feel the stiffening in his legs.

He almost loses.

Almost.

If he moves inside me even an inch more while he's touching me this way, he'll win. I don't want him to win.

Then again, I kind of *do* want him to win, and I'm thinking he *wants* to win with the way he breathes against my neck, gently lowering me back down onto him.

Miles, Miles, Miles.

He can sense that this isn't about to end in a tie, so he adds more pressure against me with his fingers at the same time as his tongue meets my ear.

Oh, wow.

I'm about to lose.

Any second now.

Oh, my word.

He lifts his hips when he pulls me against him, forcing an involuntary "Miles!" out of my mouth, along with a gasp and a moan. I lift off of him, but as soon as he realizes he just won, he exhales heavily and pulls me back onto him with more force.

"Finally," he says breathlessly against my neck. "I didn't think I could last another second."

Now that the competition is over, both of us let loose completely until we're being so loud we have to kiss again to stifle our sounds. Our bodies are moving in sync, speeding up, crashing harder together. We continue our frantic pace for a few more minutes, escalating in intensity until I'm positive I can't take another second of him.

"Tate," he says against my mouth, slowing the rhythm of my hips with his hands. "I want us to come together."

Oh, holy hell.

If he wants me to last any longer, he can't say things like that. I nod my head, unable to form a coherent response.

"Are you almost there?" he asks.

I nod again and try my best to speak this time, but nothing comes out other than another moan.

"Is that a yes?"

His lips have stopped kissing mine, and he's focused on my response now. I bring my hands to the back of his head and press my cheek to his.

"Yes," I somehow utter. "Yes, Miles. *Yes.*" I feel myself begin to tense at the same time as he sucks in a sharp breath.

I thought we were holding each other tightly before, but that doesn't begin to compare to this moment. It feels as if all our senses have magically melded together and we're feeling the exact same sensations, making the exact same noises, experiencing the exact same intensity, and sharing the exact same response.

Our rhythm gradually begins to slow, right along with the tremors in our bodies. The tight grips we have around each other begin to loosen. He buries his face into my hair and exhales heavily.

"Loser," he whispers.

I laugh and move to bite him playfully on his neck. "You cheated," I say. "You brought in illegal reinforcement when you started using your hands."

He laughs with a shake of his head. "Hands are fair game. But if you think I cheated, maybe we should have a rematch."

I raise my eyebrows. "Best two out of three?"

He lifts me by my waist and begins to push me toward the passenger door as he struggles to get behind the steering wheel. He hands me my clothes, pulls his shirt back over his head, and buttons his jeans. Once he's situated, I adjust myself in the passenger seat and finish dressing while he cranks the car. He throws it in reverse and begins backing out. "Buckle up," he says with a wink.

• • •

We barely made it out of the elevator, much less to his bed. He almost took me right there in the hallway. The sad part is, I wouldn't have minded.

He won again. I'm beginning to realize that competing for who can stay the quietest isn't really a good idea when my competitor is naturally the quietest person I've ever met.

I'll get him in round three. Just not tonight, because Corbin will more than likely be heading home soon.

Miles is staring at me. He's on his stomach, with his hands folded across his pillow and his head resting on his arms. I'm getting dressed, because I want to beat Corbin to our apartment so I don't have to lie about where I've been.

Miles follows me around his bedroom with his eyes as I dress.

"I think your bra is still in the hallway," he says with a laugh. "Might want to grab it before Corbin finds it."

I crinkle up my nose at the thought. "Good idea," I say. I kneel down on the bed and kiss him on the cheek, but he wraps his arm around my waist and pulls me forward as he rolls onto his back. He gives me an even better kiss than the one I was just giving him.

"Can I ask you a question?"

He nods, but it's a forced nod. He's nervous about my questions.

"Why don't you ever make eye contact when we're having sex?"

My question throws him for a loop. He regards me for several silent moments until I pull even farther away and sit next to him on the bed, waiting for his answer.

He pushes himself up and leans back against his headboard, staring down at his hands. "People are vulnerable during sex," he says with a shrug. "It's easy to confuse feelings and emotions for something they aren't, especially when eye contact is involved." He lifts his eyes to mine. "Does it bother you?"

I'm shaking my head no, but my heart is crying Yes! "I'll get used to it, I guess. I was just curious."

I love being with him but hate myself more and more with each new lie that passes my lips.

He smiles and pulls me back to his mouth, kissing me with more finality this time. "Good night, Tate."

I back away and walk out of his room, feeling his eyes on me the entire time. It's funny how he refuses to make eye contact during sex yet can't seem to keep his eyes off me the rest of the time.

I don't feel like going back to the apartment yet, so after retrieving my bra, I walk to the elevators and make my way down to the lobby to see if Cap is still around. I barely had a chance to wave at him earlier before Miles shoved me onto the elevator and ravished me.

Sure enough, Cap is still planted in his chair, despite the fact that it's after ten o'clock at night.

"Do you ever sleep?" I ask as I make my way to the chair next to him.

"People are more interesting at night," he says. "I like to sleep late. Avoid all the fools who are in too much of a rush in the mornings."

I sigh a lot louder than I intend to when I lean my head back into the chair. Cap notices and turns to look at me.

"Oh, no," he says. "Trouble with the boy? Looked like the two of you were getting along fine a couple of hours ago. Think I might have even seen a hint of a smile on his face when he walked in with you."

"Things are fine," I say. I pause for a few seconds, gathering my thoughts. "Have you ever been in love, Cap?"

A slow smile spreads across his face. "Oh, yes," he says. "Her name was Wanda."

"How long were you married?"

He looks at me and cocks an eyebrow. "I ain't never been married," he says. "I think Wanda's marriage lasted about forty years before she passed, though."

I tilt my head, trying to understand what he's saying. "You have to give me more than that."

He sits up straighter in his chair, the smile still on his face.

"She lived in one of the buildings I did maintenance for. She was married to a bastard of a man who was only home about two weeks out of the month. I fell in love with her when I was around thirty years old. She was in her mid-twenties. People just didn't get divorced back then once they got married. Especially women like her who came from the type of family she came from. So I spent the next twenty-five years loving her as hard as I could for two weeks out of every month."

I stare at him, not sure how to respond to that. It's not the typical love story people usually tell. I'm not even sure if it can *be* considered a love story.

"I know what you're thinking," he says. "Sounds depressing. More like a tragedy."

I nod, confirming his assumption.

"Love isn't always pretty, Tate. Sometimes you spend all your time hoping it'll eventually be something different. Something better. Then, before you know it, you're back to square one, and you lost your heart somewhere along the way."

I stop looking at him and face forward. I don't want him to see the frown that I can't seem to remove from my face.

Is that what I'm doing? Waiting for things with Miles to become something different? Something better? I contemplate his words for way too long. So long, in fact, I hear snoring. I cut my eyes in Cap's direction, and his chin has dropped to his chest. His mouth is wide open, and he's sound asleep.

chapter eighteen

MILES

Six years earlier

I rub her back reassuringly. "Two more minutes," I tell her.
She nods but keeps her face pressed into the palms of her
hands. She doesn't want to look.
I don't tell her we don't actually need the two minutes. I don't
tell her the results are already there, clear as day.
I don't tell Rachel she's pregnant yet, because she still has two
minutes left of hope.
I continue to rub her back. When the timer goes off, she
doesn't move. She doesn't turn to look at the results. I
drop my head to the side of hers until my mouth is close
to her ear.
"I'm so sorry, Rachel," I whisper. "I'm so, so sorry."
She bursts into tears.
My heart is crushed at the sound.

This is my fault. This is all my fault.

The only thing I can think to do now is figure out how to rectify it.

I turn her toward me and wrap my arms around her. "I'll tell them you don't feel well and you can't go to school today. I want you to stay here until I get back."

She doesn't even nod. She continues to cry, so I pick her up and carry her to the bed. I go back to the bathroom and package up the test, then hide it underneath the sink in the very back. I rush to my room and change clothes.

I leave.

I'm gone most of the day.

I'm rectifying.

When I finally pull back up our driveway, I still have almost an hour before my father and Lisa are due home. I grab everything from my front seat and rush inside to check on her. I left my phone behind in my rush this morning, so I haven't had a way to check on her at all, and I'd be lying if I said it wasn't killing me.

I go inside.

I go to her door.

I attempt to turn it, but it's locked.

I knock.

"Rachel?"

I hear movement. Something crashes against the door, and I jump back. When I realize what's happened, I step forward again and bang on the door. "Rachel!" I yell, frantic. "Open the door!"

I hear her crying. "Go away!"

I take two steps back, then lunge forward and shove my shoulder against the door as hard as I can. The door flies open, and I rush inside. Rachel is curled up against the headboard, crying into her hands. I reach her.

She pushes me away.

I walk back to her.

She slaps me, then scoots off the bed. She stands up, shoving me back, pushing her palms against my chest. "I hate you!" she screams through her tears. I grab her hands and try to calm her down. It makes her angrier. "Just leave!" she yells. "If you don't want anything to do with me, just leave!"

Her words stun me.

"Rachel, stop," I plead. "I'm here. I'm not going anywhere."

Her tears come harder now. She screams at me. She says I left her. I put her in bed this morning, and I left her because I couldn't handle it. I was disappointed in her.

I love you, Rachel. More than I love myself.

"Baby, no," I tell her, pulling her to me. "I didn't leave you. I told you I was coming back."

I hate that she didn't understand why I left today.

I hate that I didn't explain it to her.

I walk her back to the bed, and I position her against the headboard. "Rachel," I say, touching her tear-stained cheek, "I'm not disappointed in you," I tell her. "Not in the least. I'm disappointed in myself. Which is why I want to do everything I possibly can to turn this around for you. For *us*. That's what I've been doing today. I've been trying to find a way to make this better for us."

I stand up and grab the folders, then spread them out on the bed. I show her everything. I show her the brochures for family housing I picked up from campus. I show her the forms we need to fill out for free campus child care. I show her the financial aid brochures and the night classes and the online course review and the academic adviser list and how it will all coordinate with my flight-class schedule. All the possibilities are spread out before her, and I want her to see that even though we didn't want this, even though we didn't plan for this . . . we can *do* this.

"I know it'll be a lot harder with a baby, Rachel. I *know* that. But it's not impossible."

She stares down at everything I've laid out before her. I watch her in silence until her shoulders begin to shake and she covers her mouth with her hand. She meets my gaze as huge tears spill out of her eyes. She crawls forward and throws her arms around my neck.

She tells me she loves me.

You love me so much, Rachel.

She kisses me over and over.

"We've got this, Miles," she whispers against my ear.

I nod and hug her back. "We've got this, Rachel."

chapter nineteen

TATE

It's Thursday.

Game night.

Normally, the sound of their Thursday-night game gets under my skin. Tonight it's music to my ears, knowing that Miles should be home. I have no idea what to expect from him or this arrangement we've got going on. I haven't texted or spoken to him in the five days since he's been gone.

I know that with as much as I'm thinking about him, I shouldn't be doing this. For something that's supposed to be a casual thing, it's felt anything but casual. For me, it's been extremely involved. Intense, even. He's pretty much all I've thought about since that night in the rain, and it's quite pathetic that I'm reaching for the doorknob to walk inside my apartment and my damn hand is shaking, knowing he might be in there.

I open the door to the apartment, and Corbin is the first to look up. He nods but doesn't even say hi. Ian waves from his seat on the couch, then looks back at the TV.

Dillon's eyes roam up and down my body, and I do what I can to stop myself from rolling my eyes.

Miles doesn't do anything, because Miles isn't here.

My whole body sighs from disappointment. I drop my purse onto the empty chair in the living room and tell myself it's a good thing he isn't here, because I've got way too much homework to do anyway.

"There's pizza in the fridge," Corbin says.

"Nice." I walk into the kitchen and open the cabinet to remove a plate. I hear footsteps closing in on me, and my heart rate kicks up a notch.

A hand touches me on my lower back, and I immediately smile and turn around to face Miles.

Only it isn't Miles. It's Dillon.

"Hey, Tate," he says, reaching around me to the cabinet. The hand that first touched my lower back is still on me, but now that I've turned to face him, his hand has slid to my waist. He keeps his eyes locked with mine as he reaches past me and opens the cabinet. "Just need a cup for my beer," he says, excusing the fact that he's right here. *Touching* me. His face only inches from my face.

I hate that he saw me smiling when I turned around. I just gave him the wrong idea.

"Well, you won't find a cup in my pocket," I say, pushing his hand off of me. I look away from Dillon just as Miles steps into the kitchen. His eyes are burning holes into the part of me that Dillon was just touching.

Miles saw Dillon's hand on me.

Miles is looking at Dillon now as if he just committed murder.

"Since when do you drink beer from a cup?" Miles says.

Dillon turns around and looks at Miles, then glances back to me and smiles a very blatant, flirtatious smile. "Since Tate was standing so close to the cabinet."

Shit. He's not even hiding it. He thinks I'm into him.

Miles walks to the refrigerator and opens it. "So Dillon. How's your *wife?*"

Miles doesn't make an attempt to remove anything. He's just standing there, staring into the refrigerator, with his fingers gripping the door handle harder than it's ever been gripped, I'm sure.

Dillon is still looking at me, staring down at me. "She's at work," he says pointedly. "For at least four more hours."

Miles slams the refrigerator and takes two quick steps toward Dillon. Dillon stands up straight, and I immediately scoot two feet away from him. "Corbin specifically instructed you to keep your hands off his sister. Show him some fucking respect!"

Dillon's jaw twitches, and he doesn't back down or look away from Miles. In fact, he takes a step toward him, closing the space between them. "Sounds to me like this isn't really about *Corbin*," Dillon says, seething.

My heart is pounding in my chest. I feel guilty that I gave Dillon the wrong idea and even guiltier that they're arguing about it now. But dammit, I love that Miles hates him so much. I just wish I knew if it was because he doesn't like that Dillon is flirting when he's got a wife at home or if he doesn't like that Dillon is flirting with *me*.

And now Corbin is standing in the doorway.

Shit.

"*What* isn't really about me?" Corbin asks, watching the two of them in their standoff.

Miles backs up a step and turns so that he can face Dillon

and Corbin at the same time. His eyes remain locked hard with Dillon's. "He's trying to fuck your sister."

Jesus Christ, Miles. Ever hear of sugarcoating?

Corbin doesn't even flinch. "Go home to your wife, Dillon," he says firmly.

As embarrassing as this is, I don't do anything to step in and defend Dillon, because I get the feeling that Miles and Corbin have been looking for an excuse to defriend him for a while now. I would also never defend a man who has no respect for his marriage. Dillon stares at Corbin for several painstakingly long seconds, then turns to face me with his back to both Miles and Corbin.

This boy seriously has a death wish.

"I live in ten-twelve," he whispers with a wink. "Stop by sometime. She works weeknights." He turns away and walks between Corbin and Miles. "The two of you can go fuck yourselves."

Corbin turns, and his fists are clenched. He begins to stalk after Dillon, but Miles grabs his arm and pulls him back into the kitchen. He doesn't release Corbin's arm until the front door slams shut.

Corbin turns to face me, and he looks so angry I'm surprised steam isn't coming from his ears. His face is red, and he's popping his knuckles. I forgot how insanely protective he is of me. I feel like I'm fifteen again, only now I suddenly have *two* over-protective brothers.

"Erase that apartment number from your head, Tate," Corbin says.

I shake my head, somewhat disappointed that he would even think I'd want to remember Dillon's apartment number. "I have standards, Corbin."

He nods, but he's still making an attempt to calm himself down. He inhales a deep breath, pops his jaw, then walks back into the living room.

Miles is leaning against the counter, staring down at his feet. I watch him silently until he finally raises his eyes and looks up at me. He glances toward the living room, then kicks off the counter and walks toward me. Every step closer he takes, the more I press myself into the counter behind me, making an attempt to back away from the intensity in his eyes, even though I can't very well go anywhere.

He reaches me.

He smells good. Like apples. *Forbidden fruit.*

"Ask me if you can study at my place," he whispers.

I nod, wondering why in the hell he would make such a random request after everything that just happened. I do it anyway, though. "Can I study at your place?"

He breaks out into a huge grin and drops his forehead to the side of my head so that his lips are directly over my ear. "I meant for you to ask me in front of your brother," he says, laughing quietly. "So I have an excuse to get you over there."

Well, that's embarrassing.

Now he knows exactly how much I'm not Tate when I'm near him. I'm only liquid. Conforming. Doing what he asks, doing what I'm told, doing what he wants me to do.

"Oh," I say quietly as I watch him ease away from me. "That makes a lot more sense."

He's still smiling, and I didn't realize how much I missed seeing that smile. He should smile all the time. Forever. *At me.*

He walks out of the kitchen and heads back to the living room, so I go to my room and shower in record time.

• • •

I didn't realize I was such a good actress.

I had practice, though. Five minutes of practice. I stood in my room, trying to think of the best, most casual line for when I walked into the living room to ask Miles for his key. I decided to wait until a particularly loud moment during the game, and then I burst out of the room and yelled at all of them.

"You guys either need to mute the damn TV or go watch it next door, because I'm trying to study!"

Miles looked at me and tried to hide his smile. Ian looked at me with suspicion, and Corbin rolled his eyes. "*You* go next door," Corbin said. "We're watching the game." He looked at Miles. "She can use your place, right?"

Miles stood up immediately and said, "Sure. I'll let her in."

I grabbed my things, followed him out of my apartment, and now here we are.

Miles opens his apartment door for me, even though it isn't locked. Corbin doesn't know that, though. He walks inside, and I slip in behind him. He shuts the door, and we turn and face each other.

"I really do have homework," I say. I don't know what he's expecting to happen right this second, but I feel like I need to let him know that just because he shows up after a few days away, that doesn't mean he's my number one priority.

Even though he pretty much is.

"I really do have a game to watch," he says, pointing over his shoulder at my apartment but walking toward me at the same time. He takes my books out of my hands and walks with them to the table, where he sets them down. He starts walking back toward me and doesn't stop until his lips are pressed to mine and we can't walk any farther because my back is against the apartment door.

His hands are gripping my waist, and mine are gripping

his shoulders. His tongue slides between my lips and into my mouth, and I take it, very willingly. He groans and presses himself against me as my hands slide up his neck and through his hair. He pulls away just as fast and steps back several feet.

He's looking at me like it's somehow my fault that he has to leave. He runs two frustrated palms down his face and releases a deep breath. "You didn't get to eat earlier," he says. "I'll bring you some pizza." He walks back toward me, and I step aside without responding. He opens the door and disappears.

He's so weird.

I walk to the table and begin to lay everything out that I need in order to study. I'm pulling out my chair to sit when his apartment door flies open again. I turn around, and he's walking toward the kitchen with a plate in his hands. He puts the pizza in his microwave, presses a few buttons and starts it, and then heads straight toward me. He's doing that intimidating thing again that makes me naturally back away from him, but his table is behind me, and I can't go anywhere.

He reaches me and quickly presses his lips to mine. "I have to go back over there," he says. "You good?"

I nod.

"You need anything?"

I shake my head.

"There's juice and bottled water in the fridge."

"Thanks."

He kisses me briefly again before he releases me and walks out the door.

I fall into my chair.

He's so *nice*.

I could get used to this.

I pull my notebook in front of me and begin studying. About half an hour passes, and then I get a text from him.

Miles: How's the homework going?

I'm reading the text on my phone, smiling like an idiot. He goes nine days without seeing or texting me, and now he's texting me from twenty feet away.

Me: Good. How's the game going?

Miles: Halftime. We're losing.

Me: Bummer.

Miles: You knew I didn't have cable.

Me: ???

Miles: Earlier, when you yelled at us. You told us to go to my place to watch the game, but you already knew I didn't have cable. I think Ian's suspicious now.

Me: Oh, no. I didn't think about that.

Miles: It's cool. He's just giving me looks, like he knows something is up. Honestly, I don't care if he knows. He knows everything else about me.

Me: I'm surprised you didn't tell him already. Don't all guys kiss and tell?

Miles: Not me, Tate.

Me: I guess you're the exception. Now leave me alone, I have to study.

Miles: Don't come back until I come tell you the game is over.

I lay my phone down on the table, unable to wipe the grin from my face.

• • •

An hour later, the door to his apartment opens. I look up, and he walks in, shuts the door, and casually falls against it. "Game's over," he says.

I drop my pen. "Perfect timing. I just finished my home-work."

His eyes fall to my books, spread out across the table. "Corbin's probably expecting you."

I don't know if that's his way of telling me I should leave or if he's just making conversation. I stand up anyway and begin to gather my books, attempting to hide the disappointment on my face.

He walks straight to me and takes the books out of my hands, setting them back down. He gives them a shove, sliding them a foot away, and then he grabs my waist and pushes me onto the table.

"That doesn't mean I want you to leave," he says firmly, look-ing me hard in the eyes.

I don't smile this time, because he just made me nervous again. Every time he looks at me with this much intensity, I get nervous.

He slides me to the very edge of the table and stands between my legs. His hands are still on my waist, but his lips are now on my jaw. "I was thinking," he says softly, his breath caressing my neck, covering me in chills. "About tonight and how you've been in class all day." He slides his hands beneath me, lifting me off the table. "And how you work all weekend, every weekend." My legs are wrapped around him now. He's carrying me to his bedroom.

Now he's laying me on his bed.

Now he's on top of me, brushing my hair back, looking me in the eyes. "And I realized that you never have a day off." His mouth is back to my jaw again, kissing it softly between each sentence. "You haven't had a day off since Thanksgiving, have you?"

I shake my head, not understanding why he's talking so much but loving it just the same. His hand slides up under my shirt, and his palm meets my stomach, continuing upward until he's cupping my breast. "You must be really tired, Tate."

I shake my head. "Not really."

I'm lying.

I'm exhausted.

His lips leave my neck, and he looks me in the eyes. "You're lying," he says, brushing his thumb over the thin layer of bra covering my nipple. "I can tell you're tired." He lowers his mouth until it's pressed against mine so softly I barely even feel it. "I just want to kiss you for a few minutes, okay? Then you're going to leave and go get some rest. I don't want you to think I expect something just because we're both home."

His mouth touches mine again, but his lips can't compare to what his words do to me. I never knew thoughtfulness could be such a turn-on.

But *oh, my God*. It's so hot.

His hand slides beneath my bra, and his mouth invades me. Every time his tongue caresses mine, it makes my head spin. I wonder if that will ever get old.

I know he said he just wanted to kiss me for a few minutes, but his definition of *kiss* and my definition of *kiss* are written in two different languages. His mouth is everywhere.

So are his hands.

He pushes my shirt up above my bra, pulling one side of it down until my breast is exposed. He teases me with his tongue, looking up at me while he does it. His mouth is warm, and his tongue is even warmer, causing soft whimpers to escape from me.

He runs his hand down my stomach and lifts slightly off of me, holding his weight up on his elbow. His hand trails over my jeans until he reaches the insides of my thighs. He runs his fingers against the material between my legs, and I let my head fall back and my eyes close.

Good Lord, I love his version of kissing.

He begins to rub his hand over me, pressing firmly against my jeans until my entire body is silently begging for him. His mouth is no longer on my breast. It's on my neck now, and he's kissing, nibbling, sucking, all in one spot, as if he's trying to brand me.

I'm trying to be quiet, but it's impossible when he's creating this amazing friction between us. But that's fine, because he's not being quiet, either. Every time I moan, he groans or sighs or whispers my name. Which is why I'm being so loud, because I love his sounds.

Love them.

His hand quickly moves to the button on my jeans, and he unbuttons them, but he doesn't switch positions or move away from my neck. He pulls my zipper down and slides his hands on top of my panties. He resumes the same movements, only this time they're a million times more intense, and I can instantly tell he isn't going to have to do it for much longer.

My back arches off the bed, and it takes all I have not to pull away from his hand. It's as if he knows exactly the right places to touch that will make me react.

"Christ, Tate. You're so wet." Two of his fingers pull my panties aside. "I want to feel you."

And that's it.

I'm a goner.

His finger slips inside me, but his thumb remains outside, coaxing moans and *oh, my God*s and *don't stop*s out of me like I'm a broken record. He kisses me, swallowing all my sounds while my body begins to tremble beneath his hand.

The sensation lasts so long and is so intense I'm afraid to let go of him when it's over. I don't want his hand to leave me. I want to fall asleep like this.

I'm completely still, but we're both breathing so heavily we're unable to move. His mouth is still on mine, and our eyes are closed, but he's not kissing me. After a few moments, he finally pulls his hand out of my pants, then zips and buttons them back up. When I open my eyes, he's slowly sliding his fingers out of his mouth with a grin.

Holy shit.

I'm so glad I'm not standing up right now, or seeing him do that would have made me fall straight to the floor.

"Wow," I say as I exhale. "You're pretty damn good at this."

He smiles even wider. "Why, thank you," he says. He leans forward and kisses my forehead. "Now, go home and get some sleep, girl."

He begins to lift off the bed, and I grab his arms and pull him back down. "Wait," I tell him. I push him onto his back and slide on top of him. "That's not really fair to you."

"I'm not keeping score," he says, rolling me onto my back. "Corbin's probably wondering why you're still over here." He stands up and grabs my wrists to pull me up with him. He pulls me against him close enough for me to tell he isn't at all ready for me to leave yet.

"If Corbin says anything, I'll just tell him I didn't want to leave until I was finished with my homework."

Miles shakes his head. "You need to go back, Tate," he says. "He thanked me for protecting you from Dillon earlier. How do you think he'd feel if he knew I only did that because I was being selfish and wanted you all to myself?"

I shake my head. "I don't care how he'd feel. It's not his business."

Miles brings his hands to my cheeks. "*I* care. He's my friend. I don't want him to find out what a hypocrite I am." He kisses my forehead and pulls me out of the bedroom before I can respond. He gathers my books and hands them to me when I reach the front door, but before I walk out, he grabs my elbow and stops me. He's staring down at me, but there's something else in his expression this time.

Something in his eyes that isn't desire or want or disappointment or intimidation. It's something unspoken. Something he wants to say to me that he's too afraid to say.

His hands cup my cheeks, and he presses his mouth to mine so hard I hit the frame of the door behind me.

He kisses me so possessively and desperately it would make me sad if only I didn't love it so much. He inhales deeply and pulls away, exhaling slowly, staring me hard in the eyes. He drops his hand and steps back, waiting for me to step into the hallway before he closes his door.

I have no idea what that was, but I need more of it.

I somehow make my legs move, and I walk into Corbin's apartment. Corbin isn't in the living room, so I set my books down on the counter.

I hear Corbin's shower running.

Corbin's in the shower.

I immediately walk out the door and back across the hall and knock. His door swings open so quickly it's as if Miles was still standing in the same spot. He glances over my shoulder at my apartment door.

"Corbin's in the shower," I say.

Miles looks back at me, and before I think he even has time to process my words, he's pulling me inside his apartment. He slams the door shut and shoves me against it, and once again, his mouth is everywhere.

I waste no time, unbuttoning his jeans and pulling them down several inches. His hands take over and pull my pants down completely, along with my underwear. As soon as he slides my feet out of them, he's urging me toward his kitchen table. He spins me around, positioning me until I'm leaning across the table on my stomach.

He reaches between my legs, spreading them farther apart while freeing himself from his jeans. Both of his hands move to my waist and grip tightly. He steadies himself against me and then carefully eases himself inside me. "Oh, *God*," he groans.

I press my palms flat out on the table. There's nothing to grab hold of, and I desperately need to grab something.

He leans forward, pressing his chest against my back. His breaths are heavy and hot and crashing against my skin. "I have to get a condom."

"Okay," I breathe out.

He hasn't backed away yet, though, and my body naturally wants to take him in the rest of the way. I press myself against him, pushing him further inside me, causing him to dig his fingers into my hips so hard I wince.

"*Don't*, Tate."

His voice is a warning.

Or a dare.

I do it again, and he groans, quickly pulling out of me completely. His hands are still digging into my hips, and he's still pressed against me—he's just no longer inside me.

"I'm on the pill," I whisper.

He doesn't move.

I close my eyes, needing him to do something. Anything. I'm dying here.

"Tate," he whispers. He doesn't follow it up with anything. We stand quietly still, with him in the same position, poised right outside me.

"Dammit." He releases my waist and finds my hands palms-down on the table. He slides his fingers through mine and

squeezes, then buries his face against my neck from behind me.
"Brace yourself."

He slams into me so unexpectedly I scream. One of his hands
leaves mine, and he brings it to my mouth and covers it. "Shh,"
he warns. He holds still, giving me a moment to adjust to him
inside me.

He pulls out with a moan and slams into me again, causing
me to yell out once more. His hand muffles my noises this time.

He repeats his movements.

Harder.

Faster.

He's grunting with every thrust, and I'm making noises I
didn't even know I could make. I've never experienced anything
like this before.

I didn't know it could be this intense. This raw. This ani-
malistic.

I lower my face and press my cheek against the table.

I squeeze my eyes shut.

I let him fuck me.

• • •

It's quiet.

It's so quiet, and I don't know if it's because we were both
so loud just a few seconds ago or if he just needs a minute to
recover.

He's still inside me, but he's finished. He's just not moving.
One of his hands is still covering my mouth, the other still
squeezing my fingers. His face is still buried against my neck.

But he's so incredibly still I'm afraid to move. I don't even
feel him breathing.

The first thing to move is his hand, away from my mouth.
He unlocks his fingers from mine and straightens them, pulling

them slowly apart from mine. He presses both palms against the table and lifts his face away from my neck. He pulls out of me without a sound.

It's still too quiet, so I don't move.

I hear him as he pulls his pants back into position and zips them.

I hear his footsteps as he walks away.

He's walking away.

His bedroom door slams shut, and I flinch. My cheek and palms and stomach are still flat against his table, but now so are my tears.

They're falling.

Falling, falling, falling, and I can't stop them.

I'm embarrassed. I'm ashamed. I don't have a clue what the hell is wrong with him, but I have too much pride and too little courage to go find out.

This felt like an end. I'm not sure I was ready for this to be the end. I'm not sure I was ready for there *ever* to be an end, and I hate myself for allowing my feelings to get to that point.

I'm also angry because here I am, standing in his apartment, looking for my pants, trying to stop my ridiculous tears, still feeling the remnants of him sliding down my leg, and I have no fucking clue why he had to ruin it.

Ruin *me*.

I finish getting dressed, and I leave.

chapter twenty

MILES

Six years earlier

"You're getting an outie," I tell her. I run my fingers over her
bare stomach, and I kiss it. "It's cute."
I press my ear to her skin and close my eyes. "I bet he's lonely
in there," I say. "Are you lonely in there, buddy?"
Rachel laughs. "You keep calling him a boy. What if he's a girl?"
I tell Rachel whatever he is, I'll love him the same. I *already*
love him.
Or her.
Our parents are out of town. We're playing house again, except
this time, we aren't really playing. It's kind of serious.
"So what happens if he really does propose to her this time?"
she asks.
I tell her not to worry. I tell her he's not proposing. He would
ask me first before he did it. I know that much about him.

"We have to tell them," I say to her.

She nods. She knows we have to tell them. It's been three months. We graduate in two. She's starting to show. She's getting an outie. It's cute.

"We should tell them tomorrow," I say.

She says okay.

I move away from her stomach and lie beside her. I pull her against me. I touch her face.

"I love you, Rachel," I tell her.

She's not as scared now. She tells me she loves me, too.

"You're doing a good job," I say. She doesn't know what I'm talking about, so I grin and touch her stomach. "You're doing a good job growing him. I'm pretty sure you're gonna grow the best baby any woman has ever grown."

She laughs at my silliness.

You love me so much, Rachel.

I look at her—at the girl I gave my heart to—and I wonder how I got so lucky.

I wonder why she loves me just as much as I love her.

I wonder what my dad is going to say when he finds out about us.

I wonder if Lisa will hate me. I wonder if she'll want to take Rachel back to Phoenix.

I wonder how I can convince them that we've got this.

"What are we going to name him?" I ask her.

She's excited when I ask her this. She likes talking about names. She says if it's a girl, she wants to name her Claire. After her grandmother.

I tell her I wish I knew her grandmother. I want to know the woman my daughter will be named after. She tells me her grandmother would have loved me. I tell her I love the name Claire.

"What if he's a boy?" I ask.

"You can pick the boy name," she says.

I tell her that's a lot of pressure. I tell her he'll have to live with his name the rest of his life. She says, "Then you'd better pick a good one."

I'd better pick a good one.

"One that means something to you," she says.

One that means something to me.

I tell her I have the perfect name for him.

She wants to know what it is. I tell her I'm not telling her. I'll tell her his name after it becomes his name.

After he's born.

She tells me I'm insane. She says she refuses to give birth to our baby until she knows his name.

I laugh. I tell her she has no choice.

She tells me I'm crazy.

You love that about me, Rachel.

chapter twenty-one

TATE

I worked all weekend, so I haven't seen or spoken to Miles since Thursday night. I keep telling myself it's for the best, but it sure as hell doesn't feel like it with the way I've been letting it eat at me. Tonight is Monday, and it's the first of three days when Corbin won't be home and Miles *will* be. I know he knows Corbin is gone, but based on the way he left things Thursday, I doubt he cares much. I half expected that he would eventually explain if I did something wrong or at least tell me what upset him so much, but the last I got from him was the slam of his bedroom door after he walked away.

I can see why he hasn't been in a relationship for six years. He's obviously clueless when it comes to how a guy should treat a girl, which surprises me, because I get these vibes from him that he's really a decent guy. However, his actions during and after sex seem to contradict his character. It's as if pieces of the guy he used to be bleed over into the guy he's trying to be.

If any other man ever treated me like he did, it would be the one and only time. I don't put up with the things I've seen a lot of my friends put up with. However, I find myself continuing to make excuses for him, like something could actually justify his actions last week.

I'm beginning to fear that maybe I'm not so tough after all.

That fear is immediately confirmed with the skip of my heart as soon as I step off the elevator. There's a note taped to my apartment door, so I rush to it and pull it down. It's just a folded piece of paper without anything written on the outside of it. I open it: *I need to run an errand. I'll stop by at seven if you want to come with me.* I read the note several times. It's obviously from him, and it's obviously for me, but the note reads so incredibly casual that for a second, I begin to doubt that Thursday even happened.

He was there, though. He knows how that night ended between us. He knows I must be upset or angry, but nothing in his note reveals that at all.

I unlock my door and walk inside before I can work myself up to the point of beating on his door to scream at him.

I drop my things once I'm inside my apartment and read the note one more time, dissecting everything from his handwriting down to his selection of words. I wad it up in my hands and throw it toward the kitchen, completely pissed off.

I'm pissed because I already know I'll be going with him.

I don't know how *not* to.

• • •

There's a soft knock on the door at exactly seven o'clock. His punctuality pisses me off, and there's no reason for it. I have nothing against punctuality. I have a feeling every single thing Miles does tonight is going to piss me off.

I walk to the front door and open it.

He's standing in the hallway, several feet away. He's probably closer to his door than to mine, actually. He's looking down at his feet when I open the door, but he eventually lifts his eyes to meet mine. His hands are tucked away in his jacket pockets again, and he doesn't lift his head all the way up. I take this as a sign of submission from him, even though it's more than likely not.

"Want to come?"

His voice invades me. Weakens me. Turns me into liquid again. I nod as I step out into the hall and close the door behind me. I lock it and turn around to face him. He nods his head toward the elevators, silently telling me he'll follow behind me. I try to read the expression in his eyes, but I should know better.

I walk toward the elevator and press the down button.

He stands next to me, but neither of us speaks. It takes the elevator what seems like years to get to us. When it finally opens, we both breathe a quiet sigh of relief, but as soon as we're inside and the doors close, neither of us can breathe again.

I can feel him watching me, but I don't look at him.

I *can't*.

I feel stupid. I feel like I want to cry again. Now that I'm here and I have no idea where we're going, I feel like a fool for allowing him to even get me this far.

"I'm sorry." His voice is weak, but it's also surprisingly sincere.

I don't look at him. I don't even respond.

He takes three steps across the elevator, and then he reaches down beside me and presses the emergency stop button. His finger lingers on the button as he watches me, but I keep my eyes down. My face is level with his chest, but my jaw is tense, and I won't look up at him.

I won't.

"Tate, I'm sorry," he repeats. He's still not touching me, but he's invading again. He's standing so close to me I can feel his breath and him and how much he really is sorry, but I don't even know what I'm supposed to be forgiving him for. He never promised anything other than sex, and that's exactly what he gave me.

Sex.

Nothing less and definitely nothing more.

"I'm sorry," he says again. "You didn't deserve that."

This time, he touches my chin, lifting my eyes to meet his. The feel of his fingers on my face causes my jaw to grow even more tense. I'm doing everything I can to keep up my armor, because I'm finding it hard to fight back my tears.

The same thing I saw in his eyes when he kissed me at his door Thursday night is back. Something unspoken that he wishes he could say, but the only words that come out of his mouth are his apologies.

He winces as though he's experiencing actual physical pain, and he presses his forehead to mine. "I'm *sorry.*"

He presses his palms against the elevator wall and leans into me until our chests are touching. My arms are at my sides, and my eyes are closed, and as much as I feel like crying right now, I refuse to do it in front of him. I'm still not sure what he's apologizing for specifically, but it doesn't matter, because it sounds like he's apologizing for *everything.* For starting something with me that we knew wouldn't end well. For not being able to open up about his past. For not being able to open up about his future. For ruining me when he walked into his bedroom and slammed his door.

One of his hands wraps around the side of my head, and he pulls me against him. His other hand drops to my back, and he squeezes me, pressing his cheek against the top of my head. "I don't know what this is, Tate," he confesses. "But I swear, I didn't mean to hurt you. I just don't know what the hell I'm doing."

The apology in his voice is enough to make my arms want to hold him. I bring them up and grab the sleeves of his shirt, then press my face into his chest. We stand like this for several minutes, both of us completely lost. Completely new to this.

Completely confused.

He eventually releases me and hits the button to take us to the ground floor. I still haven't spoken, because I'm not even sure what words to use in this situation. When the elevator doors open, he takes my hand in his and holds it all the way to his car. He opens my door and waits for me to climb inside, then closes it and walks around to his side.

I've never been inside his car before.

I'm surprised by the simplicity of it. I know Corbin makes a decent amount of money and usually likes to spend it on nice things.

This car is understated, just like Miles.

He exits the parking garage, and we drive in silence for several miles. I'm tired of the quiet and tired of the curiosity, so the first thing I say to him since he ruined me is, "Where are we going?"

It's as if my voice makes the awkwardness completely disintegrate, because he exhales like he's relieved to hear it.

"To the airport," he says. "Not for work, though. I go there sometimes to watch the planes take off."

He reaches across the console and takes my hand in his. It's comforting and scary all at once. His hands are warm, and it makes me want him to hold my entire body in them, but it scares me how much I want that.

It's completely quiet again until we reach the airport. There are restricted-access signs, but he passes them like he knows exactly where he's going. We finally pull into a parking lot over-looking the runway.

Several jets are lined up, waiting to take off. He points to the left, and I look, just as one of the planes begins to accelerate. His car fills with the sound of the engines as it zooms past us. We both watch it make its ascent, until the landing gear disappears and the plane is swallowed up by the night.

"You come here a lot?" I ask him while I continue to stare out my window.

He laughs, so naturally, I turn to face him.

"That sounded like a pickup line," he says, smiling.

His smile makes me smile. His eyes drop to my mouth, and my smile makes his smile disappear.

"Yeah, I do," he says as he looks out his window again to watch the next jet prepare for takeoff.

I realize in this moment that things aren't the same between us. Something huge changed, and I can't tell if it's good or bad. He brought me here because he wants to talk.

I just don't know what he wants to talk about.

"Miles," I say, wanting him to look at me again. He doesn't.

"It's not fun," he says quietly. "This thing we're doing."

I don't like that sentence. I want him to take it back, because it feels like it's cutting me. But he's right. "I know," I say.

"If we don't stop now, it'll just get worse."

I don't verbally agree with him this time. I know he's right, but I don't want to stop. The thought of not being with him again makes my stomach feel hollow. "What did I do to upset you so much?"

He cuts his eyes to mine, and I hardly recognize them from the ice built up behind them. "That was all me, Tate," he says firmly. "Don't think for a second that my issues are because of anything you do or don't do."

I find a slight amount of relief from his answer but still have no idea what went wrong with him. We keep our eyes locked, waiting for the other to fill the silence again.

I have no idea what he's suffered through in the past, but it must have been pretty damn difficult if he can't move on after six years.

"You act like it's such a bad thing for us to like each other."

"Maybe it is," he says.

I kind of want him to stop talking now, because everything he says is just causing me more pain and making me even more confused. "So you brought me here to call it off?"

He sighs heavily. "I just wanted it to be fun, but . . . I think you might have different expectations from mine. I don't want to hurt you, and if we keep doing this . . . I *will*." He looks out his window again.

I want to hit something, but instead, I run two frustrated hands down my face and fall back heavily against my seat. I've never met anyone who can say so little when they speak. He's definitely perfected the art of evasiveness.

"You have to give me more than that, Miles. A simple explanation, maybe? What the hell happened to you?"

His jaw tightens as firmly as the grip he still has on his steering wheel. "I asked you to do two things for me. Don't ask about my past, and never expect a future. You're doing both."

I nod. "Yes, Miles. You're right. I am. Because I like you, and I know you like me, and when we're together, it's phenomenal, so that's what normal people do. When they find someone they're compatible with, they open up to them. They let them in. They want to be with them. They don't fuck them against their kitchen table and then walk away and make them feel like complete shit."

Nothing.

He gives me nothing.

No reaction whatsoever.

He faces forward and starts his car. "You were right," he says. He puts the car in reverse and prepares to pull out of the parking lot. "It's a good thing we weren't friends first. Would have made this a lot harder."

I turn away from him because I'm embarrassed at how angry his words are making me. I'm embarrassed it's hurting me like it is, but everything with Miles hurts. It hurts because I know how good our good moments are, and I know how easily the bad moments would go away if he would just stop trying to fight this.

"Tate," he says with remorse.

I want to rip his voice from his throat.

His hand meets my shoulder, and the car isn't moving anymore. "Tate, I didn't mean that."

I push his hand away. "Don't," I say. "Either admit you want me for more than just sex, or take me home."

He's quiet. Maybe he's contemplating my ultimatum.

Admit it, Miles. Admit it. Please.

The car begins moving again.

• • •

"What did you expect would happen?" Cap asks, handing me another tissue.

When Miles and I arrived back at the apartment complex, I couldn't bear riding up that elevator with him, so I took a seat next to Cap and let him go up alone. Unlike the hard exterior I try to show Miles, I completely break down while spilling all the details to Cap, whether he cares to hear them or not.

I wipe my nose again and drop the tissue, adding it to the pile next to me on the floor. "I was being delusional," I say. "I told myself I could handle it if he never wanted more. I guess I thought if I let him take his time, he'd eventually come around."

Cap reaches around to a trash can at his side and places it between us so I have somewhere to toss my tissues. "If that boy can't see what a good thing he could have with you, then he ain't worth your time."

I nod, agreeing with him. I do have a lot more important things to do with my time, but for some reason, I feel as if Miles *can* see what a good thing he has with me. I feel like he wishes he could make this work between us, but something bigger than him or me or us is holding him back. I just wish I knew what it was.

"Have I told you my favorite joke yet?" Cap asks.

I shake my head and grab another tissue from the box in his hands, relieved at the change in subject.

"Knock, knock," he says.

I didn't expect his favorite joke to be a knock-knock joke, but I play along. "Who's there?"

"Interrupting cow," he says.

"Interrupt—"

"MOO!" he yells loudly, cutting me off.

I stare at him.

Then I laugh.

I laugh harder than I've laughed in a long damn time.

chapter twenty-two

MILES

Six years earlier

My dad says he needs to speak to us.

He asks me to get Rachel and meet him and Lisa at the dining-room table. I tell him okay, that there's something we need to speak to them about, too.

Curiosity flashes in his eyes but only for a brief second. He thinks about Lisa again, and he's not curious anymore.

His everything is Lisa.

I go to Rachel's room and tell *my* everything that they want to speak to us.

We all sit down at the dining-room table.

I know what he's going to say. He's going to tell us he proposed. I don't want to care, but I do. I wonder why he didn't tell me first. This makes me sad but only a little bit. It's not going to matter after we tell them what we have to tell them.

"I asked Lisa to marry me," he says. Lisa smiles at him. He smiles at her.

Rachel and I aren't smiling.

"So we did," Lisa says, flashing her ring.

So.

We.

Did.

Rachel gasps quietly.

They're already married.

They look happy.

They're looking at us, waiting for a reaction.

Lisa is concerned. She doesn't like that Rachel looks so upset.

"Honey, it was spur-of-the-moment. We were in Vegas.

Neither of us wanted a big wedding. Please don't be mad."

Rachel begins crying into her hands. I wrap my arm around her and want to console her. I want to kiss her reassuringly, but my father and Lisa wouldn't understand it.

I need to tell them.

My dad looks confused that Rachel is so upset. "I didn't think either of you would mind," he says. "You're both leaving for college in a couple of months."

He thinks we're mad at them.

"Dad?" I say, keeping my arm around Rachel. "Lisa?"

I look at both of them.

I ruin their day.

Ruin.

"Rachel is pregnant."

Silence.

Silence.

Silence.

DEAFENING SILENCE.

Lisa is in shock.

My father is comforting Lisa. His arm is around her, and he's rubbing her back.

"You don't even have a boyfriend," Lisa says to Rachel.

Rachel looks at me.

My father stands. He's angry now. "Who's responsible?" he yells. He looks at me. "Tell me who he is, Miles. What kind of guy knocks a girl up and doesn't have the balls to be with her when she tells her own mother? What kind of guy would let a girl's brother be the one to break the news?"

"I'm not her *brother*," I say to my father.

I'm not.

He ignores my comment. He's pacing the kitchen now. He hates the person who did this to Rachel.

"Dad," I say. I stand up.

He stops pacing. He turns and looks at me.

"Dad . . ."

I'm suddenly not as confident as I was when I sat down to do this.

I've got this.

"Dad, it was me. I'm the one who got her pregnant."

My words are hard for him to swallow.

Lisa is looking back and forth between Rachel and me. She can't swallow what I'm saying, either.

"That's not possible," my father says, trying to push away all the thoughts that are telling him it *is* possible.

I wait for it to process.

His expression changes from confusion to anger. He looks at me like I'm not even his son. He's looking at me like I'm the guy who knocked up his new stepdaughter.

He hates me.

He hates me.

He *really* hates me.

UGLY LOVE | 201

"Get out of this house."

I look at Rachel. She grabs my hand and shakes her head, silently pleading for me not to leave.

"Get out," he says again.

He hates me.

I tell Rachel I should go. "Just for a little while."

She begs me not to go. My father walks around the table and shoves me. He pushes me toward the door. I release Rachel's hand.

"I'll be at Ian's," I tell her. "I love you."

Those words are obviously too much for my father, because his fist immediately comes at me. He pulls his hand back and looks almost as shocked as I do that he just punched me.

I step outside, and my father slams the door.

My father hates me.

I walk to my car and open the door. I sit in the driver's seat, but I don't crank the engine. I look in the mirror. My lip is bleeding.

I hate my father.

I get out of my car and slam the door. I walk back into the house. My father rushes to the door.

I hold my palms up. I don't want to hit him, but I will. If he touches me again, I'll hit him.

Rachel isn't at the table anymore.

Rachel is in her room.

"I'm sorry," I say to both of them. "We didn't mean for it to happen, but it happened, and now we have to deal with it."

Lisa is crying. My father hugs her. I look at Lisa.

"I love her," I say. "I'm in love with your daughter. I'll take care of them."

We've got this.

Lisa can't even look at me.

They both hate me.

"This started before I even met you, Lisa. I met her before I knew you were with my father, and we tried to stop it."

That's kind of a lie.

My father steps forward. "The entire time? This has been going on the entire time she's lived here?"

I shake my head. "It's been going on since *before* she lived here."

He hates me even more now. He wants to hit me again, but Lisa is pulling him back. She tells him they'll figure it out. She tells him she can get it "taken care of." She tells him it'll be okay.

"It's too late for that," I tell Lisa. "She's too far along."

I don't wait for my father to hit me again. I rush down the hallway and go to Rachel. I lock the door behind me.

She meets me halfway. She throws her arms around my neck and cries into my shirt.

"Well," I say. "The hard part is over with."

She laughs with her cry. She tells me the hard part isn't over yet. She tells me the hard part is getting him out.

I laugh.

I love you so much, Rachel.

"I love you so much, Miles," she whispers.

chapter twenty-three

TATE

I miss you so much, Miles.

Thoughts like that are why I'm drowning my sorrows in chocolate. It's been three weeks since he brought me home. It's been three weeks since I've laid eyes on him. Christmas came and went, but I barely noticed because I worked through it. Two Thursday game nights that Miles didn't show up to. New Year's came and went. Another semester of school began.

And Tate still misses Miles.

I take my chocolate chips and my chocolate milk and walk to the kitchen to hide them from the person knocking at the apartment door.

I already know it's not Miles, because the knock at my door belongs to Chad and Tarryn. They're the only friends I've made here, as busy as I am, and they're only my friends because we're in study group together.

Which is why they're knocking on my door right now.

I open it, and Chad is standing in the doorway sans Tarryn. "Where's Tarryn?"

"She got called in to cover a shift," he says. "She can't make it tonight."

I hold the door open further to let him in. As soon as he steps over the threshold, Miles opens his apartment door across the hall. He freezes when our eyes meet.

He holds me captive with his stare for several seconds until his gaze slides over my shoulder and lands on Chad.

I glance at Chad, who looks at me and arches an eyebrow. He can apparently tell something's up, so he respectfully retreats into my apartment. "I'll be in your room, Tate," he says.

That's nice of Chad . . . offering to give me privacy with the guy across the hall. However, announcing that he'll be waiting in my bedroom probably wasn't the respect Miles wanted to be shown, because now he's stepping back inside his apartment.

His eyes drop to the floor right before he closes his door.

The look on his face sends pangs of guilt straight to my stomach. I have to remind myself that this was his choice. I have nothing to feel guilty about, even if he is misjudging the situation he just opened his door to.

I close the front door and join Chad in my room. The silent pep talk I tried to give myself did nothing to ease the guilt. I sit on the bed, and he sits at the desk. "That was weird," he says, eyeing me. "I'm a little scared to leave your apartment now."

I shake my head. "Don't worry about Miles. He has issues, but they aren't my issues anymore."

Chad nods and doesn't question me any further. He opens the study guide and lays it across his lap as he props his feet up on the bed.

"Tarryn already made notes for chapter two, so if you get three, I'll cover four."

"Deal," I say. I scoot back against my pillow and spend the next hour preparing notes for chapter three, but I have no idea how I manage to concentrate, because the only thing I can think about is the look that crossed Miles's face right before he closed the door. I could tell I hurt him.

That makes us even now, I guess.

* * *

After Chad and I exchange notes and answer the study questions at the end of every chapter, I make copies on my printer. I realize three people divvying up three chapters and sharing answers is cheating, but who the hell cares? I never claimed to be perfect.

Once we're finished, I walk Chad back out. I can tell he's a little bit nervous after having seen the look on Miles's face earlier, so I wait for him to get on the elevator before I close the apartment door. To be honest, I was a little nervous for him, too.

I walk to the kitchen and begin making a plate of leftovers. There's no point in cooking, since Corbin won't be home until late tonight. Before I'm finished adding food to my plate, the front door opens with a knock.

Miles is the only one who opens the door and knocks at the same time.

Calm down.

Calm down, calm down, calm down.

Calm the hell down, Tate!

"Who was that?" Miles asks from behind me.

I don't even turn around. I continue making my plate of food as if his being here after weeks of silence isn't filling me with a storm of emotions. Anger being the most prominent one.

"He's in my class," I say. "We were studying."

I can feel the tension rolling off him, and I'm not even facing him. "For three hours?"

I spin around and face him, but the expletives I want to scream get caught in my throat when I see him. He's standing in the doorway to the kitchen, gripping the door frame over his head. I can tell he hasn't worked in a few days, because his jaw is lined with a thin layer of stubble. He's barefoot, and his shirt has risen up with his arms, revealing that *V*.

At first, I stare at him.

Then I yell at him.

"If I want to screw a guy in my bedroom for three hours, then good for me! You aren't at all entitled to have an opinion about what goes on in my life. You're a jerk, and you have serious issues, and I don't want to be a part of them anymore."

I'm lying. I really do want to be a part of his issues. I want to immerse myself in his issues and *become* his issues, but I'm supposed to be this independent, headstrong girl who doesn't cave just because she likes a guy.

His eyes are narrowed, and his breaths are coming hard and fast. He drops his arms and walks swiftly to me, grabbing my face, forcing me to look up at him.

His eyes are frantic, and knowing that he's scared that I've moved on feels way too good. He waits several seconds before speaking, allowing his eyes to roam over my face. His thumbs brush lightly across my cheekbones, and his hands feel protective and good, and I absolutely hate that I want them everywhere right now. I don't like who he turns me into.

"Are you sleeping with him?" he asks, finally resting his eyes on mine as they search for truth.

That's none of your business, Miles.

"No," I say instead.

"Have you kissed him?"

Still not your business, Miles.

"No."

He closes his eyes and exhales, relieved. He drops his hands to the bar on either side of me and lowers his forehead to my shoulder.

He doesn't ask me another question.

He's hurting, but I don't know what the hell to do about it. He's the only one who can change things between us, and as far as I know, he's still not willing to do that.

"Tate," he says in a pained whisper. His face moves to my neck, and one of his hands grips my waist. "*Dammit*, Tate." His other hand moves to the back of my head as his lips rest against the skin of my neck. "What do I do?" he whispers. "What the fuck do I do?"

I squeeze my eyes shut, because the confusion and pain in his voice are unbearable. I shake my head. I shake it because I don't know how to answer a question that I don't even know the meaning behind. I also shake my head because I don't know how to physically push him away.

His lips meet the spot just below my ear, and I want to pull him closer and push him as far away as I can. His mouth continues to move across my skin, and I feel my neck tilting so that he can find even more of me to kiss. His fingers tangle in my hair as he grips the back of my head to hold me still against his mouth.

"Make me leave," he says, his voice pleading and warm against my throat. "You don't need this." He's kissing his way up my throat, breaking for breath only when he speaks. "I just don't know how to stop wanting you. Tell me to go, and I'll go."

I don't tell him to go. I shake my head. "I can't."

I turn my face toward his just as he's worked his way up to my mouth, then I grab his shirt and pull him to me, knowing exactly what I'm doing to myself. I know this time won't end any prettier than the other times, but I still want it just as much. If not *more*.

He pauses and looks me hard in the eyes. "I can't give you more than this," he whispers as a warning. "I just can't."

I hate him for saying that but respect it just the same.

I respond by pulling him closer until our lips meet. We open our mouths at the exact same time and completely devour each other. We're frantic, pulling at each other, moaning, digging into each other's skin.

Sex, I remind myself. It's just sex. Nothing more. He's not giving me any other part of him.

I can tell myself that all I want, but at the same time, I'm taking, taking, taking as much as I can get. Deciphering every sound he makes and every touch, attempting to convince myself that what he's giving me is so much more than what it probably is.

I'm a fool.

At least I'm a self-aware fool.

I unbutton his jeans, and he unfastens my bra, and before we're even in my bedroom, my shirt is off. Our mouths never separate as he shuts my door, then yanks off my bra. He pushes me onto the bed and pulls off my jeans, then stands and removes his own.

It's a race.

It's Miles and me against everything else.

We're racing our consciences, our pride, our respect, the truth. He's trying to get inside me before any of the rest of that stuff catches up to us.

As soon as he's back on the bed, he's over me, against me, then inside me.

We win.

His mouth finds mine again, but that's all it does. He doesn't kiss me. Our lips touch and our breath collides and our eyes meet, but there isn't a kiss.

What our mouths are doing is so much more than that. With

every thrust inside me, his lips slide over mine, and his eyes grow hungrier, but he never once kisses me.

A kiss is so much easier than what we're doing. When you kiss, you can close your eyes. You can kiss away the thoughts. You can kiss away the pain, the doubt, the shame. When you close your eyes and kiss, you protect yourself from the vulnerability.

This isn't us protecting ourselves.

This is confrontation. This is a standoff. This is eye-to-eye combat. This is a dare, from me to Miles, from Miles to me. *I dare you to try to stop this,* we're both silently screaming.

His eyes remain focused on mine the entire time as he moves in and out of me. With each thrust, I hear his words from just a few short weeks ago repeat in my head.

It's easy to confuse feelings and emotions for something they aren't, especially when eye contact is involved.

I completely understand now. I understand so well I almost wish he'd close his eyes, because he's more than likely not feeling what his eyes are showing me right now.

"You feel so good," he whispers. The words fall into my mouth, forcing moans out of me in reciprocation. He lowers his right hand between us, placing pressure against me in a way that would normally cause my head to fall backward and my eyes to fall shut.

Not this time. I'm not backing down from this confrontation. Especially not when he's staring straight into my eyes, defying his own words.

Even though I refuse to back down, I do let him know I like what he's doing to me. I can't help but let him know that, because I don't have control over my voice right now. It's possessed by a girl who thinks she wants this from him.

"Don't stop," my voice says, becoming more possessed by him the longer this continues.

"Wasn't planning on it."

He applies more pressure, both inside and outside me. He grabs my leg behind the knee and pulls it up between our chests, finding a slightly different angle to enter me. He holds my leg firmly against his shoulder and somehow thrusts into me even deeper.

"Miles. Oh, my *God*." I moan his name and God's name and even shout out to Jesus a couple of times. I begin to shudder beneath him, and I'm not sure which one of us broke down first, but we're kissing now. We're kissing as hard and as deep as his thrusts inside me.

He's loud. *I'm louder.*

I'm shaking. *He's shaking harder.*

He's out of breath. *I'm inhaling enough for both of us.*

He pushes into me one final time and holds me firmly against the mattress with his weight. "Tate," he says, moaning my name against my mouth as his body recovers from the tremors. "*Fuck*, Tate." He slowly pulls out of me and presses his cheek against my chest. "Holy shit," he breathes. "It's so good. This. Us. So fucking good."

"I know."

He rolls onto his side and keeps his arm draped across me. We lie together quietly.

Me—not wanting to admit that I just let him use me again.

Him—not wanting to admit that it was more than just sex.

Both of us lying to ourselves.

"Where's Corbin?" he asks.

"He'll be home later tonight."

He lifts his head and looks down at me, his brows furrowed in a line of worry. "I should go." He rolls off the bed and pulls his jeans back on. "Come over later?"

I nod as I stand up and slide into my own jeans. "Grab my

shirt from the kitchen," I tell him. I pull on my bra and fasten it.
He opens my bedroom door, but he doesn't walk out. He pauses
in the doorway. He's looking at someone.

Shit.

I don't have to see him to know that Corbin is standing
there. I immediately rush to the door to stop whatever's about
to happen. When I hold it open further, Corbin is standing in
his doorway across the hall, glaring at Miles.

I make the first move. "Corbin, before you say anything—"

He holds up his hand to shut me up. His eyes drop for a
second to my bra, and he winces as if he was hoping that what
he heard didn't really happen. He looks away, and I immediately
cover myself, embarrassed that he heard everything. He looks
back at Miles, and his eyes are an equal mixture of anger and
disappointment. "How long?"

"Don't answer that, Miles," I say. I just want him to leave.
Corbin has no right to be questioning him like this. It's ridiculous.

"A while," Miles says, shamefully.

Corbin nods slowly, letting it sink in. "Do you love her?"

Miles and I look at each other. He looks back at Corbin as
if he's trying to decide which one of us he wants his answer to
please.

I'm positive the slow shake of his head pleases neither of us.

"Are you at least planning to?" Corbin asks.

I continue to study Miles as if someone is asking him what
the meaning of life is. I think I want his answer to Corbin's question more than Corbin does.

Miles exhales and shakes his head again. "No," he whispers.

No.

He's not even *planning* to love me.

I knew his answer. I expected it. However, it still hurts like
hell. The fact that he can't even lie about it to save himself from

disappointing Corbin proves that this isn't some game he's playing.

This is *Miles*. Miles isn't capable of love. Not anymore, anyway.

Corbin grips the frame of his door and presses his forehead against his arm, inhaling a slow, steady breath. He looks back up at Miles with eyes like arrows aimed at a target. In all my life, I've never seen Corbin this angry.

"You just fucked my *sister?*"

I'm waiting for Miles to fall backward from the impact of Corbin's words, but he takes a step toward him instead. "Corbin, she's a grown woman."

Corbin takes a quick step toward Miles. "Get out."

Miles glances back at me, and his eyes are apologetic and full of regret. I'm not sure if it's for me or for Corbin, but he does what Corbin asks.

He leaves.

I'm still standing in my bedroom doorway, looking at Corbin like I could fly across this hall and deck him.

Corbin pierces me with a stare as firm as his stance. "You're not a brother, Tate," he says. "Don't you dare tell me I'm not allowed to be pissed." He steps back into his bedroom and slams his door.

I blink rapidly, fighting back tears of anger because of Corbin, tears of hurt because of Miles, and tears of shame because of the selfish choices I made for myself. I refuse to cry in front of either of them.

I walk to the kitchen and retrieve my shirt, then pull it over my head as I make my way toward the front door and across the hall. I knock on his door, and Miles opens it immediately. He looks behind me as if he expects Corbin to be standing there, then he steps aside and lets me in.

"He'll get over it," I say to him after he closes his door.

"I know," he says quietly. "But it won't be the same." Miles walks to his living room and sits on his couch, so I follow him and sit down beside him. I don't have any words of advice, because he's right. Things more than likely won't be the same between him and Corbin. I feel shitty that I'm the reason for that.

Miles sighs as he pulls my hand to his lap. He threads his fingers through mine. "Tate," he says. "I'm sorry."

I look at him, and his eyes come up and meet mine. "For what?"

I don't know why I'm pretending not to know what he's talking about. I know exactly what he's talking about.

"When Corbin asked if I planned on loving you," he says. "I'm sorry I couldn't say yes. I just didn't want to lie to either of you."

I shake my head. "You've been nothing but honest about what you want from me, Miles. I can't be mad at you for that."

He inhales a deep breath as he stands and begins pacing the living room. I remain on the couch and watch him as he works to gather his thoughts. He eventually pauses and locks his hands behind his head. "I had no right to question you about that guy, either. I don't allow you to question me or my life, so I have no right to question yours."

Not about to argue with that logic.

"I just don't know how to deal with this thing between us." He steps closer to me, and I stand up. He wraps his arms around my shoulders and holds me against his chest. "I don't know an easy or even polite way to say this, but what I said to Corbin is the truth. I'll never love anyone again. It's not worth it to me. But I'm being unfair to you. I know I'm messing with your head, and I know I've hurt you, and I'm sorry for that. I just like being with you, but every time I'm with you, I'm scared you're seeing it for more than it really is."

I know I should have some sort of reaction to everything he just said, but I'm still processing his words. Every single one of his admissions should be a red flag, since they were all also coupled with the hard truth that he doesn't plan on loving me or having a relationship with me, but the red flag doesn't rise.

The green one does.

"Is it me specifically you don't want to love, or is it love in general you don't want to experience?"

He pulls me away from his chest so he can look at me while he answers my question. "It's love in general I don't want, Tate. Ever. It's you specifically that I just . . . *want*."

I fall in and out and back in love with that answer.

I'm so screwed up. Everything he says should send me running, but instead, it makes me want to wrap my arms around him and give him whatever it is he's willing to take from me. I'm lying to him, and I'm lying to myself, and I'm not doing either of us any good, but I can't stop the words that come out of my mouth.

"I can handle this as long as it stays simple," I tell him. "When you pull the shit you pulled a few weeks ago by walking away and slamming your door? That's not keeping it simple, Miles. Things like that make it complicated."

He nods, contemplating what I've said. "Simple," he says, rolling the word around in his mouth. "If you can do simple, I can do simple."

"Good," I say. "And when it becomes too hard for either of us, we'll end it for good."

"I'm not worried about it becoming too hard for me," he says. "I'm worried about it becoming too hard for *you*."

I'm worried about me, too, Miles. But I want the here and now with you a whole lot more than I care about how it will affect me in the end.

With that thought, I suddenly figure out what my one rule is. He's had his boundaries this entire time, protecting himself from the vulnerability that I've been subjected to.

"I think I finally have my one rule," I say. He looks at me and raises a brow, waiting for me to talk. "Don't give me false hope for a future," I say. "Especially if you know in your heart we'll never have one."

His posture immediately stiffens. "Have I done that?" he asks, genuinely concerned. "Have I given you false hope before?"

Yes. About thirty minutes ago, when you looked me in the eyes the entire time you were inside me.

"No," I say quickly. "Just make sure you don't do or say things that would make me believe otherwise. As long as we both see this for what it is, I think we'll be fine."

He stares at me silently for a while, studying me. Evaluating my words. "I can't tell if you're really mature for your age or really delusional."

I shrug, guarding my delusions deep inside my chest. "An unhealthy mixture of both, I'm sure."

He presses his lips against the side of my head. "This feels really fucked up to say out loud, but I promise I won't give you hope for us, Tate."

My heart frowns at his words, but my face forces a smile. "Good," I say. "You have serious issues that kind of freak me out, and I'd much rather fall in love with an emotionally stable man someday."

He laughs. Probably because he knows the odds of finding someone who can put up with this kind of relationship, if you can even call it that, are extremely low. Yet somehow, the one girl who might be fine with it just happened to move in across the hall from him. And he actually likes her.

You like me, Miles Archer.

• • •

"Corbin found out," I say as I take what has become my usual seat next to Cap.

"Uh-oh," he says. "Is the boy still alive?"

I nod. "For now. Not sure how long that'll last, though."

The doors to the lobby open, and I watch Dillon make his way inside. He pulls a hat off his head and shakes rain out of it as he walks toward the elevator.

"Sometimes I wish the flights I send up would crash," Cap says, eyeing Dillon.

I guess Cap doesn't like Dillon, either. I'm beginning to feel a little bad for Dillon.

He spots us just before he reaches the elevators. Cap is moving to press the up button, but Dillon reaches it before him. "I'm pretty capable of fetching my own elevator, old man," he says.

I vaguely remember having a brief thought ten seconds ago about Dillon and how I felt sorry for him. I take that thought back now.

Dillon looks at me and winks. "What you doing, Tate?"

"Washing elephants," I say with a straight face.

Dillon shoots me a confused look, not at all understanding my random response.

"If you don't want a sarcastic answer," Cap says to him, "don't ask a stupid question."

The elevator doors open, and Dillon rolls his eyes at both of us before walking onto the elevator.

Cap cuts his eyes to mine, and he grins. He holds a palm up in the air, and I high-five him.

chapter twenty-four

MILES

Six years earlier

"Why is everything yellow?"

My dad is standing in the doorway to Rachel's bedroom, looking at the few items we've collected in the months since he's known about the pregnancy. "It looks like Big Bird threw up in here."

Rachel laughs. She's standing at the bathroom mirror, putting the finishing touches on her makeup. I've been lying on her bed, watching her.

"We don't want to know if it's a boy or a girl, so we're buying gender-neutral colors."

Rachel answers my dad's question as if it were one of many, but we both know it's the first. He hasn't asked about the pregnancy. He doesn't ask about our plans. He usually leaves the room if Rachel and I are both in it.

Lisa isn't much different. She's not past the point of disappointment or sadness yet, so we don't push it. It'll take time, so Rachel and I are giving that to them.

Right now, Rachel only has me to talk to about the baby, and I only have her, and even though that seems like too little, it's more than enough for both of us.

"How long will the ceremony last?" my dad asks me.

"No more than two hours," I tell him.

He says we should go.

I tell him that as soon as Rachel is ready, we can go.

Rachel says she's ready.

We go.

• • •

"Congratulations," I tell Rachel.

"Congratulations," she tells me.

We both graduated three hours ago. Now we're lying on my bed, thinking about our next step. Or at least *I* am, anyway.

"Let's move in together," I tell her.

She laughs. "We kind of already live together, Miles," she points out.

I shake my head. "You know what I mean. I know we already have plans for after we start college in August, but I think we should do it now."

She rises up on her elbow and looks at me, probably trying to read my expression to see if I'm serious.

"How? Where would we go?"

I reach over to my nightstand and open the top drawer. I pull out the letter and hand it to her.

She begins reading it out loud.

Dear Mr. Archer,

She looks up at me, and her eyes are wide.

Congratulations on your summer registration. We are pleased to inform you that your application for family housing has been processed and approved.

Rachel smiles.

Enclosed you will find a return envelope and the final paperwork which will need to be returned by the postmarked date.

Rachel looks at the envelope and quickly flips through the attached paperwork. She pulls the letter back to the top.

We look forward to receiving the completed forms. Our contact information is below should you have any questions.

Sincerely,

Paige Donahue, Registrar

Rachel covers her smile with her hand and tosses the letter aside, then leans forward and hugs me.

"We get to move now?" she says.

I love how evident the excitement is in her voice.

I tell her yes. Rachel is relieved. She knows as well as I do how awkward the next several weeks would have been in the same house as our parents.

"Have you asked your father yet?"

I tell her she forgets that we're adults now. We no longer have to ask for permission. We only have to inform.

Rachel says she wants to inform them right now.

I take Rachel's hand, and we walk together to the living room and inform our parents that we're moving out.

Together.

chapter twenty-five

TATE

It's been a few weeks since Corbin found out. He hasn't ac-
cepted it, and he still hasn't spoken to Miles, but he's beginning
to adapt. He knows on the nights I leave without explanation,
only to come back a few hours later, where I've been. He
doesn't ask.

As far as things with Miles, I'm the one doing the adapting.
I've had to adapt to his rules, because there's no way Miles is
adapting to breaking them. I've learned to stop trying to figure
him out and to stop allowing things to get so tense between us.
We're doing exactly what we agreed to do in the beginning,
which was to have sex.

A lot of sex.

Shower sex. Bedroom sex. Floor sex. Kitchen-table sex.

I've still never spent the night with him, and it still hurts
sometimes how closed off he becomes right after it's over, but I
still haven't figured out a way to say no to him.

I know I want so much more than what he's giving me and he wants so much less than what I want to give him, but we're both just taking what we can get for now. I try not to think about what will happen the day I can't handle it anymore. I try not to think about all the other things I'm sacrificing by still being involved with him.

I try not to think about it at all, but the thoughts still come. Every night, when I'm in bed, I think about it. Every time I'm in the shower, I think about it. When I'm in class, in the living room, in the kitchen, at work . . . I think about what's going to happen when one of us finally comes to our senses.

"Is Tate a nickname for something else?" Miles asks me.

We're in his bed. He just got home from four days at work, and even though our arrangement is supposed to be all about sex, we're still fully dressed. We're not making out. He's just lying with me, asking me personal questions about my name, and I love it so much more than any other day we've ever spent together.

It's the first time he's ever asked me a semi-personal question. I hate that his question fills me with all these feelings of hope, and all he did was ask me if Tate was a nickname.

"Tate is my middle name," I say. "It was my grandmother's maiden name."

"What's your first name?"

"Elizabeth."

"Elizabeth Tate Collins," he says, making love to my name with his voice. My name has never sounded as beautiful as it did just now, coming out of his mouth. "That's almost twice as many syllables as my name," he says. "That's a lot of syllables."

"What's your middle name?"

"Mikel," he says. "People always mispronounce it and say 'Michael,' though. Gets annoying."

"Miles Mikel Archer," I say. "That's a strong name."

Miles rises onto his elbow and looks down at me with a peaceful expression. He brushes my hair behind my ear as his eyes roam over my face. "Anything interesting happen this week while I was working, Elizabeth Tate Collins?" There's a playfulness in his voice. One that I'm not familiar with, but I like it. I like it a lot.

"Not really, Miles Mikel Archer," I say, smiling. "I worked a lot of overtime."

"Do you still like your job?" His fingers are touching my face, sliding across my lips, trailing down my neck.

"I do like it," I say. "Do you like being a captain?" I just throw versions of his own questions back at him. I figure it's safe that way, because I know he'll only give what he's willing to take.

Miles follows his hand with his eyes as he unbuttons the top button of my shirt. "I love my job, Tate." His fingers work on the second button of my shirt. "I just don't like being gone so much, especially knowing you're right across the hall from where I live. It makes me want to be home all the time."

I try to contain it, but I can't. His words make me gasp, even though it was probably the quietest gasp to ever pass anyone's lips.

But he notices.

His eyes meet mine in a flash, and I can see him wanting to backpedal. He wants to take back what he just said, because there was hope in those words. Miles doesn't say things like that. I know he's about to apologize. He's going to remind me that he can't love me, that he didn't mean to give me that inkling of false hope.

Don't take it back, Miles. Please, let me keep that.

Our eyes remain locked for several long seconds. I continue

to stare up at him, waiting for the take-back. His fingers are still on the second button of my shirt, but they're not attempting to unbutton it anymore.

He focuses on my mouth, then back to my eyes again, then back to my mouth. "Tate," he whispers. He says my name so softly I'm not even sure if his mouth moves.

I don't have time to respond. His hand leaves the button of my shirt and slides through my hair at the same moment as his lips connect fiercely with mine. He slides his body on top of me, and his kiss instantly becomes intense. Deep. Dominating. His kiss is full of something that's never been there before. Full of feeling. Full of *hope*.

Until this moment, I thought a kiss was a kiss was a kiss. I had no idea kisses could mean different things and feel so completely opposite from one another. In the past, I've always felt passion and desire and lust . . . but this time, it's different.

This kiss is a different Miles, and I know in my heart that it's the *real* Miles. The Miles he used to be. The Miles I'm not allowed to ask about.

• • •

He rolls off of me when he's finished.

I stare up at the ceiling.

My head is full of so many questions. My heart is full of confusion. This thing between us has never been easy. One would think limiting oneself to just sex would be the simplest thing in the world, but it makes me question every move and every word that comes out of my mouth. I find myself analyzing every look he gives me.

I don't even know what move I'm supposed to make next. Do I lie here until he asks me to leave? I've never stayed the night with him before. Do I roll over and put my arms around him, hoping he'll hold me in return until we fall asleep? I'm too scared he'll reject me.

I'm stupid.

I'm a stupid, stupid girl.

Why can't this just be sex for me, too? Why can't I come over here, give him what he wants, get what I want, and leave?

I roll onto my side and slowly sit up. I reach down for my clothes, then stand up and dress myself. He's watching me. He's quiet.

I avoid looking at him until I'm fully dressed and slipping on my shoes. As much as I want to crawl back into the bed with him, I walk toward the door instead. I don't turn around to face him when I say, "See you tomorrow, Miles."

I make it all the way to his front door. He doesn't speak. He doesn't tell me he'll see me tomorrow, and he doesn't tell me good-bye.

I'm hoping his silence is proof that he doesn't like how it feels to be walked away from.

I open the door and walk across the hall and into my apartment. Corbin is seated on the couch, watching TV. He glances up at the door when he hears me enter, then shoots me a condescending look of disapproval.

"Lighten up," I say as I make my way inside. I slip off my shoes by the door. "You have to get over this eventually."

I see him shake his head, but I ignore it and walk toward my bedroom.

"He was screwing you behind my back and lying to me," Corbin says. "That's not something I'll *get over*."

I face the living room again and see that Corbin is looking at me. "Did you expect him to be open with you about it? My God, Corbin. You kicked Dillon out of your apartment for *looking* at me the wrong way."

Corbin stands up, angry now. "Exactly!" he shouts. "I thought Miles was protecting you from Dillon, when in reality, he was laying claim! He's a goddamn hypocrite, and I'll be pissed at him for as long as I want to be pissed at him, so *you* get over it!"

I laugh, because Corbin has no right to point fingers.

"What's funny, Tate?" he snaps.

I walk back to the living room and stand directly in front of him. "Miles has been nothing but honest with me about what he wants. He hasn't once fed me a line of bullshit. I'm the only girl he's been with in six years, and you're going to call *him* a hypocrite?" I don't even try to keep my voice down anymore. "You might want to look in the mirror, Corbin. How many girls have you been with since I've moved in here? How many of them do you think have brothers who would love to kick your ass if they found out about you? If anyone's the hypocrite here, it's you!"

His hands are on his hips, and he's watching me with a hardened look in his eyes. When he fails to respond, I turn to walk back toward my room, but the front door opens with a knock.

Miles.

Corbin and I both turn, just as he peeks his head inside. "Everything good over here?" he asks, stepping into the living room.

I glance at Corbin, and Corbin glares at me. I arch an eyebrow, waiting for him to respond to the question Miles posed, since he's the one with the issue.

"You okay, Tate?" Miles asks, addressing only me now.

I look back over at him and nod. "I'm fine," I say. "I'm not the one with unrealistic expectations of my sibling."

Corbin groans loudly, then turns around and kicks the couch. Miles and I watch him as he slides his hands through his hair and grips the back of his neck tightly. He turns to face Miles again, then exhales heavily.

"Why couldn't you have just been gay?"

Miles looks at him with careful concentration. I'm waiting for either of them to have a reaction, so I'll know whether or not I can breathe.

Miles begins to shake his head as soon as a smile appears on his face.

Corbin starts to laugh, but he groans at the same time, indicating that he just came to terms with our arrangement, even though he still may not agree with it.

I smile and walk quietly out of the apartment, hoping they're about to mend whatever was broken between them when I stepped into the picture.

The elevator doors open on the lobby level, and I'm prepared to step off, but Cap is poised in front of them as if he's about to step on.

"You coming for me?" he asks.

I nod and point upward. "Corbin and Miles are working things out upstairs. I was giving them a minute."

Cap steps into the elevator and presses the button for the twentieth floor. "Well, I suppose you can walk me home," he says. He grabs the bars behind him for support. I stand next to him and lean against the wall behind me.

"Can I ask you a question, Cap?"

He gives me the all clear with a nod. "I love being asked them as much as I love asking them."

I look down at my shoes, crossing one foot over the other. "What do you think would make a man never want to experience love again?"

Cap doesn't answer my question for at least five floors. I eventually look at him, and he's looking right at me, his eyes narrowed, producing even more wrinkles between them. "I suppose if a man lived through the ugliest side of love, he might never want to experience it again."

I contemplate his answer, but it doesn't help much. I don't see how love could get ugly enough for a person to just shut himself off from it completely.

The elevator doors open to the twentieth floor, and I let him step off first. I walk with him to his apartment door and wait for him to open it. "Tate," he says. He's facing his door, and he doesn't turn around to finish his sentence. "Sometimes a man's spirit just ain't strong enough to withstand the ghosts from his past." He opens his apartment door and walks inside. "Maybe that boy just lost his spirit somewhere along the way." He closes his door and leaves me attempting to decipher even more confusion.

chapter twenty-six

MILES

Six years earlier

My room is Rachel's now. Rachel's room is my room.
We graduated. We moved in together. We're in college now.
See? We've got this.
Ian brings in the last of the boxes from the car. "Where do you
want this one?" he asks.
"What is it?" Rachel asks him.
He tells her it looks like a box full of her bras and underwear.
She laughs and tells him to set it next to my dresser. Ian does.
Ian likes Rachel. Ian likes that she's not holding me back. Ian
likes that she wants me to get my degree and finish flight
school.
Rachel wants me to be happy. I tell Rachel I'll be happy as long
as I have her.
She tells me, "Then you'll always be happy."

My dad still hates me. My dad doesn't want to hate me. They're trying to accept it, but it's hard. It's hard for everyone. Rachel doesn't care what everyone thinks. She only cares what I think, and I only think about Rachel.

I'm learning that no matter how difficult a situation is, people learn how to adapt to it. My dad and her mom may not approve, but they'll adapt.

Rachel may not be ready to be a mom, and I may not be ready to be a dad, but we're adapting.

It's what has to happen. If people want peace within themselves, it's necessary.

Vital, even.

• • •

"Miles."

I love my name when it comes out of her mouth. She doesn't waste it. She only says it when she needs something. She only says it when it needs to be said.

"Miles."

She said it twice.

She must really need something.

I roll over, and she's sitting up in bed. She looks at me, wide-eyed.

"Miles." *Three times.* "Miles." *Four.* "It hurts."

Shit.

I jump out of bed and grab our bag. I help Rachel change clothes. I help her to the car.

She's scared.

I might be more scared than she is.

I hold her hand while we drive. I tell her to breathe. I don't know why I tell her this. Of course, she knows to breathe.

I don't know what else to tell her.

I feel helpless.

Maybe she wants her mom.

"Do you want me to call them?"

She shakes her head. "Not yet," she says. "After."

She just wants it to be us. I like this. I just want it to be us, too.

A nurse helps her out of the car. They take us to a room. I get Rachel whatever she needs.

"Do you need ice?"

I get it for her.

"Do you want a cold rag?"

I get it for her.

"Do you want me to turn off the TV?"

I turn it off.

"Do you want another blanket, Rachel? You look cold."

I don't get her a blanket. She's not cold.

"Do you want more ice?"

She doesn't want more ice.

She wants me to shut up.

I shut up.

"Give me your hand, Miles."

I give it to her.

I want it back.

She's hurting it.

I let her keep it anyway.

She's quiet. She never makes a sound. She just breathes. She's incredible.

I'm crying. I don't know why.

I love you so goddamn much, Rachel.

The doctor tells her she's almost done. I kiss her on the forehead.

It happens.

I'm a dad.

She's a mom.

"It's a boy," the doctor says.

She's holding him. She's holding my heart.

He stops crying. He tries to open his eyes.

Rachel cries.

Rachel laughs.

Rachel tells me thank you.

Rachel tells *me* thank you. Like she wasn't the one who created this.

Rachel is crazy.

"I love him so much, Miles," she says. She's still crying. "I love him so, so much."

"I love him, too," I tell her. I touch him. I want to hold him, but I want her to hold him even more. She looks beautiful holding him.

Rachel looks up at me. "Will you please tell me his name now?"

I was hoping he would be a boy so I could have this moment. I was hoping I could tell her what her son's name is, because I know she'll love it.

I hope she remembers the moment

she

became

my

everything.

Miles is going to show you the way to Mr. Clayton's class, Rachel.

"His name is Clayton."

She begins to sob.

She remembers.

"It's perfect," she says, her words mixed with tears.

She's crying too hard now. She wants me to hold him.

I sit on the bed with her and take him.

I'm holding him.

I'm holding my son.

Rachel rests her head on my arm, and we stare at him. We stare at him for so long. I tell Rachel he has her red hair. Rachel says he has my lips. I tell Rachel I hope he has her personality. She disagrees and says she hopes he's just like me.

"He makes life so much better," she says.

"He sure does."

"We're so lucky, Miles."

"We sure are."

Rachel squeezes my hand.

"We've got this," Rachel whispers.

"We've *so* got this," I tell her.

Clayton yawns, and it makes us both laugh. Since when did yawns become so incredible?

I touch his fingers.

We love you so much, Clayton.

chapter twenty-seven

TATE

I drop down into the chair beside Cap, still dressed from head to toe in my scrubs. As soon as I got home from work, I studied for two hours straight. It's already after ten, and I haven't even had supper yet, which is why I'm sitting next to Cap right now, because he's getting to know my habits and had a pizza ordered for the two of us.

I hand him a slice and grab my own, then shut the lid and set it on the floor in front of me. I shove a huge bite into my mouth, but Cap is staring down at the slice in his hand.

"It's really sad when pizza can make it to you faster than the police," he says. "I just ordered this ten minutes ago." He takes a bite and closes his eyes like it's the best thing he's ever tasted.

We both finish our slices, and I reach for another one. He shakes his head when I offer him a second slice, so I put it back in the box.

"So?" he says. "Any progress between the boy and his friend?"

It makes me laugh that he constantly refers to Miles as *the boy*. I nod and respond with a mouthful. "Kind of," I say. "They had a successful game night, but I think it was only successful because Miles pretended I wasn't there the whole time. I know he's trying to respect Corbin, but it kind of makes me feel like shit in the process, you know?"

Cap nods like he understands. I'm not sure that he does, but I like that he always listens so attentively anyway. "Of course, he texted me the entire time he was in the living room sitting next to Corbin, so I guess I have that. But then there are weeks like this week when he's not even in the same state, and it's like I don't even exist to him. No texts. No phone calls. I'm pretty sure he only thinks about me when I'm within ten feet of him."

Cap shakes his head. "I doubt that. I bet that boy thinks about you a lot more than he lets on."

I'd like to believe those words to be true, but I'm not so sure they are.

"But if he doesn't," Cap says, "you can't be mad at him for it. Wasn't part of the agreement, now, was it?"

I roll my eyes. I hate that he always brings me back to the fact that Miles isn't the one breaking rules or agreements. I'm the one with the problems in our arrangement, and that's no one's fault but my own.

"How did I get myself into this mess?" I ask, not even needing an answer. I know how I got myself into this mess. I also know how to get out of it . . . I just don't want to.

"You ever heard that expression, 'When life gives you lemons . . .'?"

"Make lemonade," I say, finishing his quote.

Cap looks at me and shakes his head. "That's not how it goes," he says. "When life gives you lemons, make sure you know whose eyes you need to squeeze them in."

I laugh, grab another slice of pizza, and wonder how in the hell I ended up with an eighty-year-old man as my best friend.

• • •

Corbin's home phone never rings. Especially after midnight. I throw the covers off and grab a T-shirt, then pull it over my head. I don't know why I bother getting dressed. Corbin's gone, and Miles isn't due back until tomorrow.

I make it to the kitchen on the fifth ring, right as the answering machine picks up. I cancel the message, then put the phone to my ear.

"Hello?"

"Tate!" my mother says. "Oh, my God, Tate."

Her voice is panicked, which immediately causes me to panic. "What is it?"

"A plane. A plane crashed about half an hour ago, and I can't get through to the airline. Have you talked to your brother?"

My knees meet the floor. "Are you sure it was his airline?" I ask her. My voice sounds so terrified I don't even recognize it. It sounds as terrified as hers did the last time this happened.

I was only six, but I remember every single detail as if it happened yesterday, down to the moon-and-star pajamas I was wearing. My father was on a domestic flight, and we had turned on the news right after dinner and saw that one of the planes had gone down due to engine failure. Everyone on board was killed. I remember watching my mother on the phone with the airline, hysterical, trying to find out information on who the pilot was. We found out it wasn't him within the hour, but that hour was one of the scariest of our lives.

Until now.

I rush to my room and grab my cell phone off my nightstand and immediately dial his number. "Have you tried calling him?"

I ask my mother as I make my way back to the living room. I try to make it to the couch, but for some reason, the floor seems more comforting. I kneel down again, almost as if I'm in prayer mode.

I guess I am.

"Yes, I've been calling his phone nonstop. It's just going to voice mail."

It's a stupid question. Of course, she's tried calling him. I try again anyway, but his phone goes directly to voice mail.

I try to reassure her, but I know it's pointless. Until we hear his voice, reassurance won't help. "I'll call the airline," I tell her. "I'll call you back if I hear anything."

She doesn't even say good-bye.

I use the home phone to call the airline and my cell phone to call Miles. It's the first time I've ever dialed his number.

I pray that he answers, because as much as I'm scared to death for Corbin, it's also running through my head that Miles works for the same airline.

My stomach is sick.

"Hello?" Miles says on the second ring. His voice sounds hesitant, like he's unsure why I'm calling.

"Miles!" I say, both frantic and relieved. "Is he okay? Is Corbin okay?"

There's a pause.

Why is there a pause?

"What do you mean?"

"A plane," I say immediately. "My mom called. There was a plane crash. He's not answering his phone."

"Where are you?" he says quickly.

"The apartment."

"Let me in."

I walk to the door and unlock it. He pushes the door open

and still has the phone to his ear. When he sees me, he pulls the phone away, immediately rushes to the couch, grabs the remote, and turns on the television.

He flips through the channels until he finds the TV news report. He dials numbers on his cell phone, then turns and rushes toward me. He takes my hand in his. "Come here," he says, pulling me to him. "I'm sure he's fine."

I nod against his chest, but his reassurance is pointless.

"Gary?" he says when someone answers on the other end. "It's Miles. Yeah. Yeah, I heard," he says. "Who was the crew?"

There's a long pause. I'm terrified to look at him. *Terrified.*

"Thank you." He hangs up the phone. "He's okay, Tate," he says immediately. "Corbin's fine. Ian, too."

I break down into tears of relief.

Miles walks me to the couch and sits down, then pulls me to him. He takes my cell phone out of my hands and presses several buttons before putting the phone to his ear.

"Hey, it's Miles. Corbin is fine." He pauses for a few seconds. "Yeah, she's fine. I'll tell her to call you in the morning." A few more seconds pass, and he says good-bye. He sets the phone on the couch beside him. "Your mom."

I nod. I already knew.

And that simple gesture, him calling my mother, just made me fall for him even harder.

Now he's kissing the top of my head, rubbing his hand up and down my arm reassuringly.

"Thank you, Miles," I tell him.

He doesn't say *you're welcome*, because he doesn't think he did anything that deserves thanking.

"Did you know them?" I ask. "The crew on board?"

"No. They were out of a different hub. The names didn't sound familiar."

My phone vibrates, so Miles hands it back to me. I look at it, and it's a text from Corbin.

> Corbin: In case you've heard about the plane, just want you to know I'm fine. I called headquarters, and Miles is, too. Please let Mom know if she hears about it. Love you.

Receiving his text fills me with even more relief, now that I know with one hundred percent certainty that he's okay.

"It's a text from Corbin," I tell Miles. "He says you're okay. In case you were worried."

Miles laughs. "So he checked up on me?" he says with a grin. "I knew he couldn't hate me forever."

I smile. I love that Corbin wanted me to know that Miles was okay.

Miles continues to hold me, and I savor every second of it.

"When is he scheduled to come home?"

"Not for two more days," I say. "How long have you been home?"

"About two minutes," he says. "I had just plugged my phone in to charge when you called."

"I'm glad you're back."

He doesn't respond. He doesn't tell me he's glad to *be* back. Instead of saying something that might give me false hope, he just kisses me.

"You know," he says, pulling me onto his lap, "I hate the circumstances surrounding the reason you probably didn't have time to put on pants, but I love that you don't have on pants." His hands slide up my thighs, and he pulls me closer until we're flush together. He kisses the tip of my nose, then kisses my chin.

"Miles?" I run my hands through his hair and down his neck,

then pause with them on his shoulders. "I was also scared it could have been you," I whisper. "That's why I'm glad you're back."

His eyes grow soft, and the worry lines between them disappear. I may not know anything about his past or his life, but I definitely notice that he hasn't called anyone to let them know he's okay. That makes me sad for him.

His eyes fall away from mine and land on my chest. He fingers the bottom edges of my shirt, then slowly pulls it over my head. I have nothing but a pair of panties on now.

He leans forward, wraps his arms around my back, and pulls me against his mouth. His lips close softly over my nipple, and my eyes shut involuntarily. Chills erupt over my skin as his hands begin to explore every bare part of my back and my thighs. His mouth works its way to my other breast, just as his hands slip inside my panties at my hips.

"I think I have to rip these off you, because I sure don't want you to move off my lap," he says.

I smile. "Fine with me. I have more where these came from."

I can feel him grin against my skin as his hands pull at the elastic band of my underwear. He pulls on one side but fails to tear them. He tries ripping the other side to pull them off me, but nothing gives.

"You're giving me a wedgie," I say, laughing.

He lets out a frustrated sigh. "It's always so much sexier when they do this on TV."

I readjust myself and sit up straighter. "Try it again," I encourage. "You can do it, Miles."

He grabs the left side of my panties and yanks them hard.

"Ouch!" I yell, scooting in the direction of his pull to lessen the pain of the elastic digging into my right side.

He laughs again and drops his face to my neck. "Sorry," he says. "Got any scissors?"

I cringe at the thought of him coming at me with a pair of scissors. I scoot off of him and stand up, then pull my underwear down, kicking them off and away from me.

"Watching you do that was totally worth my failed attempt at being sexy," he says.

I smile. "Your failed attempt at being sexy actually *made* you sexy."

My comment makes him laugh again. I walk toward him and climb back onto his lap. He repositions me so that I'm straddling him again. "My failures are a turn-on for you?" he asks teasingly.

"Oh, yeah," I murmur. "*So* hot."

His hands are on me again, roaming across my back and down my arms. "You would have loved me from the ages of thirteen to sixteen," he says. "I failed at pretty much everything. Especially football."

I grin. "Now we're talking. Tell me more."

"Baseball," he says, right before he presses his mouth to my neck. He kisses his way up to my ear. "And one semester of world geography."

"Holy shit." I moan. "Now, that's hot."

He moves his lips to my mouth and pulls me in for a soft kiss. He barely touches his mouth to mine. "I failed at kissing, too. Terribly. I almost choked a girl with my tongue once."

I laugh.

"Want me to show you?"

As soon as I nod, he's repositioning us on the couch until I'm lying on my back and he's on top of me. "Open your mouth."

I open it. He drops his mouth to mine and shoves his tongue inside, giving me what is quite possibly the worst kiss I've ever experienced. I push against his chest, attempting to get his tongue out of my mouth, but he doesn't budge. I turn my face to the left, and he begins licking my cheek, causing me to laugh even harder.

"Oh, my God, that was terrible, Miles!"

He pulls his mouth away and lowers himself on top of me. "I got better."

I nod. "That's a fact," I say, agreeing wholeheartedly.

We're both smiling. The relaxed look on his face fills me with so many emotions I can't even begin to classify them. I'm happy, because we're having fun together. I'm sad, because we're having fun together. I'm angry, because we're having fun together and it makes me want so much more of this. So much more of him.

We quietly stare at each other, until he slowly dips his head, pressing a long kiss against my lips. He begins placing soft kisses all over my mouth until the kisses become longer and more intense. His tongue eventually parts my lips, and the playfulness disappears.

It's quite serious now, as our kisses grow more hurried and his clothes begin to join mine on the floor, piece by piece.

"The couch or your bed?" he whispers.

"Both," I reply.

He obliges.

• • •

I fell asleep in my bed.

Next to Miles.

Neither of us has ever fallen asleep afterward before. One of us always leaves. As much as I'm trying to convince myself that it means nothing, I know it does. Every time we're together, I get a little bit more of him. Whether it's a glimpse of his past or time spent without the sex or even time spent sleeping, he's giving me more and more of himself, little by little. I feel like this is both good and bad. It's good, because I want and need so much more of him, so every little bit I get is enough to satisfy me when I begin worrying about everything I *don't* get from him. But it's also bad, because every time I get a little bit more of him, another part of him grows more distant. I can see it in his eyes. He's worried he's giving me hope, and I'm afraid he'll eventually just pull away completely.

Everything with Miles will come crashing down.

It's inevitable. He's so adamant about the things he doesn't want out of life, and I'm starting to understand just how serious he is. So as much as I try to protect my heart from him, it's pointless. He's going to break it eventually, yet I continue to allow him to fill it. Every time I'm with him, he fills my heart up more and more, and the more it's filled with pieces of him, the more painful it'll be when he rips it out of my chest as though it never belonged there in the first place.

I hear the vibration of his phone and feel him roll over and reach for it on the nightstand next to him. He thinks I'm asleep, so I don't give him reason to think otherwise.

"Hey," he whispers. There's a long pause, and I start to panic internally, wondering who he's talking to. "Yeah, I'm sorry. I should have called you. I figured you'd be asleep."

My heart is in my throat now, crawling its way up, trying to escape from Miles and me and this entire situation. My heart knows by my reaction to this phone call that it's in trouble. My heart has just gone into fight-or-flight mode, and right now, it's doing everything it can to run.

I don't blame my heart one bit.

"Love you, too, Dad."

My heart slides back down my throat and finds its normal home in my chest again. It's happy for now. *I'm* happy. Happy that he actually does have someone to call.

In the same moment, I'm also reminded of how little I know about him. How little he shows me. How much he hides himself from me, so that when I finally break, it won't be his fault.

It won't be a quick break, either. It'll be slow and painful, filled with so many moments like these that tear me up from the inside out. Moments when he thinks I'm asleep and he slides out of my bed. Moments when I keep my eyes closed but listen as he puts on his clothes. Moments when I make sure my breathing remains regular in case he's watching me when he leans over to kiss me on the forehead.

Moments when he leaves.

Because he always leaves.

chapter twenty-eight

MILES

Six years earlier

"What if he turns out to be gay?" Rachel asks me. "Would that bother you?"

She's holding Clayton, and we're both sitting on the hospital bed. I'm on the foot of the bed facing her, watching her stare at him.

She keeps asking me random questions. Playing devil's advocate again.

She says we need to work these things out now so we don't run into any parenting issues in the future.

"It would only bother me if he felt like he couldn't talk to us about it. I want him to know he can talk to us about anything."

Rachel smiles at Clayton, but I know her smile is for me. Because she loved my answer.

"What if he doesn't believe in God?" she asks.

"He can believe whatever he wants. I just want his beliefs—or lack thereof—to make him happy."

She smiles again.

"What if he commits an awful, heinous, heartless crime and gets sent to prison for life?"

"I would question where I went wrong as a father," I tell her.

She looks up at me. "Well, based on this interrogation, I'm convinced he'll never commit a crime, because you're already the best dad I've ever known."

Now she's making *me* smile.

We both look at the door when it opens and a nurse walks in.

She flashes a regretful smile. "It's time," she says.

Rachel groans, but I have no idea what the nurse is referring to. Rachel sees the confusion on my face.

"His circumcision."

My stomach clenches. I know we discussed this during the pregnancy, but I'm suddenly having second thoughts, knowing what he's about to go through.

"It's not so bad," the nurse says. "We numb him first."

She walks over to Rachel and begins to lift him from Rachel's arms, but I lean forward.

"Wait," I tell her. "Let me hold him first."

The nurse backs up a step, and Rachel hands Clayton to me. I pull him in front of me and look down on him.

"I'm so sorry, Clayton. I know it'll hurt, and I know it's emasculating, but—"

"He's a day old," Rachel interjects with a laugh. "There's hardly anything that can emasculate him yet."

I tell her to hush. I tell her I'm having a father-son moment, and she needs to pretend she's not here.

"Don't worry, your mom left the room," I say to Clayton, giving Rachel a wink. "I was saying, I know it's emasculating, but you'll thank me later for it. Especially when you're older and you get involved with girls. Hopefully not until after you're eighteen, but it'll more than likely be around the age of sixteen. It was for me, anyway."

Rachel leans forward and holds her arms out for him. "That's enough bonding," she says, laughing. "I think we need to review the boundaries of father-son conversation while he's being emasculated."

I give him a quick kiss on his forehead and hand him back to Rachel. She does the same and passes him on to the nurse.

We both watch as the nurse leaves the room with him.

I look back at Rachel and crawl toward her until I'm lying next to her on the bed.

"We have the place to ourselves," I whisper. "Let's make out."

She grimaces. "I don't feel sexy right now," she says. "My stomach is flabby, and my boobs are engorged, and I need a shower so bad, but it hurts too much to try to take one right now."

I look down at her chest and pull at the collar on her hospital gown. I peer down her shirt and grin. "How long do they stay like this?"

She laughs and pushes my hand away.

"Well, how does your mouth feel?" I ask her.

She looks at me like she doesn't understand my question, so I elaborate.

"I'm just wondering if your mouth hurts like the rest of you hurts, because if it doesn't, I want to kiss you."

She grins. "My mouth feels great."

I rise up on my elbow so she doesn't have to roll toward me. I look down on her, and seeing her beneath me feels different now.

It feels *real*.

Until yesterday, it really did feel like we had been playing house. Of course, our love is real, and our relationship is real, but until I witnessed her give life to my son yesterday, everything I felt before that moment was like child's play compared to what I feel for her now.

"I love you, Rachel. More than I loved you yesterday."

Her eyes are looking up at me like she knows exactly what I'm talking about. "If you love me more today than you loved me yesterday, then I can't wait for tomorrow," she says.

My lips fall to hers, and I kiss her. Not because I should but because I need to.

• • •

I'm standing outside Rachel's hospital room. She and Clayton are both in the room, napping.

The nurse said he hardly even cried. I'm sure she tells all the parents that, but I believe her anyway.

I take out my phone to text Ian.

Me: He got snipped a few hours ago. Took it like a champ.

Ian: Ouch. I'm coming to meet him tonight. I'll be there after seven.

Me: See you then.

My father is walking toward me with two coffees in his hands, so I slide my phone into my back pocket.

He hands me one of the coffees.

"He looks like you," he says.

He's trying to accept it.

"Well, I look just like you," I say. "Cheers to strong genes."

I hold my coffee up, and my dad bumps his against it, smiling.

He's trying.

He leans against the wall for support and looks down at his coffee. He wants to say something, but it's hard for him.

"What is it?" I ask, giving him the opening he needs. He lifts his eyes from their focus on the coffee, and he meets my gaze.

"I'm proud of you," he says with sincerity.

It's a simple statement.

Four words.

Four of the most impactful words I've ever heard.

"Of course, it's not what I wanted for you. No one wants to see his son become a dad at the age of eighteen, but . . . I'm proud of you. For how you've handled it. For how you've treated Rachel." He smiles. "You made the best of a difficult situation, and that's honestly more than most adults would do."

I smile. I tell him thank you.

I think the conversation is over, but it's not.

"Miles," he says, wanting to add more. "About Lisa . . . and your mom?"

I hold my hand up to stop him. I don't want to have this conversation today. I don't want this day to become his defense for what he did to my mother.

"It's fine, Dad. We'll discuss it another time."

He tells me no. He says he needs to discuss it with me now.

He tells me it's important.

I want to tell him it's not important.

I want to tell him Clayton is important.

I want to focus on Clayton and Rachel and forget all about the fact that my father is human and makes awful choices like the rest of us.

But I don't say any of that.

I listen.

Because he's my father.

chapter twenty-nine

TATE

Miles: What are you doing?

Me: Homework.

Miles: Feel like taking a swim break?

Me: ??? It's February.

Miles: The rooftop pool is heated. It doesn't close for
another hour.

I stare at the text, then immediately look up at Corbin. "There's a rooftop pool here?"

Corbin nods his head but doesn't look away from the TV. "Yep."

I sit up straight. "Are you kidding me? I've lived here this long, and you fail to tell me there's a heated rooftop pool?"

He faces me now and shrugs. "I hate pools."

Ugh. I could slap him.

250 | COLLEEN HOOVER

> **Me:** Corbin never mentioned there was a pool. Let me change, and I'll head over there.
>
> **Miles:** ;)

• • •

I realize I forgot to knock as soon as I close the door to his apartment. I always knock. I guess my mentioning in a text that I was coming over after I changed seemed good enough to me, but the way Miles is staring at me from the doorway of his bedroom makes me think he doesn't like the fact that I didn't knock.

I pause in his living room and look at him, waiting to see what mood he's in today.

"You're in a bikini," he says pointedly.

I look down at my attire. "And shorts," I say defensively. I look back up at him. "What are people supposed to wear when they swim in February?"

He's still standing frozen in his doorway, staring at my attire. I fold my towel across my arms and over my stomach. I suddenly feel extremely awkward and underdressed.

He shakes his head and finally begins moving toward me. "I just . . ." He's still staring at my bikini. "I hope no one is up there, because if you're wearing that bikini, these swim shorts are going to be really embarrassing." He looks down at his shorts. At the obvious bulge in them.

I laugh. So he actually *likes* the bikini.

He takes another step forward and slides his hands around to the back of my shorts, then pulls me against him. "I changed my mind," he says with a grin. "I want to stay here."

I immediately shake my head. "I'm going swimming," I say. "You can stay here if you want, but you'll be alone."

He kisses me, then backs me toward his apartment door. "Then I guess I'm going swimming," he says.

• • •

Miles enters the passcode for rooftop access, then opens the door for me. I'm relieved to see that no one else is out here, and I am taken by how breathtakingly beautiful it is. It's an infinity pool, overlooking the city, and it's lined with patio chairs, all the way to the opposite end, where it's capped off with an attached hot tub.

"I can't believe neither of you thought to mention this before now," I say. "All these months, and I've been missing out."

Miles takes my towel and lays it on one of the tables surrounding the pool. He walks back over to me and drops his hands to the button on my shorts. "This is actually the first time I've ever been out here." He unzips my shorts and pushes them over my hips. His lips are close to mine, and his expression is playful. "Come on," he whispers. "Let's get wet."

I kick off the shorts at the same time as he takes off his shirt. The air is incredibly cold, but the steam rising from the water is promising. I walk to the shallow end to descend the steps, but Miles dives headfirst into the deep end of the pool. I step in, and my feet are swallowed up in the warmth of the water, so I quickly step in the rest of the way. I make my way toward the middle of the pool and walk to the edge, then rest my arms on the concrete ledge looking out over the city.

Miles swims up behind me and cages me in by pressing his chest against my back and placing his hands on either side of the ledge. He rests his head against mine as we both take in the view.

"It's beautiful," I whisper.

He's quiet.

We watch the city in silence for what seems like forever. Every now and then, he'll cup his hands and bring water up to my shoulders to warm my chills away.

"Have you always lived in San Francisco?" I ask him. I turn so that my back is against the ledge now and I'm facing him. He keeps his arms on either side of me and nods.

"Close to it," he says, still looking at the city over my shoulder.

I want to ask him where, but I don't. I can tell by his body language that he doesn't want to talk about himself. He never wants to talk about himself.

"Are you an only child?" I ask, trying to see what I can get away with. "Any brothers or sisters?"

He looks me in the eyes now. His lips are pressed into a firm, agitated line. "What are you doing, Tate?" He doesn't ask it in a rude way, but there's no other way his question can come across.

"Just making conversation," I say. My voice is soft and sounds offended.

"I can think of a lot more things I'd rather talk about than myself."

But that's all I want to know about, Miles.

I nod, understanding that although I'm technically not breaking his rules, I'm bending them. He doesn't feel comfortable with that.

I turn around and face the ledge again. He's still in the same position, pressed against me, but it's different now. He's stiff. Guarded. Defensive.

I don't know anything about him. I don't know a single thing about his family, and he's already met mine. I don't know a single thing about his past, but he's slept in my childhood bed. I don't know what subjects I bring up or what actions I take that will cause him to close off, but I've got nothing to hide from him.

He sees me for exactly who I am.

I don't see him at *all*.

I quickly bring a hand up and wipe away a tear that somehow

just escaped down my cheek. The absolute last thing I want is for him to see me cry. As much as I know I'm too far gone to continue treating this as casual sex, I'm also too far gone to stop it. I'm terrified to lose him for good, so I sell myself short and take what I can from him, even though I know I deserve better.

Miles places a hand on my shoulder and turns me around to face him. When I choose to stare down at the water instead, he hooks a finger under my chin and makes me look up at him. I allow him to tilt my face up to his, but I don't make eye contact. I look up and to the right, attempting to blink back the tears.

"I'm sorry."

I don't even know what he's apologizing for. I don't even know if *he* knows what he's apologizing for. But we both know my tears have everything to do with him, so he's more than likely just apologizing for that simple reason alone. Because he knows he's incapable of giving me what I want.

He stops making me look at him and instead pulls me to his chest. I rest my ear against his heart, and he rests his chin on top of my head.

"Do you think we should stop?" he asks quietly. His voice is fearful, like he's hoping my answer is no, yet he feels compelled to ask me anyway.

"No," I whisper.

He sighs heavily. It sounds like it could be a sigh of relief, but I'm not sure. "If I ask you something, will you be honest with me?"

I shrug, because there's no way I'm answering that with a yes until I hear his question first.

"Are you still doing this with me because you think I'll change my mind? Because you think there's a chance I'll fall in love with you?"

That's the only *reason I'm still doing this, Miles.*

I don't say that out loud, though. I don't say anything.

"Because I *can't*, Tate. I just . . ." His voice fades away, and he grows quiet. I analyze his words and the fact that he said *I can't* rather than *I won't*. I want to ask him *why* he can't. Is he scared? Is it because I'm not right for him? Is he afraid he'll break my heart? I don't ask him, because none of his answers to these questions would reassure me. None of these scenarios is reason enough to absolutely deny a heart happiness.

Which is why I don't question him, because I feel like maybe I'm not prepared for the truth. Maybe I'm underestimating whatever it was that happened in his past to make him this way. Because *something* happened. Something I more than likely couldn't relate to, even if I found out what it was. Something that stole the spirit right out of him, just like Cap said.

His arms pull me in tighter, and the hold he has on me speaks volumes. It's more than an embrace. More than a hug. He's holding me like he's terrified I'd drown if he were to release me.

"Tate," he whispers. "I know I'll regret saying this, but I want you to hear it." He pulls back just enough for his lips to meet my hair, then grips me tightly again. "If I were capable of loving someone . . . it would be you." My heart cracks with his words, and I feel the hope seep in and leak right back out again. "But I'm not capable. So if it's too hard—"

"It's not," I interrupt, doing whatever I can to stop him from ending this. I somehow find it in me to look him in the eyes and tell the best lie I've ever told in my whole life. "I like things exactly how they are."

He knows I'm lying. I can see the doubt in his concerned eyes, but he nods anyway. I try to get his mind off of it before he sees right through me. I wrap my arms loosely around his neck, but his attention is pulled to the door, which is now opening. I turn, too, and see Cap slowly shuffling his way onto the rooftop deck. He walks toward the switch on the wall that turns off the jets to the hot tub. He flips it off and slowly turns back toward the door but not before noticing us out of the corner of his eye. He turns and faces us full on, standing no more than five feet away.

"That you, Tate?" he says, squinting.

"It's me," I say, still in the same position with Miles.

"Hmm," Cap says, taking us both in. "Anyone ever told the two of you that you make a pretty darn good-looking couple?"

I wince, because I know this isn't the best moment for Miles to hear that, especially after the awkward conversation we just had. I also know what Cap is up to with that comment.

"We'll shut the lights off when we leave, Cap," Miles says, ignoring Cap's question and redirecting the conversation.

Cap narrows his eyes at him, shakes his head as though he's disappointed, and begins to turn back to the door. "It was a rhetorical question anyway," he mumbles. I see his hand go up to his forehead, and he salutes the air in front of him. "Good night, Tate," he says loudly.

"Good night, Cap."

Miles and I both watch until the door closes behind Cap. I pull my hands away from his neck and gently push against his chest until he steps back in order for me to make my way around him. I swim backward toward the other side of the pool.

"Why are you always so rude to him?" I ask.

Miles lowers himself in the water, parting his arms in front of him and kicking off the wall behind him. He swims toward me, and I watch as his eyes remain focused on mine. I swim backward until my back is against the opposite wall of the pool. He continues toward me, almost crashing into me, but he stops himself by gripping the ledge on both sides of my head, sending waves of water against my chest.

"I'm not rude to him." His lips meet my neck, and he kisses it softly, trailing slowly upward until his mouth is close to my ear. "I just don't like answering questions."

I think we've established that already.

I pull my neck away a few inches in order to see his face. I try to focus on his eyes, but there are drops of water on his lips, and it's hard not to stare. "He's an old man, though. You're not supposed to be rude to old people. And he's pretty damn funny, if you'd just get to know him."

Miles laughs a little. "You like him, huh?" He seems amused.

I nod. "Yeah. I like him a lot. Sometimes I like him more than I like *you*."

He laughs loudly this time and leans in again, planting a kiss on my cheek. His hand conforms to the nape of my neck, and his eyes drop to my mouth. "I like that you like him," he says, bringing his eyes up to mine. "I won't be rude to him again. Promise."

I bite my lip so that he doesn't see how much I want to smile at the fact that he just made me a promise. It was a simple promise. But it still feels good.

He slides his hand around to my jaw, and his thumb meets my lip. He pulls it away from my teeth. "What did I tell you about hiding that smile?" He takes my bottom lip between his teeth and bites it gently, then releases it.

It feels as if the temperature in the pool just shot up twenty degrees.

His mouth meets my throat, and he breathes out a heavy sigh against my skin. I tilt my head back and let it rest against the ledge of the pool as he kisses his way down my neck.

"I don't want to swim any more," he says, sliding his lips from the base of my throat all the way up to my mouth again.

"Well, then, what do you want to do?" I whisper weakly.

"You," he says without hesitation. "In my shower. From behind."

I swallow a huge gulp of air and feel it fall all the way to the pit of my stomach. "Wow. That's very specific."

"And also in my bed," he whispers. "With you on top, still soaking wet from the shower."

I inhale sharply, and we can both hear the tremble of my breath as I exhale. "Okay," I try to say, but his mouth is on mine before the word is even all the way out.

And once again, what should have been an eye-opening conversation for me is shoved aside to make room for the only thing he's willing to give me.

chapter thirty

MILES

Six years earlier

We quietly walk to an empty waiting area. My father sits first,
and I reluctantly sit across from him.
I wait for his confession, but he doesn't know I don't need it. I
know about his relationship with Lisa.
I know how long it's been going on.
"Your mother and I . . ." He's looking at the floor.
He can't even make eye contact with me.
"We decided to separate when you were sixteen. However,
with as much as I traveled, it made financial sense for us to wait
until you graduated before filing for divorce, so that's what we
decided to do."
Sixteen?
She got sick when I was sixteen.
"We had been split up for almost a year when I met Lisa."

He's looking at me now. He's being honest.

"When she found out she was sick, it was the right thing to do, Miles. She was your mother, and I wasn't going to leave her when she needed me the most."

My chest hurts.

"I know you've put two and two together," he says. "I know you've done the math. I know you've been hating me, thinking I was having an affair while she was sick, and I hated allowing you to think that."

"Then why did you?" I ask him. "Why did you let me think that?"

He looks at the floor again. "I don't know," he says. "I thought maybe there was a chance that you didn't realize I'd been dating Lisa for longer than I let on, so I thought bringing it up would do more harm than good. I didn't like the thought of you knowing my marriage with your mother had failed. I didn't want you to think she died unhappy."

"She didn't," I reassure him. "You were there for her, Dad. We both were."

He appreciates that I say this, because he knows it's true.

My mother was happy with her life.

Happy with me.

It makes me wonder if she'd be disappointed now, seeing how things have turned out.

"She would be proud of you, Miles," he says to me. "With how you've handled yourself."

I hug him.

I needed to hear that more than I knew.

chapter thirty-one

TATE

I'm trying to listen to Corbin go on about his conversation with Mom, but all I can think about is the fact that Miles is due home any minute now. It's been ten days since he's been home, and that's the longest we've gone without seeing each other since the weeks we spent not speaking.

"Have you told Miles yet?" Corbin asks.

"Told him what?"

Corbin faces me. "That you're moving out." He points at the potholder on the counter next to me.

I toss him the potholder and shake my head. "I haven't talked to him since last week. I'll probably tell him tonight."

Honestly, I've wanted to tell him I found my own apartment all week, but that would involve either calling or texting him, two things we don't do. The only times we text each other are when we're both home. I think we do this because it helps us maintain our boundaries.

It's not like the move is a big deal anyway. I'm only moving a few blocks away. I found an apartment that's closer to both work and school. It's definitely no downtown high-rise, but I love it.

I do wonder, though, how it will affect things between Miles and me. I think that's one of the reasons I haven't mentioned that I was even looking for my own place. There's a fear in the back of my mind that not being right across the hall from him will become too inconvenient, and he'll just call off whatever is going on between us.

Corbin and I both look up as soon as the apartment door opens and there's a quick knock on it. I glance at Corbin, and he rolls his eyes.

He's still adapting.

Miles walks into the kitchen, and I see the smile that wants to spread across his face when he sees me, but he keeps it in check when he sees Corbin.

"What are you cooking?" Miles asks him. He leans against the wall and folds his arms across his chest, but his eyes are scrolling up my legs. They pause when he sees I'm wearing a skirt, and then he smiles in my direction. Luckily, Corbin is still facing the stove.

"Dinner," Corbin says with a clipped voice.

He takes a while to adapt.

Miles looks at me again and stares for a few silent seconds. "Hey, Tate," he says.

I grin. "Hey."

"How were midterms?" His eyes are everywhere on me but my face.

"Good," I say.

He mouths, *You look pretty.*

I smile and wish more than anything that Corbin wasn't

standing here right now, because it's taking all I have not to throw my arms around Miles and kiss the hell out of him.

Corbin knows why Miles is here. Miles and I just try to respect the fact that Corbin still doesn't like what's going on between us, so we keep it behind closed doors.

Miles is chewing on the inside of his cheek, fidgeting with his shirtsleeve, watching me. It's quiet in the kitchen, and Corbin still hasn't turned around to acknowledge him. Miles looks like he's about to burst at the seams.

"Fuck it," he says, gliding across the kitchen toward me. He takes my face in his hands and kisses me, hard, in front of Corbin.

He's kissing me.

In front of Corbin.

Don't analyze this, Tate.

He's pulling my hands, dragging me out of the kitchen. As far as I know, Corbin is still facing the stove, trying his best to ignore us.

Still adapting.

We get to the living room, and Miles separates his mouth from mine. "I haven't been able to think about anything else today," he says. "At all."

"Me, neither."

He pulls me by the hand toward the front door. I follow. He opens it, walks to his apartment, and pulls his keys out of his pocket. His luggage is still outside in the hallway.

"Why is your luggage out here?"

Miles pushes open his apartment door. "I haven't been home yet," he says. He turns around and grabs his things from the hallway, then holds the door open for me.

"You came to my apartment first?"

He nods, then tosses his duffel bag onto the couch and

pushes his suitcase against the wall. "Yep," he says. He grabs my hand and pulls me to him. "I told you, Tate. Haven't thought about anything else." He smiles and lowers his head to kiss me.

I laugh. "Aw, you missed me," I say teasingly.

He pulls back. You would think I'd just told him I loved him with the way his body tenses up.

"Relax," I say. "You're allowed to miss me, Miles. It doesn't break your rules."

He backs up a few steps. "You thirsty?" he asks, changing the subject like he always does. He turns and heads toward the kitchen, but everything about him just changed. His demeanor, his smile, his excitement over finally seeing me after ten days.

I stand in the living room and watch it all crumble.

I'm hit by a reality check, but it feels more like a meteor.

This man can't even admit that he misses me.

I've been holding out hope that if I take it slowly enough with him, he'll eventually break through whatever it is that's holding him back. The entire past few months, I've been under the assumption that maybe he just can't handle the way things have developed between us and he needs time, but it's clear now. It's not him.

It's *me*.

I'm the one who can't handle this thing between us.

"You okay?" Miles says from the kitchen. He walks out from behind the obstructed view of the cabinets so he can see me. He waits for me to answer him, but I can't.

"Did you miss me, Miles?"

And up comes the armor again, shielding him. He looks away and walks back into the kitchen. "We don't say things like that, Tate," he says. The hardness is back in his voice.

Is he serious?

"We don't?" I take a few steps toward the kitchen. "Miles. It's a common phrase. It doesn't mean commitment. It doesn't even mean love. Friends say it to friends."

He leans against the bar in the kitchen and calmly looks up at me. "But we were never friends. And I don't want to break your one and only rule by giving you false hope, so I'm not saying it."

I can't explain what happens to me, because I don't know. But it's as if every single thing he's ever said and done that's hurt me impales me all at once. I want to scream at him. I want to hate him. I want to know what the hell happened that made him capable of saying things that can hurt me more than any other words have ever come close to doing.

I'm tired of treading water.

I'm tired of pretending it's not killing me to want to know everything about him.

I'm tired of pretending he's not everywhere. Everything. My *only* thing.

"What did she do to you?" I whisper.

"Don't," he says. The word is a warning. A threat.

I'm so tired of seeing the pain in his eyes and not knowing the reason for it. I'm tired of not knowing what words are off-limits with him.

"Tell me."

He looks away from me. "Go home, Tate." He turns around and grips the edge of the counter, dropping his head between his shoulders.

"Fuck you." I turn and exit the kitchen. When I reach the living room, I hear him coming after me, so I speed up. I make it to the front door and open it, but his palm meets the door above my head, and he slams it shut.

I squeeze my eyes tightly, bracing for whatever words are about to completely slay me, because I know they will.

His face is right next to my ear, and his chest is pressed

against my back. "That's what we've been doing, Tate. *Fucking*. I've made that clear from day one."

I laugh, because I don't know what else to do. I turn around and look up at him. He doesn't back away, and he's so much more intimidating in this moment than I've ever seen him be before.

"You think you've made that clear?" I ask him. "You are so full of shit, Miles."

He still doesn't move, but his jaw tenses. "How have I not been clear? Two rules. Can't get any simpler than that."

I laugh incredulously, then get everything off my chest at once. "There's a huge difference between fucking someone and making love to them. You haven't *fucked* me in more than a month. Every time you're inside me, you're making love to me. I can see it in the way you look at me. You miss me when we aren't together. You think about me all the time. You can't even wait ten seconds to walk in your own front door before coming to see me. So don't you dare try to tell me you've been clear from day one, because you are the murkiest goddamn man I've ever met."

I breathe.

I breathe for the first time in what feels like a month.

He can do what he wants with all that. I'm done trying.

He blows out a steady, controlled breath while he backs several steps away from me. He winces and turns around as if he doesn't want me to read the emotions that are obviously present somewhere deep within him. His hands grip the back of his neck tightly, and he remains in this position for a solid minute without moving. He begins to blow out steady breath after steady breath, as if he's doing everything in his power to pull himself together and not cry. My heart begins to ache when I realize what's happening.

He's breaking.

"Oh, God," he whispers. His voice is completely pain-ridden. "What am I doing to you, Tate?"

He walks to the wall and falls against it, then slides to the floor. His knees come up, and he rests his elbows on them, covering his face with his hands to stop his emotions. His shoulders begin to shake, but he's not making a sound.

He's crying.

Miles Archer is crying.

It's the same heart-wrenching cry that came from him the night I met him.

This grown man, this wall of intimidation, this solid veil of armor, he's completely crumbling right in front of my eyes.

"Miles?" I whisper. My voice is weak compared with his massive silence. I walk to him and lower myself to my knees in front of him. I wrap my arm around his shoulders and lower my head to his.

I don't ask him what's wrong again, because now I'm terrified to know.

chapter thirty-two

MILES

Six years earlier

Lisa loves Clayton.

My dad loves Clayton.

Clayton fixes families.

He's already my hero, and he's only two days old.

Shortly after my dad and Lisa leave, Ian arrives. He says he
doesn't want to hold Clayton, but Rachel makes him. He's
uncomfortable, because he's never held a baby before, but he
holds him.

"Thank God he looks like Rachel," Ian says.

I agree with him.

Ian asks Rachel if I ever told her what I said to him after I met
her.

I don't know what he's talking about.

Ian laughs.

"After he walked you to class that first day, he took a picture of you from his seat," Ian tells her. "He texted it to me and said, 'She's gonna have all my babies.'"

Rachel looks at me.

I shrug.

I'm embarrassed.

Rachel loves that I said that to Ian. I love that Ian told her that. The doctor comes in and tells us we can go home now. Ian helps me take everything to the car and pull it up to the exit. Before I go back to Rachel's room, Ian touches my shoulder. I turn around and face him.

I get the feeling he wants to tell me congratulations, but instead, he just hugs me.

It's awkward, but it's not. I like that he's proud of me.

It makes me feel good. Like I'm doing this right.

Ian leaves.

So do we.

Me and Rachel and Clayton.

My family.

I want Rachel in the front seat with me, but I love that she's riding in the back with him. I love how much she loves him. I love that I'm attracted to her even more now that she's a mom. I want to kiss her. I want to tell her I love her again, but I think I tell her way too much. I don't ever want her to get tired of hearing it.

"Thank you for this baby," she says from the backseat. "He's beautiful."

I laugh. "You're responsible for the beautiful part, Rachel. The only thing he got from me was his balls."

She laughs. She laughs hard. "Oh, my God, I know," she says. "They're so big."

We both laugh at our son's big balls.

She sighs.

"Rest," I tell her. "You haven't slept in two days."

I see her smile in the rearview mirror. "But I can't stop staring at him," she whispers.

I can't stop staring at you, Rachel.

But I do stop, because the oncoming traffic is brighter than it should be.

My hands grip the steering wheel.

Too bright.

I've always heard your life flashes before your eyes in the moments before you die.

In a sense, that's true.

However, it doesn't come at you in sequence or even in random order.

It's just one picture that

STICKS

in your head and becomes *everything* you feel and *everything* you see.

It's not your *actual* life that flashes before your eyes.

What flashes before your eyes are the people who *are* your life.

Rachel and Clayton.

All I see is the two of them—*my whole life*—flash before my eyes.

The sound becomes everything.

Everything.

Inside me, outside me, through me, under me, over me.

RACHEL, RACHEL, **RACHEL.**

I can't find her.

CLAYTON, CLAYTON, **CLAYTON.**

I'm wet. It's cold. My head hurts. My arms hurt.

I can't see her, I can't see her, I can't see her, I can't see him.

Silence.

Silence.

Silence.

DEAFENING SILENCE.

"Miles!"

I open my eyes.

It's wet, it's wet, there's water, it's wet.

Water is in the car.

I unbuckle my seat belt and turn around. Her hands are on his car seat. "Miles, help me! It's stuck!"

I try.

I try again.

But she needs to get out, too.

She needs to get out, too.

I kick my window and break the glass. I saw it in a movie once.

Make sure there's a way out before there's too much pressure on the windows.

"Rachel, get out! I've got him!"

She tells me no. She won't stop trying to get him out.

I'll get him, Rachel.

She can't get out. Her seat belt is stuck. It's too tight.

I let go of the car seat and reach for her seat belt. My hands are underwater when I find it.

She slaps at my arms and attempts to push me away from her. "Get him first!" she screams. "Get him out first!"

I can't.

They're both stuck.

You're stuck, Rachel.

Oh, God.

I'm scared.

Rachel is scared.

The water is everywhere. I can't see him anymore.

I can't see her.

I can't hear him.

I reach for her seat belt again.

I get it off her.

I grab her hands. Her window isn't broken.

Mine is.

I pull her forward. She's fighting me.

She's fighting me.

She stops fighting me.

Fight me, Rachel.

Fight me.

Move.

Someone is reaching in through my window.

"Give me her hand!" I hear him yell.

The water is coming in through my window now.

The entire backseat is water.

Everything is water.

I give him Rachel's hand. He helps me get her out.

Everything is water.

I try to find him.

I can't breathe.

I try to find him.

I can't breathe.

I try to save him.

I want to be his hero.

I can't breathe.

So I just stop.

Silence.

Silence.

Silence.

Silence.

Silence.

Silence.

Silence.

Silence.

Silence.

DEAFENING SCREAM.

I cover my ears with my hands.

I cover my heart with armor.

I cough until I can breathe again.

I open my eyes. *We're in a boat.*

I look around. *We're on a lake.*

I bring my hand up to my jaw.

My hand is red.

Covered in blood as red as Rachel's hair.

Rachel.

I find Rachel.

Clayton.

I don't find Clayton.

I push up on my hands and move to the edge of the boat.

I need to find him.

Someone stops me. Someone pulls me back.

Someone won't let me.

Someone is telling me it's too late.

Someone tells me he's sorry.

Someone tells me we can't get to him.

Someone tells me we went over the bridge after the impact.

Someone tells me he's *so* sorry.

I move to Rachel, instead.

I try to hold her, but she won't let me. She's screaming.

Sobbing. CRYING. WAILING.

She hits me.

She kicks me.

She says I should have saved him instead.

But I tried to save you both, Rachel.

"You should have saved *him*, Miles!" she cries.

You should have saved *him*.

You should have saved *him*.

I should have saved *HIM*.

She's screaming.

Sobbing. CRYING. **WAILING.**

I hold her anyway.

I let her hit me.

I let her hate me.

Rachel hates me.

I hold her anyway.

Rachel cries, but she's quiet. She's crying so hard her throat can't even make a sound. Her body is crying, but her voice is not.

Ruined.

Ruined.

RUINED.

I cry with her. I cry and I cry and I cry and I cry and we cry and we cry and we cry.

Ruined.

The water is everything now.

I look at Rachel. *I only see water.*

I close my eyes. *I only see water.*

I look up at the sky. *I only see water.*

It hurts so much. I never knew a heart could hold the weight of the entire world.

I don't make Rachel's life better anymore.

I ruined you, Rachel.

My family.

Me and you and Clayton.

RUINED.

You can't love me after this, Rachel.

chapter thirty-three

TATE

My hands are on him, rubbing his back, touching his hair. He's crying, and the only thing I can do is tell him never mind. I want to tell him to forget everything I said tonight. I want to do whatever I can to take this pain away from him, because whatever happened shouldn't matter. Whatever happened, no one deserves to feel the way he's feeling right now.

I move his arms from his face, then slide onto his lap. I hold his face in my hands and tilt it to mine. He keeps his eyes closed. "I don't have to know, Miles."

His arms wrap around my back, and he buries his face against my chest. His labored breaths come faster as he tries to push back his emotions. My arms are wrapped around his head, and I kiss his hair, then trail kisses down the side of his head until he pulls back and looks up at me.

No amount of armor in the world and no wall no matter how thick could hide the devastation in his eyes right now. It's so prominent, and there's so much of it, I have to hold my breath so I don't cry with him.

What happened to you, Miles?

"I don't have to know," I whisper again, shaking my head.

His hands move to the back of my head, and he presses his mouth to mine, hard and painfully. He moves forward until my back is against the floor. His hands pull at my shirt, and he's kissing me desperately, furiously, filling my mouth with the taste of his tears.

I let him use me to get rid of his pain.

I'll do whatever he wants me to do as long as he stops hurting like he's hurting.

He slips his hand beneath my skirt and begins to pull down my underwear at the same time as I hook my thumbs onto the hips of his jeans and push them down. My panties make it to my ankles, and I kick them off, just as he takes both my hands and pushes them above my head, pressing them to the floor.

He drops his forehead to mine but doesn't kiss me. He closes his eyes, but I keep mine open. He wastes no time pushing himself between my legs, spreading them wider. He moves his forehead to the side of my head, then slides into me slowly. When he's all the way inside me, he exhales, releasing some of his pain. Taking his mind away from whatever horror he just went through.

He pulls out, then thrusts inside me again, this time with all his strength.

It hurts.

Give me your pain, Miles.

"My God, Rachel," he whispers.

My God, Rachel . . .

Rachel, Rachel, Rachel.

That word gets put on repeat inside my head.

My.

God.

Rachel.

I turn my head away from his. It's the worst pain I've ever felt. The absolute worst.

His body immediately stills inside mine when he realizes what he said. The only thing moving between us right now are the tears falling from my eyes.

"Tate," he whispers, shattering the silence between us. "Tate, I'm so sorry."

I shake my head, but the tears won't stop. Somewhere deep inside me, I feel something harden. Something that was once liquid completely freezes, and it's in this moment that I know this is it.

That name.

It said it all. I'll never have his past, because *she* has it.

I'll never have his future, because he refuses to give it to anyone who isn't her.

And I'll never know why, because he'll never tell me.

He begins to pull out of me, but I tighten my legs around his. He sighs heavily against my cheek. "I swear to God, Tate. I wasn't thinking about—"

"Stop," I whisper. I don't want to hear him defend what just happened. "Just finish, Miles."

He lifts his head and looks down at me. I see the apology, clear as day, hiding behind fresh tears. I don't know if it's my words that have just cut him again or the fact that we both know this is it, but it looks like his heart just broke again.

If that's even possible.

A tear falls from his eyes and lands on my cheek. I feel it roll down and combine with one of my own.

I just want this to be over.

I wrap my hand around the back of his head and pull his mouth to mine. He's not moving inside me anymore, so I arch my back, pressing my hips harder against him. He moans in my mouth and moves against me once, then stops again. "Tate," he says against my lips.

"Just finish, Miles," I say to him through my tears. "Just finish."

He places a palm against my cheek and he presses his lips to my ear. We're both crying harder now, and I can see that I'm more than this to him. I *know* I am. I feel how much he wants to love me, but whatever is stopping him is more than I'm able to conquer. I wrap my arms around his neck. "Please," I beg him. "*Please*, Miles." I'm crying, begging for something, but I don't even know what it is anymore.

He thrusts against me. Hard this time. So hard I scoot away from him, so he wraps his arms under my shoulders and cups his hands upward, holding me in place against him as he repeatedly pushes into me. Hard, long, deep thrusts that force moans out of both of us with every movement.

"Harder," I beg.

He pushes harder.

"Faster."

He moves faster.

We're both gasping for breath between our tears. It's intense. It's heartbreaking. It's devastating.

It's ugly.

It's over.

As soon as his body is motionless on top of mine, I push against his shoulders. He rolls off of me. I sit up and wipe my eyes with my hands, then stand up and pull on my underwear. His fingers wrap around my ankle. The same fingers that wrapped around the same ankle the first night I met him.

"Tate," he says, his voice riddled with *everything*. Every single emotion wraps itself around each letter of my name as it comes out of his mouth.

I pull away from his grasp.

I walk to the door, still feeling him inside me. Still tasting his mouth on mine. Still feeling the stains of his tears against my cheek.

I open the door and walk out.

I close the door behind me, and it's the hardest thing I've ever done.

I can't even walk the three feet back to my apartment.

I collapse in the hallway.

I'm liquid.

Nothing but tears.

chapter thirty-four

MILES

Six years earlier

We went home. Not to *our* home.

Rachel wanted Lisa. Rachel needs her mother.

I kind of need my father.

Every night I hold her. Every night I tell her I'm sorry. Every night we just cry.

I don't understand how it can be so perfect. How life and love and people can be so perfect and beautiful.

Then it's not.

It's so ugly.

Life and love and people become ugly.

It all becomes water.

Tonight is different. This night is the first night in three weeks when she's not crying. I hold her anyway. I want to be happy that she's not crying, but it scares me. Her tears mean she feels something. Even if that something is devastation, it's still *something*. There aren't any tears tonight.

I hold her anyway. I tell her I'm sorry again.

She never tells me it's okay.

She never tells me it's not my fault.

She never tells me she forgives me.

She does kiss me tonight, though. She kisses me and takes off her shirt. She tells me to make love to her. I tell her we shouldn't. I tell her we're supposed to wait two more weeks. She kisses me so I'll stop talking.

I kiss her back.

Rachel loves me again.

I think.

She's kissing me like she loves me.

I'm gentle with her.

I go slow.

She's touching my skin like she loves me.

I don't want to hurt her.

She cries.

Please don't cry, Rachel.

I stop.

She tells me not to stop.

She tells me to finish.

Finish.

I don't like that word.

Like this is a job.

I kiss her again.

I *finish*.

* * *

Miles,
Rachel wrote me a letter.

I'm sorry.

No.

I can't do this. It hurts too much.

No, no, no.

My mother is taking me back to Phoenix. We're both staying there. It's all too complicated, even between the two of them now. Your father already knows.

Clayton brings families together.

Miles rips them apart.

I tried to stay. I tried to love you. Every time I look at you, I see him. Everything is him. If I stay, everything will always be him. You know that. I know you understand that. I shouldn't blame you.

But you do.

I'm so sorry.

You stopped loving me with a letter, Rachel?

Love,

I feel it. All the ugly parts of it. It's in my pores. My veins. My memories. My future.

Rachel.

The difference between the ugly side of love and the beautiful side of love is that the beautiful side is much lighter. It makes you feel like you're floating. It lifts you up. Carries you.

The beautiful parts of love hold you above the rest of the world. They hold you so high above all the bad stuff, and you just look down on everything else and think, *Wow. I'm so glad I'm up here.*

Sometimes the beautiful parts of love move back to Phoenix.

The ugly parts of love are too heavy to move back to Phoenix. The ugly parts of love can't lift you up.

They bring you

D
  O
    W
      N.

They hold you under.

Drown you.

You look up and think, *I wish I was up there.*

But you're not.

Ugly love *becomes* you.

Consumes you.

Makes you *hate it all.*

Makes you realize that all the beautiful parts aren't even worth it. Without the beautiful, you'll never risk feeling *this.*

You'll never risk feeling the *ugly.*

So you give it up. You give it all up. You never want love again, no matter what kind it is, because no type of love will ever be worth living through the ugly love again.

I'll never let myself love anyone again, Rachel.

Ever.

chapter thirty-five

TATE

"Last load," Corbin says, picking up the remaining two boxes.

I hand Corbin the key to my new place. "I'll make one more walk-through and meet you over there." I open the door for Corbin, and he exits the apartment. I'm left staring at the door across the hall.

I haven't seen or spoken to him since last week. I've been selfishly hoping he would show up and apologize, but then again, what would he even be apologizing for? He never lied to me. He never verbalized promises that he broke.

The only times he wasn't brutally honest with me were the times he didn't speak. The times he looked at me and I assumed the feelings I saw in his eyes were more than what he was able to verbalize.

It's apparent now that I more than likely invented those feelings from him in order to match them to my own. The occasional emotion behind his eyes when we were together was obviously a figment of my own imagination. A figment of my hope.

I scan the apartment one last time to make sure I packed everything. When I step outside and lock Corbin's door behind me, my movements are taken over by something I'm unfamiliar with.

I can't tell if it's braveness or desperation, but my hand is balled into a fist, and that fist is knocking on his door.

I tell myself that I'm free to escape to the elevator if ten seconds pass and the door doesn't open.

Unfortunately, it opens after seven.

My thoughts begin to riot with rationalization as the door opens wider. Before rationalization wins and I dart away, Ian appears in the doorway. His eyes change from complacent to sympathetic when he sees me standing here.

"Tate," he says, capping my name off with a smile. I notice the shift of his gaze toward Miles's bedroom before his eyes fall back on mine. "Let me get him," he says.

I feel the ascent in the nod of my head, but my heart is making a descent, scaling down my chest, through my stomach, and straight to the floor.

"Tate's at the door," I hear Ian say. I inspect every word, every syllable, searching for a clue wherever I can find one. I want to know if he rolled his eyes when he said that or if he said it hopefully. If anyone knows how Miles would feel about me standing in his doorway, it would be Ian. Unfortunately, Ian's voice gives no indication of what Miles may feel about my presence.

I hear footsteps. I dissect the sound of the footsteps as they close in on the living room. Are they hurried footsteps? Are they hesitant? Are they angry?

When he reaches the door, my eyes fall to his feet first.

I get nothing from them. No clues that will help me find the confidence I so desperately need in this moment.

I can already tell my words will come out raspy and weak, but I force them up anyway. "I'm leaving," I say, still staring down at his feet. "I just wanted to say good-bye."

There's no immediate reaction from him, physically *or* verbally. My eyes finally make the brave journey up to his. When I see the stoic look on his face, I want to step back, but I'm afraid I'll trip over my heart.

I don't want him to watch me fall.

My regret over making the choice to knock consumes me with the brevity in his response.

"Good-bye, Tate."

chapter thirty-six

MILES

Present day

Her eyes finally find the courage to meet mine, but I try not to
see her. When I really look at her, it's too much. Every time I'm
with her, her eyes and her mouth and her voice and her smile
find every vulnerable spot on me to breach. To seize. To conquer.
Every time I'm around her, I have to fight it, so I try not to see
her with anything other than my eyes this time.

She says she's here to say good-bye, but that's not why she's
here, and she knows it. She's here because she fell in love with
me, even though I told her not to. She's here because she still has
hope that I can love her back.

I want to, Tate. I want to love you so much it fucking hurts.

I don't even recognize my own voice when I tell her good-
bye. The lack of emotion behind my words could be miscon-
strued as hateful. A far cry from the apathy I'm attempting to

convey and an even farther cry from the urge I have to beg her not to go.

She immediately looks down at her feet. I can tell my response just killed her, but I've given her enough false hope. Every time I ever allowed her in, it hurts her that much more when I have to push her away.

But it's hard to feel bad for her, because as much as she's hurting, she doesn't know pain. She doesn't know it like I know it. I keep pain alive. I keep it in business. I keep it thriving with as much as I experience it.

She inhales and then looks back up at me with slightly redder, glossier eyes. "You deserve so much more than what you're allowing yourself to have." She stands on the tips of her toes and places her hands on my shoulders, then presses her lips to my cheek. "Good-bye, Miles."

She turns and walks toward the elevator, just as Corbin steps out to meet her. I see her lift one of her hands to wipe away her tears.

I watch her walk away.

I shut my door, expecting to feel even the slightest ripple of relief over the fact that I was able to let her walk away. Instead, I'm met with the only familiar sensation my heart is capable of feeling: *pain.*

"You're a goddamn idiot," Ian says from behind me. I turn around, and he's sitting on the arm of the couch, staring at me. "Why are you not going after her right now?"

Because, Ian, I hate this feeling. I hate every feeling she evokes in me, because it fills me with all the things I've spent the last six years avoiding.

"Why would I do that?" I ask as I head toward my room. I pause with the knock at my front door. I expel a frustrated breath before turning back to the door, not wanting to have to turn her

288 | COLLEEN HOOVER

away for a second time. I will, though. Even if I have to lay it out in terms that will hurt her even more, she needs to accept the fact that it's over. I let it go too far. Hell, I never should have allowed it to even begin, with us knowing it would more than likely end this way.

I open the door but find Corbin in my line of sight rather than Tate. I want to feel relieved by the fact that it's him standing here rather than her, but the fuming look on his face makes it impossible to feel relieved.

Before I can react, his fist connects with my mouth, and I stumble backward toward the couch. Ian breaks my fall, and I steady myself before turning to face the door again.

"What the hell, Corbin?" Ian yells. He's holding me back, assuming I want retaliation.

I don't. I deserved that.

Corbin trades looks between the two of us, finally settling on me. He pulls his fist up to his chest and rubs it with his other hand. "We all know I should have done that a long time ago." He grips the doorknob and pulls the door shut, disappearing back out into the hallway.

I shrug out of Ian's grasp and bring my hand up to my lip. I pull my fingers back, and they're tinged with blood.

"How about now?" Ian says, hopeful. "You gonna go after her now?"

I glare at him before turning to stalk off to my bedroom.

Ian laughs loudly. It's the kind of laugh that says, *You're a goddamn idiot.* Only he already said that, so he's kind of just repeating himself.

He follows me to my bedroom.

I'm really not in the mood for this conversation. Good thing I know how to look at people without actually seeing them.

I take a seat on my bed, and he walks into my room and leans against the door. "I'm tired of this, Miles. Six fucking years I've watched this zombie walk around in your place."

"I'm not a zombie," I say flatly. "Zombies can't fly."

Ian rolls his eyes, obviously not in the mood for jokes. Good thing, because I'm not really in the mood to make them.

He continues to glare at me, so I pick up my phone and lie back on the bed in order to pretend he isn't here.

"She's the first thing to breathe life back into you since the night you drowned in that fucking lake."

I'll hurt him. If he doesn't leave right this second, I'll fucking hurt him.

"Get out."

"No."

I look at him. I *see* him. "Get the hell out, Ian."

He walks to my desk, pulls out the chair, and sits in it. "Fuck you, Miles," he says. "I'm not finished."

"Get out!"

"No!"

I stop fighting him. I get up and walk out myself.

He follows me. "Let me ask you one question," he says, trailing me into the living room.

"And then you'll get out?"

He nods. "And then I'll get out."

"Fine."

He regards me silently for a few moments.

I patiently wait for his question so he can leave before I hurt him.

"What if someone told you they could erase that entire night from your memory, but in doing so, they also have to erase every single good thing. All the moments with Rachel. Every word, every kiss, every *I love you*. Every moment you had with your son, no matter how brief. The first moment you saw Rachel holding him. The first moment *you* held him. The first time you heard him cry or watched him sleep. All of it. Gone. Forever. If someone told you they could get rid of the ugly stuff, but you'd lose all the other stuff, too . . . would you do it?"

He thinks he's asking me something I've never asked myself before. Does he think I don't sit and wonder about this stuff every fucking day of my life?

"You didn't say I had to answer your question. You just asked if you could ask it. You can leave now."

I'm the worst kind of person.

"You *can't* answer it," he says. "You can't say yes."

"I also can't say no," I tell him. "Congratulations, Ian. You stumped me. Good-bye."

I begin to walk back to my room, but he says my name again. I stop and put my hands on my hips and drop my head. Why won't he stop with it, already? It's been six damn years. He should know that night made me who I am now. He should know I'm not changing.

"If I would have asked you that a few months ago, you would have said yes before the question even left my mouth," he says. "Your answer has always been yes. You would have given up anything to not have to relive that night."

I turn around, and he's heading toward the door. He opens it, then pauses and faces me again. "If being with Tate for a few short months can make that pain bearable enough for you to answer with *maybe*, imagine what a lifetime with her could do for you."

He closes the door.

I close my eyes.

Something happens. Something inside me. It's as if his words have created an avalanche out of the glacier surrounding my heart. I feel chunks of hardened ice break off and fall next to all the other pieces that have detached since the moment I met Tate.

• • •

I step off the elevator and walk over to the empty chair next to Cap. He doesn't even acknowledge my presence with eye contact. He's staring across the lobby toward the exit.

"You just let her go," he says, not even attempting to hide the disappointment in his voice.

I don't respond.

He pushes on the arms of his chair with his hands, repositioning himself. "Some people . . . they grow wiser as they grow older. Unfortunately, most people just grow older." He turns to face me. "You're one of the ones just been growing older, because you are as stupid as you were the day you were born."

Cap knows me well enough to know this is what had to happen. He's known me all my life; having worked maintenance on my father's apartment buildings since before I was born. Before that, he worked for my grandfather doing the same thing. This pretty much guarantees he knows more about me and my family than even I do. "It had to happen, Cap," I say, excusing the fact that I let the only girl who has been able to reach me in more than six years just walk away.

"Had to happen, huh?" he grumbles.

As long as I've known him and as many nights as I've spent down here talking to him, he's never once given me an opinion about the decisions I've made for myself. He knows the life I chose after Rachel. He spouts off tidbits of wisdom here and there but never his opinion. He's listened to me vent about the situation with Tate for months, and he always sits quietly, patiently hearing me out, never giving me advice. That's what I like about him.

I feel that's all about to change.

"Before you give me a lecture, Cap," I say, interrupting him before he has the chance to continue. "You know she's better off." I turn and face him. "You *know* she is."

Cap chuckles, nodding his head. "That's for damn sure."

I look at him disbelievingly. *Did he just agree with me?*

"Are you saying I made the right choice?"

He's quiet for a second before blowing out a quick breath. His expression contorts as if his thoughts aren't something he necessarily wants to share. He relaxes into his chair and folds his arms loosely over his chest. "I told myself to never get involved in your problems, boy, because in order for a man to give advice, he'd better know what the hell he's talkin' about. And Lord knows in all my eighty years, I ain't never been through nothing like what you went through. I don't know the first thing about what that was like or what that did to you. Just thinking 'bout that night makes my gut hurt, so I know you feel it in your gut, too. And your heart. And your bones. And your soul."

I close my eyes, wishing I could close my ears instead. I don't want to hear this.

"None of the people in your life knows what it feels like to be you. Not me. Not your father. Not those friends of yours. Not even Tate. There's only one person who feels what you feel. Only one person who hurts like you hurt. Only one other parent to that baby boy who misses him the same way you do."

My eyes are closed tightly now, and I'm doing all I can to respect his end of the conversation, but it's taking all I have not to get up and walk away. He has no right bringing Rachel into this conversation.

"Miles," he says quietly. There's determination in his voice, like he needs me to take him seriously. I always do. "You believe you took away that girl's chance at happiness, and until you confront that past, you won't ever move forward. You're gonna be reliving that day every single day until the day you die, unless you go see for your own eyes that she's okay. Then maybe you'll see that it's okay for you to be happy, too."

I lean forward and run my hands over my face, then rest my elbows on my knees and look down. I watch as a single tear falls from my eye and drops to the floor beneath my feet. "And what happens if she's not okay?" I whisper.

Cap leans forward and clasps his hands between his knees. I turn and look at him, seeing tears in his eyes for the first time in the twenty-four years I've known him. "Then I guess nothing changes. You can keep on feeling like you don't deserve a life for ruining hers. You can keep on avoiding everything that might make you *feel* again." He leans in toward me and lowers his voice. "I know the thought of confronting your past terrifies you. It terrifies every man. But sometimes we don't do it for ourselves. We do it for the people we love *more* than ourselves."

chapter thirty-seven

RACHEL

"Brad!" I yell. "Someone's at the door!" I grab a dish towel and dry my hands.

"Got it," he says, passing through the kitchen. I take a quick inventory of the kitchen to make sure there isn't anything my mother can insult. Counters are clean. Floors are clean.

Bring it on, Mom.

"Wait here," Brad says to whoever is at the door.

Wait here?

Brad wouldn't say that to my mother.

"Rachel," Brad says from the kitchen entryway. I turn around to face him, and I immediately tense. The look on his face is one I rarely ever see. It's reserved for preparation. When he's about to tell me something I don't want to hear or something he's afraid will hurt me. My immediate thoughts fall to my mother, and I'm gripped with worry.

"Brad," I whisper. "What is it?" I'm holding the counter next to me. The familiar fear washes over me that used to live and breathe inside me, but now it's something that only grips me on occasion.

Like right now, when my husband is too afraid to tell me something he's not sure I want to hear. "Someone's here to see you," he says.

I don't know of anyone who could make Brad as concerned as he is right now. "Who?"

He slowly walks toward me and cups my face in his hands when he reaches me. He looks into my eyes as if he's trying to brace me for a fall. "It's Miles."

I don't move.

I don't fall, but Brad holds me up anyway. He wraps his arms around me and pulls me against his chest.

"Why is he here?" My voice trembles.

Brad shakes his head. "I don't know." He pulls away and looks down on me. "I'll ask him to leave if you need me to."

I immediately shake my head. I wouldn't do that to him. Not if he came all the way to Phoenix.

Not after almost seven years.

"Do you need a few minutes? I can take him to the living room."

I don't deserve this man. I don't know what I'd do without him. He knows my history with Miles. He knows everything we went through. It took me a while to be able to tell him the whole story. He knows all of this, and he's still standing here, offering to invite the only other man I've ever loved into our home.

"I'm okay," I tell him, even though I'm not. I don't know if I want to see Miles. I have no idea why he's here. "Are *you* okay?"

He nods. "He looks upset. I think you should talk to him." He leans in and kisses me on the forehead. "He's in the foyer. I'll be in my office if you need me."

I nod, and then I kiss him. I kiss him hard.

He walks away, and I'm left standing silently in the kitchen, my heart beating erratically within my chest. I take a deep breath, but it does nothing to calm me. I brush my hands down my shirt and walk toward the foyer.

Miles's back is to me, but he hears me round the corner. He turns his head slightly over his shoulder, almost as if he's just as afraid to turn around and look at me as I am to see him.

He does it carefully. Slowly. Suddenly, my eyes are locked with his.

I know it's been six years, but in that six years, he's somehow completely changed, without changing at all. He's still Miles, but he's a man now. This makes me wonder what he's seeing, looking at me for the first time since the day I left him.

"Hey," he says, treading carefully. His voice is different. It isn't the voice of a teenager anymore.

"Hi."

I lose his gaze as his eyes travel around the foyer. He takes in my home. A home I never expected to see him in. We both stand in silence for a whole minute. Maybe two.

"Rachel, I . . ." He looks back at me again. "I don't know why I'm here."

I do.

I can see it in his eyes. I got to know those eyes so well when we were together. I knew all his thoughts. All his emotions. He wasn't able to hide how he felt, because he felt so much. He's always felt so much.

He's here because he needs something. I don't know what. Answers, maybe? Closure? I'm glad he waited until now to get it, because I think I'm finally ready to give it.

"It's good to see you," I tell him.

Our voices are weak and timid. It's weird, seeing someone

for the first time under different circumstances from when you parted.

I loved this man. I loved him with all my heart and soul. I loved him like I love Brad.

I also hated him.

"Come in," I say, motioning toward the living room. "Let's talk."

He takes two hesitant steps toward the living room. I turn around and let him follow me.

We both take a seat on the sofa. He doesn't get comfortable. Instead, he sits on the edge of it and leans forward, resting his elbows on his knees. He's looking around, taking in my home once more. My life.

"You're brave," I say. He looks at me, waiting for me to continue. "I've thought about this, Miles. About seeing you again. I just . . ." I look down. "I just couldn't."

"Why not?" he says almost immediately.

I make eye contact with him again. "The same reason you haven't. We don't know what to say."

He smiles, but it's not the smile I used to love on Miles. This one is guarded, and I wonder if I did this to him. If I'm responsible for all the sad parts of him. There are so many sad parts of him now.

He picks up a photo of Brad and me from the end table. His eyes study the picture in his hands for a moment. "Do you love him?" he asks, continuing to stare at the picture. "Like you loved me?" He's not asking in a bitter or jealous way. He's asking in a curious way.

"Yes," I reply. "Just as much."

He places the picture back on the end table but continues to stare at it.

"How?" he whispers. "How did you do that?"

His words bring tears to my eyes, because I know exactly what he's asking me. I asked myself the same question for several years, until I met Brad. I didn't think I'd ever be able to love someone again. I didn't think I'd *want* to love someone again. Why would anyone want to put themselves in a position that could bring back the type of pain that makes a person envious of death?

"I want to show you something, Miles."

I stand up and reach out for his hand. He watches my hand cautiously for a moment before finally reaching for it. His fingers slide through mine, and he squeezes my hand as he stands up. I begin making my way toward the bedroom, and he follows closely behind me.

We reach the bedroom door, and my fingers pause on the doorknob. My heart is heavy. The emotions and everything we went through are surfacing, but I know I have to allow them to surface if I want to help him. I push the door open and walk inside, pulling Miles behind me.

As soon as we're inside the room, I feel his fingers tighten around mine. "Rachel," he whispers. His voice is a plea for me not to do this. I feel him try to pull back toward the door, but I don't let him. I make him walk to her crib with me.

He's standing by my side, but I can feel him struggling because he doesn't want to be in here right now.

He's squeezing my hand so tightly I can feel the hurt in his heart. He blows out a quick breath as he looks down on her. I see the roll of his throat when he swallows, then blows out another steadying breath.

I watch as his free hand comes up and grips the edge of her crib, holding on to it as tightly as the hand that's wrapped around mine. "What's her name?" he whispers.

"Claire."

His whole body reacts with my response. His shoulders immediately begin to shake, and he tries to hold in his breath, but nothing can stop it. Nothing can stop him from feeling what he's feeling, so I just allow him to feel it. He pulls his hand from mine and covers his mouth to conceal the quick rush of air released from his lungs. He turns and walks swiftly out of the room. I follow him just as fast, in time to see his back hit the hallway wall across from her nursery. He slides to the floor, and the tears begin to fall hard.

He doesn't try to cover them. He pulls his hands through his hair, and he leans his head back against the wall and looks up at me. "That's . . ." He points to Claire's nursery and tries to speak, but it takes him several tries to get his sentence out. "That's his sister," he finally says, blowing out an unsteady breath. "Rachel. You gave him a sister."

I sink to the floor next to him and wrap my arm around his shoulders, stroking his hair with my other hand. He presses his palms to his forehead and squeezes his eyes shut, crying quietly to himself.

"Miles." I don't even try to disguise the tears in my voice. "Look at me."

He leans his head back against the wall, but he can't look me in the eyes. "I'm sorry I blamed you. You lost him, too. I didn't know how else to deal with it back then."

My words completely break him, and I'm consumed with guilt over allowing six years to pass without letting him hear those words. He leans over and wraps his arms tightly around me, pulling me against him. I let him hold me.

He holds me for a long time, until all the apologies and forgiveness are absorbed and it's just us again. No tears.

I would be lying if I said I never think about what I did to him. I think about it every day. But I was eighteen and devastated, and nothing mattered to me after that night.

Nothing.

I just wanted to forget, but every morning I woke up and didn't feel Clayton by my side, I blamed Miles. I blamed him for saving me, because I had no reason left to live. I also knew in my heart that Miles did what he could. I knew in my heart that it was never his fault, but at that point in my life, I wasn't capable of rational thought or even forgiveness. At that point in my life, I was convinced I wouldn't be capable of anything at all but feeling pain.

Those feelings never wavered for more than three years.

Until the day I met Brad.

I don't know who Miles has, but the familiar struggle in his eyes proves there's someone. I used to see the same struggle every time I looked in the mirror, unsure if I had it in me to love again.

"Do you love her?" I ask him. I don't need to know her name. We're beyond that now. I know he isn't here because he's still in love with me. He's here because he doesn't know how to love at *all*.

He sighs and rests his chin on top of my head. "I'm scared I won't be able to."

Miles kisses the top of my head, and I close my eyes. I listen to his heart beating inside his chest. A heart he's claiming isn't capable of knowing how to love, but in actuality, it's a heart that loves too much. He loved so much, and that one night took it away from us. Changed our worlds. Changed his heart.

"I used to cry all the time," I tell him. "All the time. In the shower. In the car. In my bed. Every time I was alone, I would cry. For those first couple of years, my life was constant sadness, penetrated by nothing. Not even good moments."

I feel his arms wrap tighter around me, silently telling me he knows. He knows exactly what I'm talking about.

"Then when I met Brad, I found myself having these brief moments where my life wasn't sad every second of the day. I would go somewhere with him in a car, and I'd realize it was my first time in a car without crying at least one tear. The nights we would spend together were the only nights I wouldn't cry myself to sleep. For the first time, this impenetrable sadness that had become me was being broken by the brief, good moments I spent with Brad."

I pause, needing a moment. I haven't had to think about this in a while, and the emotions and feelings are too fresh. Too real. I pull away from Miles and lean back against the wall, then rest my head on his shoulder. He tilts his head until it's resting against mine and grabs my hand, intertwining our fingers.

"After a while, I began to notice that the good moments with Brad began to outweigh all the sadness. The sadness that was my life became the *moments*, and my happiness with Brad became my *life*."

I feel him exhale, and I know he knows what I'm talking about. I know that whoever she is, he's had those good moments with her.

"For the entire nine months I was pregnant with Claire, I was so scared I wouldn't be able to cry from happiness when I saw her. Right after she was born, they handed her to me, just like they did when Clayton was born. Claire looked just like him, Miles. Just *like* him. I was staring down at her, holding her in my arms, and tears were running down my cheeks. But I was crying good tears, and I realized at that moment that they were the first tears of happiness I had cried since the day I held Clayton in my arms."

I wipe my eyes and let go of his hand, then lift my head off his shoulder. "You deserve that, too," I tell him. "You deserve to feel that again."

He nods. "I want to love her so much, Rachel," he says, breathing out the words like they've been pent up forever. "I want that with her so much. I'm just scared the rest of it will never go away."

"The pain will never go away, Miles. Ever. But if you let yourself love her, you'll only feel it sometimes, instead of allowing it to consume your entire life."

He wraps his arm around me and pulls my forehead against his lips. He kisses me, long and hard, before pulling back. He nods, letting me know that he understands what I'm trying to explain to him.

"You've got this, Miles," I say, repeating the same words he used to comfort me with. "You've got this."

He laughs, and it's as if I can feel some of the heaviness lift away from him.

"You know what I was most afraid of tonight?" he asks. "I was afraid that when I got here, you'd be just like me." He brushes my hair back and smiles. "I'm so happy you're not. It makes me feel good to see you happy."

He pulls me to him and hugs me tightly. "Thank you, Rachel," he whispers. He kisses me gently on the cheek before releasing me to stand up. "I should probably go now. I have a million things I want to tell her."

He makes his way down the hallway toward the living room, then turns to face me one last time. I no longer see all the sad parts of him. Now I just see a calmness when I look in his eyes.

"Rachel?" He pauses, watching me quietly for a moment. A peaceful smile slowly spreads across his face. "I'm so proud of you."

He disappears from the hallway, and I remain on the floor until I hear the front door close behind him.

I'm proud of you, too, Miles.

chapter thirty-eight

TATE

I close the door to my car and walk to the stairs leading up to the second floor of my apartment complex. I'm relieved not to have to use the elevator anymore, but I can't help but miss Cap a little bit, even if his advice didn't make a whole lot of sense to me the majority of the time. It was nice just having him there to vent to. I've been keeping myself busy with work and school, trying to stay focused, but it's been hard.

I've been in my new apartment for two weeks now, and even though I wish I were alone, I never am. Every time I walk in through my front door, Miles is still everywhere. He's still in everything, and I keep waiting until he's not. I keep waiting for the day when it will hurt less. When I won't miss him as much.

I would say my heart is broken, but it's not. I don't think it is. Actually, I wouldn't know, because my heart hasn't been in my chest since I left it lying in front of his apartment the day I told him good-bye.

I tell myself to take it one day at a time, but it's so much easier said than done. Especially when those days turn into nights, and I have to lie in my bed alone, listening to the silence.

The silence was never so loud until I told Miles good-bye.

I'm already dreading opening my apartment door, and I'm not even halfway up the stairwell yet. I can already tell this night isn't going to be any different from all the other nights since Miles. I reach the top of the stairs and turn left toward my apartment, but my feet stop working.

My legs stop working.

I can feel the thumping of a heart somewhere in my chest again for the first time in two weeks.

"Miles?"

He doesn't move. He's sitting on the floor in front of my apartment, propped up against the door. I walk slowly toward him, not sure what to make of his appearance. He's not in uniform. He's casually dressed, and the stubble on his face proves he hasn't worked in a few days. There's also what looks like a fresh bruise under his right eye. I'm scared to wake him up, because if he's as belligerent as he was the first time I met him, I don't want to deal with it. But once again, there's no way I can get around him and inside my apartment without waking him up.

I look up and inhale a deep breath, wondering what to do. I'm afraid if I wake him up, I'll cave. I'll let him inside, and I'll give him what he's here for, which definitely isn't the part of me I want to give him.

"Tate," he says. I look down at him, and he's awake now, pulling himself up, watching me nervously. I take a step back once he's standing, because I forgot how tall he is. How much he becomes everything when he's standing right in front of me.

"How long have you been here?" I ask him.

He glances down to the cell phone in his hand. "Six hours."

He looks back up at me. "I need to use your restroom pretty bad."

I want to laugh, but I can't remember how.

I turn to my door, and he steps out of the way for me to unlock it.

My trembling hand pushes open the door to my apartment, and I walk inside, then point to the hallway. "On the right."

I don't look back at him while he walks in that direction. I wait until the bathroom door closes, and I fall onto the couch and bury my face in my hands.

I hate that he's here. I hate that I let him in without question. I hate that as soon as he walks out of the bathroom, I'm going to have to make him leave. But I just can't do this to myself anymore.

I'm still trying to gather myself when the bathroom door opens and he walks back into the living room. I look up at him and can't look away.

Something is different.

He's different.

The smile on his face . . . the peacefulness in his eyes . . . the way he carries himself like he's floating.

It's only been two weeks, but he looks so different.

He takes a seat on the couch and doesn't even bother putting space between us. He sits right next to me and leans into me, so I close my eyes and wait for whatever words he's about to say that will hurt me again. That's all he knows how to do.

"Tate," he whispers. "I *miss* you."

Whoa.

I was absolutely not expecting to hear those three words, but they just became my new favorite words.

I and *miss* and *you.*

"Say it again, Miles."

"I miss you, Tate," he says immediately. "So much. And it's not the first time. I've missed you every single day we weren't together since the moment I met you."

He wraps his arm around my shoulders and pulls me to him. I go.

I fall to his chest and grab hold of his shirt, squeezing my eyes shut when I feel his lips press against the top of my head.

"Look at me," he says softly, pulling me onto his lap to face him.

I do. I look at him. I actually see him this time. There's no guard up. There's no invisible wall blocking me from learning and exploring everything about him. He's allowing me to see him this time, and he's beautiful.

So much more beautiful than before. Whatever changed in him, it was huge.

"I want to tell you something," he says. "This is so hard for me to say, because you're the first person I've ever wanted to say it to."

I'm scared to move. His words are terrifying me, but I nod.

"I had a son," he says quietly, looking down at our hands now laced together. Those three words are delivered with more pain than any three words I've ever heard.

I inhale. He looks up at me with tears in his eyes, but I remain quiet for him, even though his words just knocked the breath out of me.

"He died six years ago." His voice is soft and distant, but it's still his voice.

I can tell those words are some of the hardest he's ever had to say. It hurts him so much to admit this. I want to tell him to stop. I want to tell him I don't need to hear it if it hurts. I want to wrap my arms around him and rip the sadness from his soul with my bare hands, but instead, I let him finish.

Miles looks back down at our interlocked fingers. "I'm not ready to tell you about him yet. I need to do it at my own pace."

I nod and squeeze his hands reassuringly.

"I will tell you about him, though. I promise. I also want to tell you about Rachel. I want you to know everything about my past."

I don't even know if he's finished, but I lean forward and press my lips to his. He pulls me against him so tightly and pushes back against my mouth so hard it's as if he's telling me he's sorry without using words.

"Tate," he whispers against my mouth. I can feel him smiling. "I'm not finished."

He lifts me and adjusts me next to him on the couch. His thumb circles my shoulder as he looks down at his lap, forming whatever words he's needing to say to me.

"I was born and raised in a small suburb just outside of San Francisco," he says, bringing his eyes back up to meet mine. "I'm an only child. I don't really have any favorite foods, because I like almost everything. I've wanted to be a pilot for as long as I can remember. My mother passed away from cancer when I was seventeen. My father has been married for about a year to a woman who works for him. She's nice, and they're happy together. I've always kind of wanted a dog, but I've never had one . . ."

I watch him, mesmerized. I watch his eyes as they roam around my face while he talks. While he tells me all about his childhood and his past and how he met my brother and his relationship with Ian.

His hand finds mine, and he covers it as though he's becoming my shield. My armor. "The night I met you," he finally says. "The night you found me in the hallway?" His eyes dart toward his lap, unable to hold contact with mine. "My son would have been six that day."

I know he said he wants me to listen to him, but right now, I just need to hug him. I lean forward and wrap my arms around him, and he lies back on the couch, pulling me on top of him.

"It took everything I had to try to convince myself that I wasn't falling for you, Tate. Every single time I was around you, the things I would feel terrified me. I had gone six years thinking I had control of my life and my heart and that nothing could ever hurt me again. But when we were together, there were moments I didn't care if I ever hurt again, because being with you almost felt worth the potential pain. Every time I began to feel that way, I would just push you farther away out of guilt and fear. I felt like I didn't deserve you. I didn't deserve happiness at all, because I'd taken it away from the only two people I had ever loved."

His arms tighten around me when he feels my shoulders shaking from the tears making their way out of my eyes. His lips meet the top of my head, and he inhales a steady breath as he kisses me, long and hard.

"I'm sorry it took me so long," he says with a voice full of remorse. "But I'll never be able to thank you enough for not giving up on me. You saw something in me that gave you hope in us, and you didn't give up on that. And Tate? That means more to me than anything anyone's ever done."

His hands meet my cheeks, and he lifts me away from his chest so he can see me face-to-face. "It may be a small piece at a time, but my past is yours now. All of it. Anything you want to know, I want to tell you. But only if you promise me I can also have your future."

The tears cascade down my cheeks, and he wipes them away, even though I don't need him to. I don't care that I'm crying, because they aren't sad tears. Not in the least.

We kiss for so long my mouth starts to hurt as much as my

heart. My heart isn't hurting from pain this time, though. It hurts because it's never felt this full.

I trace my fingers across the scar on his jaw, knowing he'll eventually tell me how he got it. I also touch the tender area beneath his eye, relieved that I can finally ask him questions without being scared I'll upset him.

"What happened to your eye?"

He laughs and lets his head fall back against the couch. "I had to ask Corbin for your address. He gave it to me, but it took a lot of convincing."

I immediately lean forward and gently kiss his eye. "I can't believe he hit you."

"Not the first time," he admits. "But I'm pretty sure it'll be the last. I think he's finally okay with us being together after I agreed to a few of his rules."

This makes me nervous. "What rules?"

"Well, for one, I'm not allowed to break your heart," he says. "Second, I'm also not allowed to break your *damn* heart. And last, I'm not allowed to *fucking* break your damn heart."

I can't contain my laughter, because that sounds exactly like something Corbin would say to him. Miles laughs with me, and we take each other in for several quiet moments. I can see everything in his eyes now. Every single emotion.

"Miles," I say with a smile, "you're looking at me like you fell in love with me."

He shakes his head. "I didn't *fall* in love with you, Tate. I *flew*."

He pulls me back to him and gives me the only part of himself that he's never been able to give me until now.

His heart.

chapter thirty-nine

MILES

I stand in the doorway of my bedroom and watch her sleep. She doesn't know it, but I do this every morning she's here with me. She's what starts my day off right.

The first time I did this was the morning after I met her. I couldn't remember much from the night before. The only thing I remembered was her. I was on the couch, and she was stroking my hair, whispering, telling me to go to sleep. When I woke up in Corbin's apartment the next morning, I couldn't get her out of my head. I thought she had been a dream until I saw her purse in the living room.

I peeked inside her bedroom just to see if anyone was in the apartment with me. What I felt the moment I laid eyes on her was something I hadn't felt since the moment I first laid eyes on Rachel.

I felt like I was floating. Her skin and her hair and her lips and the way she looked like an angel while I stood there and watched her brought back so many feelings that had become foreign to me over the past six years.

I had gone so long refusing to allow myself to feel anything for anyone.

Not that I could have controlled the feelings I was experiencing toward Tate that day. I couldn't control them if I'd wanted to.

I know, because I tried.

I tried like hell.

But the second she opened her eyes and looked at me, I knew. She was either going to be the death of me . . . or she was going to be the one who finally brought me back to life.

The only problem I had with that was the fact that I didn't *want* to be brought back to life. I was comfortable. Protecting myself from the possibility of experiencing what I had experienced in the past was my only priority. However, there were so many moments when I forgot what my only priority was supposed to be.

When I finally caved and kissed her, that was the point at which everything changed. I wanted so much more after experiencing that kiss with her. I wanted her mouth and her body and her mind, and the only reason I stopped was that I felt myself also wanting her heart. I was good at lying to myself, though. Convincing myself that I was strong enough to have her physically and no other way. I didn't want to get hurt again, and I sure as hell didn't want to hurt her.

I did anyway, though. I hurt her so much. More than once. Now I plan to spend a lifetime making it up to her.

I walk to my bed and sit on the edge of it. She feels the bed shift, and she opens her eyes but not all the way. A hint of a smile plays on her lips before she pulls the covers over her head and rolls over.

We officially began dating six months ago, and that's been plenty long enough for me to realize she's not at all a morning person. I lean forward and kiss the area of blanket covering up her ear.

"Wake up, sleepyhead," I whisper.

She groans, so I lift the covers up and slide in behind her, wrapping myself around her. Her groan eventually turns into a soft moan.

"Tate, you need to get up. We have a plane to catch."

That gets her attention.

She rolls over cautiously and pulls the covers from over our heads. "What the hell do you mean we have a *plane* to catch?"

I'm grinning, trying to contain my anticipation. "Get up, get dressed, let's go."

She's eyeing me suspiciously, which makes total sense, considering it's not even five o'clock in the morning yet. "I know you know how rare it is for me to have an entire day off, so this better be worth it."

I laugh and give her a quick kiss. "That all depends on our ability to be punctual." I stand up and pat the mattress several times with the palms of my hands. "So get up, get up, get up."

She laughs and throws the covers off of her completely. She scoots to the edge of the bed, and I help her stand up. "It's hard to stay irritated with you when you're this giddy, Miles."

• • •

We reach the lobby, and Cap is waiting at the elevator just as I asked him to. He has her juice in a to-go cup and our breakfast. I love the relationship they have. I was a little worried to reveal to Tate that I had known Cap all my life. When I finally told her, she was irritated with both of us. Mostly because she assumed Cap was telling me everything she confessed to him.

I assured her Cap wouldn't do that.

I *know* he wouldn't, because Cap is one of the few people in this world I trust.

He knew just the right things to say to me without appearing as though he were lecturing me or giving me advice. He'd always say just enough to make me think long and hard about my situation with Tate. Luckily, he's one of the few people who grow wiser with age. He knew what he was doing with both of us all along.

"Morning, Tate," he says to her, grinning from ear to ear. He holds out his arm for her to take, and she looks back and forth between us.

"What's going on?" she asks Cap as he begins to walk her toward the lobby exit.

He smiles. "The boy is about to take me on my first-ever ride in an airplane. I wanted you to come along, too."

She tells him she doesn't believe this is his first time in an airplane.

"It's true," he says. "Just 'cause I have the moniker don't mean I've ever been on a real plane."

The look of appreciation she shoots me over her shoulder is enough to declare this day one of my favorites, and it's not even daylight yet.

• • •

"You okay back there, Cap?" I say into the headset. He's seated right behind Tate, staring out his window. He gives me a thumbs-up but doesn't take his eyes off the window. The sun hasn't even broken through the clouds yet, and there's not very much to see at this point. We've only been in the plane ten minutes, but I'm pretty sure he's just as fascinated and mesmerized as I hoped he would be.

I return my attention to the controls until I reach optimal altitude, and then I mute Cap's headset. I glance at Tate, and she's staring at me, watching me with an appreciative smile spread across her lips.

"Want to know why we're here?" I ask her.

She glances over her shoulder at Cap and then looks back at me. "Because he's never done this before."

I shake my head, timing it just right. "Remember the day we were driving back from your parents' house after Thanksgiving?"

She nods, but her eyes are curious now.

"You asked what it was like to experience the sunrise from up here. It's not something that can be described, Tate." I point out her window. "You just have to experience it for yourself."

She immediately turns and looks out her window. Her palms press against the glass, and for five minutes straight, she doesn't move a muscle. She watches it the entire time, and I don't know how, but I fall even more in love with her in this moment.

When the sun has broken through the clouds and the airplane is completely filled with sunlight, she finally turns back to face me. Her eyes are filled with tears, and she doesn't speak a word. She just reaches for my hand and holds it.

• • •

"Wait here," I tell her. "I want to help Cap out first. A driver is taking him back to the apartment, because you and I are going to breakfast after this."

She tells Cap good-bye and waits patiently in the plane as I help him down the steps. He reaches into his pocket and hands me the boxes, then flashes me one of his approving smiles. I shove the boxes into the pocket of my jacket and turn back toward the steps.

"Hey, boy!" Cap yells, right before climbing into the car. I pause and turn around to face him. He looks at the plane behind me. "Thank you," he says, waving his hand down the length of the plane. "For this."

I nod, but he disappears inside the vehicle before I can tell him thank you in return.

I climb back up the steps and into the plane. She's unbuckling her safety belt, getting prepared to exit the plane, but I slide back into my seat.

She smiles at me warmly. "You're incredible, Miles Mikel Archer. And I have to say, you look pretty damn hot flying an airplane. We should do this more often."

She gives me a quick peck on the mouth and begins to get up out of her seat.

I push her back down. "We're not finished," I say, turning and facing her full on. I take her hands in mine and look down at them, inhaling slowly, preparing to say everything she deserves to hear. "That day you asked me about watching the sunrise?" I look her in the eyes again. "I need to thank you for that. It was the first moment in more than six years I felt like I wanted to love someone again."

She blows out a quick breath with her smile and pulls in her bottom lip to try to hide it. I lift a hand to her face and pull her lip out from beneath her teeth with the pressure of my thumb. "I told you not to do that. I love your smile almost as much as I love you."

I lean forward to kiss her again, but I keep my eyes open so I can make sure that I'm retrieving the black box first. When I have it in my hand, I stop kissing her and pull away. Her eyes fall to the box and immediately grow wide, moving back and forth between the box and my face. Her hand comes up to her mouth, and she covers her gasp.

"Miles," she says, continuing to trade glances between me and the box in my hands.

I cut her off. "It's not what you think," I say, immediately opening the box to reveal the key. "It's *kind of* not what you think," I hesitantly add.

Her eyes are wide and hopeful, and I'm relieved by her reaction. I can tell by her smile that she wants this.

I pull the key out and flip her hand over, then place it in her palm. She stares at the key for several seconds and looks back up at me. "Tate," I say, looking at her with hope. "Will you move in with me?"

She looks down at the key one more time, then says two words that bring an immediate smile to my face.

Hell and *yes*.

I lean forward and kiss her. Our legs and arms and mouths become two pieces of a puzzle, fitting together effortlessly. She winds up in my lap, straddling me in the cockpit of the airplane.

It's cramped and tight.

It's perfect.

"I'm not a very good cook, though," she warns. "And you do laundry way better than I do. I just throw all the whites and colors together. And you know I'm not very nice in the morning." She's holding my face, spouting off every warning she can, as if I don't know what I'm getting myself into.

"Listen, Tate," I tell her. "I *want* your mess. I want your clothes on my bedroom floor. I want your toothbrush in my bathroom. I want your shoes in my closet. I want your mediocre leftovers in my fridge."

She laughs at that.

"Oh, and I almost forgot," I say, pulling the other box from my pocket. I hold it up between us and open it, revealing the ring. "I also want you in my future. Forever."

Her mouth is open in shock, and she's staring at the ring. She's frozen. I hope she doesn't have doubts, because I have absolutely none when it comes to wanting to spend the rest of my life with her. I know it's only been six months, but when you know, you know.

Her silence makes me nervous, so I quickly remove the ring and pick up her hand. "Will you break rule number two with me, Tate? Because I really want to marry you."

She doesn't even have to say yes. Her tears and her kiss and her laugh say it for her.

She pulls back and looks at me with so much love and appreciation it makes my chest hurt.

She's absolutely beautiful. Her hope is beautiful. The smile on her face is beautiful. The tears streaming down her cheeks are beautiful.

Her

love

is

beautiful.

She exhales a soft breath and leans in slowly, gently pressing her lips to mine. Her kiss is filled with tenderness and affection and an unspoken promise that she's mine now.

Forever.

"Miles," she whispers against my mouth, teasing my lips with hers. "I've never made love in an airplane before."

A smile immediately forms on my lips. It's as if she somehow infiltrated my thoughts.

"I've never made love to my *fiancée* before," I say in response.

Her hands slowly slide down my neck and shirt until her fingers meet the button on my jeans.

"Well, I think we need to rectify that," she says, ending her sentence with a kiss.

When her mouth meets mine again, it's as if every last piece of my armor disintegrates and every last piece of ice surrounding the glacier that was my heart melts and evaporates.

Whoever coined the phrase, *I love you to death* obviously never experienced the kind of love Tate and I share.

If that were the case, the phrase would be *I love you to life*.

Because that's exactly what Tate did.

She loved me back to life.

The

end.

EPILOGUE

I think back to the day I married her.

It was one of the best days of my life.

I remember standing next to Ian and Corbin at the end of the
aisle. We were waiting for her to walk through the doors when
Corbin leaned over and whispered something to me.

He said, "You're the only one who could have ever met my
standards for her, Miles. I'm happy it's you."

I was happy it was me, too.

That was more than two years ago, and every day since then,
I've somehow fallen in love with her a little bit more.

Or *flew*, rather.

I didn't cry the day I married her, though.

Her tears were

falling

falling

falling

that day,

but mine weren't.

I was convinced they never would.

Not in the way I wished they could.

It was eight months ago when we found out we were having a baby.

We weren't trying to have a baby, but we also weren't *not* trying.

"If it happens it happens," Tate said.

It happened.

When we found out, we were both excited.

She cried.

Her tears were

falling

falling

falling,

but mine weren't.

As excited as I was, I was also scared.

I was scared of the fear that comes along with loving someone that much.

Scared of everything bad that could happen.

I was scared that my memories would take away from the day I became a father again.

Well, it just happened.

And I'm still scared.

Terrified.

"It's a girl," the doctor says.

A girl.

We just had a baby girl.

I just became a father again.

Tate just became a mother.

Feel something, Miles.

Tate looks up at me.

I know she can see the fear in my eyes. I also know how much pain she's in right now, but she still somehow manages a smile.

"Sam," she whispers, saying her name out loud for the first time. Tate insisted we name her Sam in honor of Cap's real name, Samuel.

I wouldn't have had it any other way.

The nurse walks over to Tate and lays Sam in her arms.

Tate begins to cry.

My eyes are still dry.

I'm still too scared to look away from Tate and down at our daughter.

I'm not afraid of what I'll feel when I look at her.

I'm afraid of what I *won't* feel.

I'm terrified my past experiences have ruined any ability I have to feel what every father should feel in this moment.

"Come here," Tate says, wanting me closer.

I sit down next to them on the bed.

She hands Sam to me, and my hands are shaking, but I take her anyway.

I close my eyes and release a slow breath before finding the courage to open them again.

I feel Tate's hand fall gently to my arm.

"She's beautiful, Miles," she whispers. "Look at her."

I open my eyes and inhale sharply when I see her.

She looks just like he did, except that she has Tate's brown hair.

Her eyes are blue.

She has my eyes.

I

feel

it.

It's all there.

Everything I felt the first time I held him in my arms is every single thing I'm feeling now as I look down at her.

Believing that I lacked the ability to love someone in this capacity again was the only fear I had left to conquer.

One look at Sam, and she just helped me conquer that fear.

She's already my hero, and she's only two minutes old.

"She's so beautiful, Tate," I whisper. "So beautiful."

My voice cracks.

My face is covered in tears.

Falling

Falling

Falling.

For the first time since the moment I held Clayton in my arms, I'm crying tears of joy.

Rachel was right. The pain will always be there.

So will the fear.

But the pain and fear are no longer my life. They're only moments.

Moments that are constantly overshadowed with every minute I spend with Tate.

And now with every minute I spend with Sam.

Me and Tate and Sam.

My family.

I kiss her on the forehead, and then I lean over and kiss Tate for giving me something this beautiful again.

Tate lays her head on my arm, and we both watch her.

Our daughter.

I love you so much, Sam.

I'm looking down at the perfection we created when it hits me.

It's all worth it.

It's the beautiful moments like these that make up for the ugly love.

If you loved *Ugly Love*,
read on for a sneak peek of

Colleen Hoover's
HOPELESS

Available in both paperback and eBook

Sunday, October 28, 2012
7:29 p.m.

I stand up and look down at the bed, holding my breath in fear of the sounds that are escalating from deep within my throat.

I will not cry.

I will not cry.

Slowly sinking to my knees, I place my hands on the edge of the bed and run my fingers over the yellow stars poured across the deep blue background of the comforter. I stare at the stars until they begin to blur from the tears that are clouding my vision.

I squeeze my eyes shut and bury my head into the bed, grabbing fistfuls of the blanket. My shoulders begin to shake as the sobs I've been trying to contain violently break out of me. With one swift movement, I stand up, scream, and rip the blanket off the bed, throwing it across the room.

I ball my fists and frantically look around for something else to throw. I grab the pillows off the bed and chuck them at the reflection in the mirror of the girl I no longer know. I watch as the girl in the mirror stares back at me, sobbing pathetically. The weakness in her tears infuriates me. We begin to run toward each other until our fists collide against the glass, smashing the mirror. I watch as she falls into a million shiny pieces onto the carpet.

I grip the edges of the dresser and push it sideways, letting out another scream that has been pent up for way too long. When the dresser comes to rest on its back, I rip open the drawers and throw the contents across the room, spinning and throwing and kicking at everything in my path. I grab at the sheer blue curtain panels and yank them until the rod snaps and the curtains fall around me. I reach over to the boxes piled high in the corner, and without even knowing what's inside, I take the top one and throw it against the wall with as much force as my five-foot, three-inch frame can muster.

"I hate you!" I cry. "I hate you, I hate you, I hate you!"

I'm throwing whatever I can find in front of me at whatever else I can find in front of me. Every time I open my mouth to scream, I taste the salt from the tears that are streaming down my cheeks.

Holder's arms suddenly engulf me from behind and grip me so tightly I become immobile. I jerk and toss and scream some more until my actions are no longer thought out. They're just reactions.

"Stop," he says calmly against my ear, unwilling to release me. I hear him, but I pretend not to. Or I just don't care. I continue to struggle against his grasp but he only tightens his grip.

"Don't touch me!" I yell at the top of my lungs, clawing at his arms. Again, it doesn't faze him.

Don't touch me. Please, please, please.

The small voice echoes in my mind and I immediately become limp in his arms. I become weaker as my tears grow stronger, consuming me. I become nothing more than a vessel for the tears that won't stop shedding.

I am weak, and I'm letting *him* win.

Holder loosens his grip around me and places his hands on my shoulders, then turns me around to face him. I can't even look at him. I melt against his chest from exhaustion and defeat, taking in fistfuls of his shirt as I sob, my cheek pressed against his heart. He places his hand on the back of my head and lowers his mouth to my ear.

"Sky." His voice is steady and unaffected. "You need to leave. Now."

Saturday, August 25, 2012
11:50 p.m.

Two months earlier . . .

I'd like to think most of the decisions I've made throughout my seventeen years have been smart ones. Hopefully intelligence is measured by weight, and the few dumb decisions I've made will be outweighed by the intelligent ones. If that's the case, I'll need to make a shitload of smart decisions tomorrow because sneaking Grayson into my bedroom window for the third time this month weighs pretty heavily on the dumb side of the scale. However, the only accurate measurement of a decision's level of stupidity is time . . . so I guess I'll wait and see if I get caught before I break out the gavel.

Despite what this may look like, I am not a slut. Unless, of course, the definition of slut is based on the fact that I make out with lots of people, regardless of my lack of attraction to them. In that case, one might have grounds for debate.

"Hurry," Grayson mouths behind the closed window, obviously irritated at my lack of urgency.

I unlock the latch and slide the window up as quietly as possible. Karen may be an unconventional parent, but when it comes to boys sneaking through bedroom windows at midnight, she's your typical, disapproving mother.

"Quiet," I whisper. Grayson hoists himself up and throws

one leg over the ledge, then climbs into my bedroom. It helps that the windows on this side of the house are barely three feet from the ground; it's almost like having my own door. In fact, Six and I have probably used our windows to go back and forth to each other's houses more than we've used actual doors. Karen has become so used to it, she doesn't even question my window being open the majority of the time.

Before I close the curtain, I glance to Six's bedroom window. She waves at me with one hand while pulling on Jaxon's arm with the other as he climbs into her bedroom. As soon as Jaxon is safely inside, he turns and sticks his head back out the window. "Meet me at your truck in an hour," he whispers loudly to Grayson. He closes Six's window and shuts her curtains.

Six and I have been joined at the hip since the day she moved in next door four years ago. Our bedroom windows are adjacent to each other, which has proven to be extremely convenient. Things started out innocently enough. When we were fourteen, I would sneak into her room at night and we would steal ice cream from the freezer and watch movies. When we were fifteen, we started sneaking boys in to eat ice cream and watch movies *with* us. By the time we were sixteen, the ice cream and movies took a backseat to the boys. Now, at seventeen, we don't even bother leaving our respective bedrooms until *after* the boys go home. That's when the ice cream and movies take precedence again.

Six goes through boyfriends like I go through flavors of ice cream. Right now her flavor of the month is Jaxon. Mine is Rocky Road. Grayson and Jaxon are best friends, which is how Grayson and I were initially thrown together. When Six's flavor of the month has a hot best friend, she eases him into my graces. Grayson is definitely hot. He's got an undeniably great body, perfectly sloppy hair, piercing dark eyes . . . the works. The majority of girls I know would feel privileged just to be in the same room as him.

It's too bad I don't.

I close the curtains and spin around to find Grayson inches from my face, ready to get the show started. He places his hands on my cheeks and flashes his panty-dropping grin. "Hey, beautiful." He doesn't give me a chance to respond before his lips greet mine in a sloppy introduction. He continues kissing me while slipping off his shoes. He slides them off effortlessly while we both walk toward my bed, mouths still meshed together. The ease with which he does both things simultaneously is impressive *and* disturbing. He slowly eases me back onto my bed. "Is your door locked?"

"Go double check," I say. He gives me a quick peck on the lips before he hops up to ensure the door is locked. I've made it thirteen years with Karen and have never been grounded; I don't want to give her any reason to start now. I'll be eighteen in a few weeks and even then, I doubt she'll change her parenting style as long as I'm under her roof.

Not that her parenting style is a negative one. It's just . . . very contradictory. She's been strict my whole life. We've never had access to the internet, cell phones, or even a television because she believes technology is the root of all evil in the world. Yet, she's extremely lenient in other regards. She allows me to go out with Six whenever I want, and as long as she knows where I am, I don't even really have a curfew. I've never pushed that one too far, though, so maybe I do have a curfew and I just don't realize it.

She doesn't care if I cuss, even though I rarely do. She even lets me have wine with dinner every now and then. She talks to me more like I'm her friend than her daughter (even though she adopted me thirteen years ago) and has somehow even warped me into being (almost) completely honest with her about everything that goes on in my life.

There is no middle ground with her. She's either extremely lenient or extremely strict. She's like a conservative liberal. Or a liberal conservative. Whatever she is, she's hard to figure out, which is why I stopped trying years ago.

The only thing we've ever really butted heads on was the issue of public school. She has homeschooled me my whole life (public school is another root of evil) and I've been begging to be enrolled since Six planted the idea in my head. I've been applying to colleges and feel like I'll have a better chance at getting into the schools that I want if I can add a few extracurricular activities to the applications. After months of incessant pleas from Six and me, Karen finally conceded and allowed me to enroll for my senior year. I could have enough credits to graduate from my home study program in just a couple of months, but a small part of me has always had a desire to experience life as a normal teenager.

Of course, if I had known then that Six would be leaving for a foreign exchange the same week as what was supposed to be our first day of senior year together, I never would have entertained the idea of public school. But I'm unforgivably stubborn and would rather stab myself in the meaty part of my hand with a fork than tell Karen I've changed my mind.

I've tried to avoid thinking about the fact that I won't have Six this year. I know how much she was hoping the exchange would work out, but the selfish part of me was really hoping it wouldn't. The idea of having to walk through those doors without her terrifies me. But I realize that our separation is inevitable and I can only go so long before I'm forced into the real world where other people besides Six and Karen live.

My lack of access to the real world has been replaced completely by books, and it can't be healthy to live in a land of happily-ever-afters. Reading has also introduced me to the (perhaps dramatized) horrors of high school and first days and cliques and mean girls. It doesn't help that, according to Six, I've already got a bit of a reputation just being associated with her. Six doesn't have the best track record for celibacy, and apparently some of the guys I've made out with don't have the best track record for secrecy. The combination should make for a pretty interesting first day of school.

Not that I care. I didn't enroll to make friends or impress anyone, so as long as my unwarranted reputation doesn't interfere with my ultimate goal, I'll get along just fine.

I hope.

Grayson walks back toward the bed after ensuring my door is locked, and he shoots me a seductive grin. "How about a little striptease?" He sways his hips and inches his shirt up, revealing his hard-earned set of abs. I'm beginning to notice he flashes them any chance he gets. He's pretty much your typical, self-absorbed bad boy.

I laugh when he twirls the shirt around his head and throws it at me, then slides on top of me again. He slips his hand behind my neck, pulling my mouth back into position.

The first time Grayson snuck into my room was a little over a month ago, and he made it clear from the beginning that he wasn't looking for a relationship. I made it clear that I wasn't looking for *him*, so naturally we hit it off right away. Of course, he'll be one of the few people I know at school, so I'm worried it might mess up the good thing we've got going—which is absolutely nothing.

He's been here less than three minutes and he's already got his hand up my shirt. I think it's safe to say he's not here for my stimulating conversation. His lips move from my mouth in favor of my neck, so I use the moment of respite to inhale deeply and try again to feel something.

Anything.

I fix my eyes on the plastic glow-in-the-dark stars adhered to the ceiling above my bed, vaguely aware of the lips that have inched their way to my chest. There are seventy-six of them. Stars, that is. I know this because for the last few weeks I've had ample time to count them while I've been in this same predicament. Me, lying unnoticeably unresponsive, while Grayson explores my face and neck, and sometimes my chest, with his curious, overexcited lips.

Why, if I'm not into this, do I let him do it?

I've never had any emotional connection to the guys I make out with. Or rather, the guys that make out with me. It's unfortunately mostly one-sided. I've only had one guy come close to provoking a physical or emotional response from me once, and that turned out to be a self-induced delusion. His name was Matt and we ended up dating for less than a month before his idiosyncrasies got the best of me. Like how he refused to drink bottled water unless it was through a straw. Or the way his nostrils flared right before he leaned in to kiss me. Or the way he said, "I love you," after only three weeks of declaring ourselves exclusive.

Yeah. That last one was the kicker. Buh-bye Matty boy.

Six and I have analyzed my lack of physical response to guys many times in the past. For a while she suspected I might be gay. After a very brief and awkward "theorytesting" kiss between us when we were sixteen, we both concluded that wasn't the case. It's not that I don't enjoy making out with guys. I do enjoy it—otherwise, I wouldn't do it. I just don't enjoy it for the same reasons as other girls. I've never been swept off my feet. I don't get butterflies. In fact, the whole idea of being swooned by anyone is foreign to me. The real reason I enjoy making out with guys is simply that it makes me feel completely and comfortably numb. It's situations like the one I'm in right now with Grayson when it's nice for my mind to shut down. It just completely stops, and I like that feeling.

My eyes are focused on the seventeen stars in the upper right quadrant of the cluster on my ceiling, when I suddenly snap back to reality. Grayson's hands have ventured further than I've allowed them to in the past and I quickly become aware of the fact that he has unbuttoned my jeans and his fingers are working their way around the cotton edge of my panties.

"No, Grayson," I whisper, pushing his hand away.

He pulls his hand back and groans, then presses his forehead into my pillow. "Come on, Sky." He's breathing heavily against my neck. He adjusts his weight to his right arm and looks down at me, attempting to play me with his smile.

Did I mention I'm immune to his panty-dropping grin?

"How much longer are you gonna keep this up?" He slides his hand over my stomach and inches his fingertips into my jeans again.

My skin crawls. "Keep *what* up?" I attempt to ease out from under him.

He pushes up on his hands and looks down at me like I'm clueless. "This 'good girl' act you've been trying to put on. I'm over it, Sky. Let's just do this already."

This brings me back to the fact that, contrary to popular belief, I am *not* a slut. I've never had sex with any of the boys I've made out with, including the currently pouting Grayson. I'm aware that my lack of sexual response would probably make it easier on an emotional level to have sex with random people. However, I'm also aware that it might be the very reason I *shouldn't* have sex. I know that once I cross that line, the rumors about me will no longer be rumors. They'll all be fact. The last thing I want is for the things people say about me to be validated. I guess I can chalk my almost eighteen years of virginity up to sheer stubbornness.

For the first time in the ten minutes he's been here, I notice the smell of alcohol reeking from him. "You're drunk." I push against his chest. "I told you not to come over here drunk again." He rolls off me and I stand up to button my pants and pull my shirt back into place. I'm relieved he's drunk. I'm beyond ready for him to leave.

He sits up on the edge of the bed and grabs my waist, pulling me toward him. He wraps his arms around me and rests his head against my stomach. "I'm sorry," he says. "It's just that I want you so bad I don't think I can take coming over here again if you don't let me have you." He lowers his hands and cups my butt, then presses his lips against the area of skin where my shirt meets my jeans.

"Then don't come over here." I roll my eyes and back away from him, then head to the window. When I pull the curtain back, Jaxon is already making his way out of Six's window. Somehow we both managed to condense this hour-long visit into ten minutes. I glance at Six and she gives me the all-knowing "time for a new flavor" look.

She follows Jaxon out of her window and walks over to me. "Is Grayson drunk, too?"

I nod. "Strike three." I turn and look at Grayson, who's lying back on the bed, ignorant of the fact that he's no longer welcome. I walk over to the bed and pick his shirt up, tossing it at his face. "Leave," I say. He looks up at me and cocks an eyebrow, then begrudgingly slides off the bed when he sees I'm not making a joke. He slips his shoes back on, pouting like a four-year-old. I step aside to let him out.

Six waits until Grayson has cleared the window, then she climbs inside when one of the guys mumbles the word "whores." Once inside, Six rolls her eyes and turns around to stick her head out.

"Funny how we're whores because you *didn't* get laid. Assholes." She shuts the window and walks over to the bed, plopping down on it and crossing her hands behind her head. "And another one bites the dust."

I laugh, but my laugh is cut short by a loud bang on my bedroom door. I immediately go unlock it, then step aside, preparing for Karen to barge in. Her motherly instincts don't let me down. She looks around the room frantically until she eyes Six on the bed.

"Dammit," she says, spinning around to face me. She puts her hands on her hips and frowns. "I could have sworn I heard boys in here."

I walk over to the bed and attempt to hide the sheer panic coursing throughout my body. "And you seem disappointed *because* . . ." I absolutely don't understand her reaction to things sometimes. Like I said before . . . *contradictory*.

"You turn eighteen in a month. I'm running out of time to ground you for the first time ever. You need to start screwing up a little more, kid."

I breathe a sigh of relief, seeing she's only kidding. I almost feel guilty that she doesn't actually suspect her daughter was being felt up five minutes earlier in this very room. My heart is pounding against my chest so incredibly loud, I'm afraid she might hear it.

"Karen?" Six says from behind us. "If it makes you feel better, two hotties just made out with us, but we kicked them out right before you walked in because they were drunk."

My jaw drops and I spin around to shoot Six a look that I'm hoping will let her know that sarcasm isn't at all funny when it's the *truth*.

Karen laughs. "Well, maybe tomorrow night you'll get some cute *sober* boys."

I don't think I have to worry about Karen hearing my heartbeat anymore, because it just completely stopped.

"Sober boys, huh? I think I can arrange that," Six says, winking at me.

"Are you staying the night?" Karen says to Six as she makes her way back to the bedroom door.

Six shrugs her shoulders. "I think we'll stay at my house tonight. It's my last week in my own bed for six months. Plus, I've got Channing Tatum on the flat-screen."

I glance back at Karen and see it starting.

"Don't, Mom." I begin walking toward her, but I can see the mist forming in her eyes. "No, no, no." By the time I reach her, it's too late. She's bawling. If there's one thing I can't stand, it's crying. Not because it makes me emotional, but because it annoys the hell out of me. And it's awkward.

"Just one more," she says, rushing toward Six. She's already hugged her no less than ten times today. I almost think she's sadder than I am that Six is leaving in a few days. Six obliges her request for the eleventh hug and winks at me over Karen's shoulder. I practically have to pry them apart, just so Karen will get out of my room.

She walks back to the door and turns around one last time. "I hope you meet a hot Italian boy," she says to Six.

"I better meet more than just one," Six deadpans.

When the door closes behind Karen, I spin around and jump

on the bed, then punch Six in the arm. "You're such a bitch," I say. "That wasn't funny. I thought I got caught."

She laughs and grabs my hand, then stands up. "Come. I've got Rocky Road."

She doesn't have to ask twice.

ACKNOWLEDGMENTS

I have no idea how I came into the position of writing acknowledgments for my eighth book. It's definitely a surreal moment, and one I would never have been able to experience if it weren't for the following people.

The entire Dystel & Goderich team, for your continued support and encouragement.

Johanna Castillo, Judith Curr, and the entire Atria Books family. You guys keep it fun, and I'm forever grateful to be part of one of the coolest publishing teams in the industry.

To all my friends and beta-readers, you guys know who you are. Your feedback and support continue to baffle me. Know that I love you and thank you and couldn't do this without any of you.

My amazing family. I don't know how I lucked out and got the best one, but I'll never take any of you for granted. Especially my four boys.

FP gals, y'all always know exactly when to fire the glitter cannons and release the unicorns. We make a great team.

To my Weblichs. We may not know how to properly pronounce *Weblich*, but we wear the name with pride. I don't even know what to say, other than thank you for giving me a place to go when I need encouragement, a good laugh, and a nice reality check.

To the CoHorts for your unrivaled support. You make this job not a job at all.

And last but definitely not least, to my NPTBF. I will forever be grateful for being disorganized and not knowing how to pack jewelry. Otherwise, I would have missed out on one of the greatest, oddest, most unethical and random relationships of my life.

ABOUT THE AUTHOR

COLLEEN HOOVER is the No.1 bestselling author of *Slammed*, *Point of Retreat*, *This Girl*, *Hopeless*, *Losing Hope*, *Finding Cinderella*, and *Maybe Someday*. She lives in Texas with her husband and their three boys. Please visit ColleenHoover.com.

'Unique, unlike anything else out there . . .
Go out and buy it already' – Tammara Webber

COLLEEN HOOVER
Slammed

Layken's father died suddenly, leaving her to gather
every ounce of strength to be a pillar for her family, in
order to prevent their world from falling apart. Now
her life is taking another unexpected turn . . .

Layken's mother gets a job which leads to an
unwanted move across the country. However, a new
home means new neighbours . . . and Layken's new
neighbour is the very attractive Will Cooper.

Will has an intriguing passion for slam poetry, and a
matching passion for life. The two feel an irresistible
attraction but are rocked to the core when a shocking
revelation brings their romance to a screeching halt.

Layken and Will must find a way to fight the forces
that threaten to tear them apart . . . or learn to
live without each other.

Available in eBook and paperback

Paperback ISBN: 978-1-47112-567-6
eBook ISBN: 978-1-47112-555-3

Before *It Ends With Us*
it started with Atlas...

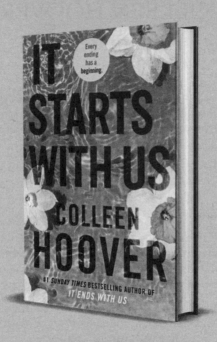

18 OCTOBER 2022

Available to pre-order now at
itstartswithusbook.com

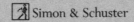